PRAISE FOR CB SAMET

Four-time award winning author

GRAY HORIZON: 2019 Readers' Favorite Bronze Winner in Thriller category

MASTERS FILE: 2018 Readers' Favorite Honorable Mention in Romantic Suspense category

"... a fast-paced tale of crime and unexpected humor.... a combination of romance and suspense that lures the reader in, making it a one-sitting read."

— Readers' Favorite Reviewer on Masters File

"CB Samet is a master of the craft."

— Readers' Favorite Reviewer on Whyte Knight

STORM FILE

THE RIDER FILES, BOOK 5

CB SAMET

1
____

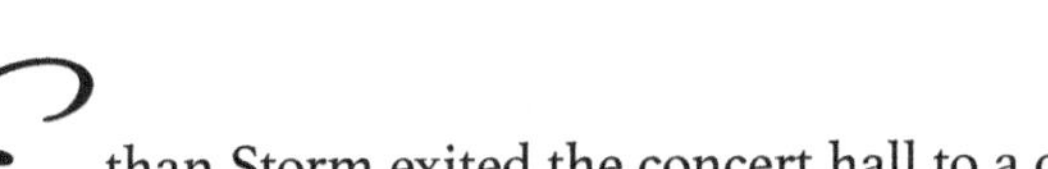

*E*than Storm exited the concert hall to a crowd of
enthusiastic fans lining the sidewalk. He wove
through the throng of people, signing autographs on
photos and CDs with a permanent marker.

The flash of camera lights was blinding, and the
sound of cheering and hollering was deafening. Fans
screamed his name as if competing for who could be
loudest—or the first to shatter glass with their pitch.

Three of his bodyguards kept groping female hands
and gloss-painted lips off Ethan as he made his way to the
rented limousine.

He was still twenty feet from the limo when his security detail began struggling to move the crowd aside
without the use of force. The largest of his bodyguards,

Claude, dressed in a snug T-shirt and black fatigues, tried to lead the way, sweating and grunting through the effort.

Ethan wanted nothing more than to sit in the quiet comfort of the car and drive back to his hotel. He appreciated the fans' fervor, but after a three-hour concert, he needed rest and hydration, not after-parties and intoxicated women. When he was in his twenties, sure. Now, nearing forty, he preferred evenings alone to wind down after his shows.

As they neared the limo parked on the curb, Ethan's phone vibrated in his pocket, and he fished in his blue jeans to retrieve it. He always checked his phone calls in case it was Alyssa, his eight-year-old daughter.

Someone bumped into him, causing the phone to fly from his hand. He bent to the ground in a hurry, not wanting his phone to get trampled.

A shot rang out.

The glass window of Ethan's waiting vehicle shattered as fans screamed in panic.

"We gotta move!" Claude yelled.

Ethan's grip closed over his phone. As he stood, Claude—his longtime friend and bodyguard, who was the size of a linebacker—shoved him into the back seat of his limo, clamored into the backseat beside him, and slammed the door shut.

"Go! Go!" he yelled to the driver.

Pope pulled the limo away from the curb. "Are you hurt?"

"What?"

"Were you shot, Ethan?" Pope, another man he'd known forever, was glancing at him through the rearview mirror as he drove. His tall, lanky friend looked wide-eyed and pale.

Ethan looked over himself, patting his body. "No."

Someone had shot at him? He looked at the shattered window as his heart raced. Cold March air blasted into the car as it gained speed.

"How'd you know to duck?" Claude asked.

Ethan stared at the phone in his hand. "I didn't."

Alyssa had called.

BILLY KNOCKED on the door of the old house. Had the place always been so dilapidated? The porch stairs creaked. The wooden exterior was weather-beaten and peeling, and dark green mold covered one side of the house where a large oak shaded it. Shingles on the roof had abandoned their post in patches.

No one answered.

Billy stepped off the porch, and her boots crunched through the overgrown Kentucky bluegrass which brushed against her jeans as she walked around to the back of the house. When she passed the large oak, she remembered the swing that used to hang there.

"Higher! Higher!" Her small-child's voice echoed in her memory.

Art, the brother closest to her in age, had robustly pushed her on the swing.

"My turn!" Without warning, Mac, the eldest, had shoved her hard, thrusting her out of the swing.

Billy remembered her fear as she'd soared through

the air and the pain of landing on her elbow. She'd sat on the dirt, clutching her injured arm.

"You going to cry, Crybaby?" Mac had asked.

Her dad had stood on the porch, silently watching them as he puffed his twentieth cigarette of the day.

Billy walked through the memory and around to the back porch where her father now sat. The spot overlooked the small pond on the three-acre plot of land.

"Ed," she said tersely.

He squinted at her before adjusting the oxygen tubing running to his nose. He was wearing it all the time now? His black lung must be worse. One of the doctors Billy knew had explained coal-workers' pneumoconiosis to her when she'd asked about the disease. Fifty years of smoking on top of that hadn't helped his lung health either. He looked frail with hollowed cheeks and spidery veins slinking around bony fingers.

"Is Mom around?" Billy tucked her hands in her blue jeans' pockets. A light breeze ruffled her navy-blue T-shirt.

"You should've called first."

"I did call first. You either didn't hear the phone ring or chose not to answer it."

"We don't answer unlisted calls."

"I work in security, Ed. I'm always unlisted." Billy stared at him, recalling the first time she'd visited him after enlisting—the first time she no longer feared him. She'd been stronger, but even by that time he was becoming a shell of the man he once was.

"What makes you so damn special?"

Sure as hell not being born into this family, she wanted to say. But she hadn't come here for a fight. Not another one.

"Is Mom here?" she repeated

Before her father could answer her question, the roar of an ATV split the silence. Mac approached, driving his four-wheeler through the bumpy land, his fishing rod sticking up out of the back of the ATV like a flimsy antenna.

He came to a halt near the backyard picnic table and hopped off the vehicle. "You got a *helluva* lot of nerve coming back here," he snapped at Billy.

She clenched her fists as the hair on her neck stood on end. She could be as cool as a cucumber taking enemy fire in a military tactical armored vehicle, but face-to-face with her oldest brother, she had to resist the urge not to punch him. He always could push her buttons.

"I've a few days off before my next assignment. I came to see Mom."

Mac had lost most of his hair with age and tried to compensate by growing an untamed beard that touched his chest.

He walked closer, swaggering in his camo pants—not that he'd served a day in the military. She supposed he'd been wearing them while duck hunting, and a glance at his ATV confirmed the presence of his shotgun near his fishing pole.

"You ain't welcome here," he snarled.

"So you told me last time. Where's Mom?"

"Grocery shopping." He approached her, cheeks beet red. Once in her face, his breath smelled like beer and dipping tobacco.

"Don't crowd me, Mac," Billy warned. She didn't step back from his attempt to intimidate her. "It won't end well for you."

"Why, because you think you're some badass marine?"

She moved fast—a single, quick jab to his stomach. When he doubled over, she stepped to the side before driving him down, face first, into the table with an elbow between his shoulder blades. He let out a grunt of shock and pain as she kept him pinned.

"I *am* a badass Marine. Show some respect."

"Billy," a familiar woman's voice called to her.

She looked up to see her mom standing on the back porch, staring at her with a look of horrified shock. Billy let Mac up. He stumbled back and stood, holding his abdomen with one hand and bruised cheekbone with other.

Damn, she'd lost her temper.

Who's the bully now, Billy?

Those had been Art's last words to her when she'd come home after ten years of military service and caught him dealing drugs. She'd roughed him up, and when he still didn't quit, she sent him to jail—helped the cops bust him for selling meth to a twelve-year-old girl.

"Some hero you turned out to be," Mac sneered, rubbing his abdomen where she'd struck him.

"Screw you." She spoke the words quietly enough that they'd only be heard by her brother. And she hadn't hurt much more than his pride anyway.

"Billy, what are you doing?" her mother demanded.

Billy didn't like her mom's heated tone and accusatory

glare—as if all this was Billy's fault, as if Mac hadn't done far worse year after year while they were growing up in this house.

"Leaving," Billy replied.

"Billy Jean, you come back here and apologize to your brother."

When hell freezes over, Billy thought.

She looked at her mother who appeared more frail and withered each time she saw her. Scrawny arms and legs protruded from her simple, pale-pink dress. Seeing how she'd aged broke Billy's heart.

"I came to check on you, and I see that you're fine." She started to walk back around front where her rental car was parked.

"Where are you going?" her mother asked.

"I'll be at the motel down the road tonight. One night. If you want to see me away from these two"—she indicated Ed and Mac—"I'll be there."

Mica Rider finished compiling her brief, converted it to pdf, and sent it in an email to Billy. She stood from her desk and stretched in her blouse and skirt. The week had been busy—rearranging people's roles on her team, checking in with Mr. Sharp's security detail, meeting with prospective clients (turning one down because the job sounded shady), and putting a brief together for a client she'd accepted.

Running a business was a new challenge for her. After a few years in the FBI, she'd been a one-woman show as a fugitive recovery agent. Now, she was owner and operator of a security business. People working for Rider SI depended on her for a paycheck. She had company bills to cover and employee health insurance to maintain.

Fortunately, her predecessor and now mother-in-law, Maxine Rider, had built a firm foundation for the company. Rider Security and Investigation was respected, and clients approached them for help because of the company's renowned reputation. Mica didn't need a large advertising budget.

She checked her watch. Her husband was using his day off to get supplies to paint their nursery. Mica wanted to make it an early day.

Billy first.

She picked up her mobile from beside her keyboard and dialed her employee's number.

Billy answered on the second ring. "Mica, I'm ready for the job."

Wow, Billy had already checked her email. She knew Billy had planned to go home to West Virginia for a few days on her down time between jobs. The family visit must not have gone well if she was so eager to get back to work.

"Hello, Billy. The client is a high-profile celebrity. A singer and musician."

"Yeah, I've heard of him. I'm looking over the brief now."

Who hadn't heard of Ethan Storm—singer, song-writer, thirtysomething heartthrob?

Mica switched to speaker phone and tidied her desk

as she spoke. "He was shot at and wants to bolster his security and get his team better trained. Not because they did anything wrong but because he's worried about their safety. He actually said that by the way—he was worried about the safety *of his crew*."

"Okay. Enhance his team," Billy said. "And you have a section in your brief about investigating, finding the perpetrator? Claire's doing that, right?"

"Yes, but she'll need help from you," Mica said. Claire could uncover amazing facts with her internet searches, but electronic investigation needed to be augmented by on scene investigation. "You'll be the on-the-ground investigator. Barry will take the lead on training Mr. Storm's existing crew."

"Me?"

Mica smiled at the incredulity in Billy's voice. "Yes, you."

"I've never done investigative work. Max—"

"Maxine let you stay in your comfort zone. I'm pushing you out of it. I know you'd never want to become complacent. And I think you'll discover a new skill set."

"Did I do something wrong?" Billy asked.

Mica chuckled as she grabbed her keys and walked out of her office. "This isn't punishment, Billy. This is opportunity. You've seen how Ryan and Reece work." They were Rider SI's lead investigative team and had solved numerous cases. "You know how to be the on site investigator." She had a feeling Billy would rather parachute into enemy territory than be lead investigator.

"Which government agency is investigating? Police or FBI?" Billy asked.

"New Jersey PD, where the incident happened. It's not a hate crime or organized crime, so the FBI won't get involved unless the local PD requests assistance."

"Shouldn't I cut my investigative teeth on a less high-profile client?"

Mica appreciated Billy's concern about screwing-up a case. What the marine didn't realize was that she'd already cut her teeth. She was beyond ready to take the next step. She'd been on the Rider team for seven years.

"I'll walk you through it, and Claire will be helping." Mica gave her a little extra reassurance. "You're already a lion, not a cub."

BILLY WATCHED dark clouds in the distance from the hotel rooftop. She held a glass of unconsumed champagne in one hand and adjusted her black cocktail dress with the other. The heels she wore were growing uncomfortable.

She silently cursed Mica, who must have been having a good laugh at forcing Billy undercover. She had explained that Billy needed to conduct a night of observation when Ethan was in public and covertly watch his security team. If the men didn't know they were being monitored, Billy could identify all of the chinks in their armor.

As such, Billy joined Ethan, unbeknownst to him and his bodyguards, for a rooftop party—some other celebrity's engagement celebration, for which they'd rented the swanky spot in downtown Washington, DC. Guests socialized under the pavilion and around a pool. Some people even waded into the water—clothing optional—after several disinhibiting alcoholic beverages.

One of Ethan's bodyguards, Claude, roamed the perimeter, desperately attempting to portray a no-nonsense protector in his snug suit over a sumo-wrestler body. Instead, his expression looked more like a bad case of indigestion.

Billy's partner, Barry Howell, was downstairs observing two of Ethan's bodyguards: JJ, who was in charge keeping Ethan's exit route secure and clear of paparazzi, and Pope, who was the driver.

Billy stayed near Ethan as she leaned against the balcony and watched unobtrusively while eavesdropping. Despite all of the champagne in overflowing flutes, Ethan drank club soda. He looked dashing in his tuxedo—more movie star than rock star. She wasn't the only woman who noticed. Every female on the rooftop seemed drawn to him. And they all had to touch him—a hug, a kiss, a lingering hand on his shoulder.

She didn't interfere; she was here to observe only. None of the women were threats. Their skin-tight dresses couldn't conceal a weapon. They typically had a clutch in one hand and champagne glass in the other—hardly dangerous.

If the women became too clingy or started pushing alcoholic beverages on Ethan, Claude stepped in to put some distance between them and his boss.

To Ethan's credit and Billy's surprise, the celebrity kept his hands to himself. Through all the flirtatious pecks, doting, and proximity of barely concealed body parts, he touched nothing, even when offered to him. He returned the occasional hug, but nothing more. Nonetheless, his magnetism kept Billy on her toes. And on high alert.

ETHAN WAITED for an opportunity to politely excuse himself from the party. He'd intended to only stay an hour or two, but, to his dismay, midnight approached. An endless stream of people seemed to bombard him. He was fairly certain the invitation had mentioned a "small, intimate" gathering, but the number of people mulling about probably exceeded the fire code limit.

Then the sky opened and rain began to fall—not ideal for a rooftop party. He'd noticed dark clouds rolling in earlier and the change in barometric pressure. Well, at least he had his reason for leaving.

People gasped in surprise and made a mad dash for the enclosure by the elevators.

Ethan shook his head. *It's just water not acid rain, people.*

Claude started to usher him toward the rest of the crowd.

A woman in a black dress materialized out of nowhere and placed a hand on Ethan's back, angling him away from the crowd.

"This way," she said with such command, confidence, and reassurance that Ethan obeyed.

"Hey!" Claude snapped, trailing after them.

She led Ethan through the main enclosure and

around the side through a door that said "EMPLOYEES ONLY." Claude scurried to keep up with them.

She glanced back at Claude. "You want to take your boss into a packed foyer and force him into an elevator with a dozen people you can't control? Think, Claude. That's reckless."

Ethan gaped at her. Claude fell silent.

As she moved one hand from Ethan's back to his arm, she pressed the down button on the service elevator. She blew strands of short, wet hair out of her eyes. They didn't cooperate and fell back down over her forehead. The woman had a lovely oval face, full lips, and large brown eyes.

She continued to address Claude. "You need to know every back route to get the asset to safety."

A streak of lightning lit the sky behind them followed by a crash of thunder that reverberated throughout the building. Gasps echoed from the crowd in the other room where six dozen inebriated people waited to board two elevators.

"Who are you?" Ethan asked.

"I'm your new bodyguard."

2

When the door to the service elevator opened, Billy frowned.

"That's a small elevator," Ethan remarked as he stepped inside and turned around.

Billy entered next, facing her new client. "I didn't realize it was so small from the schematics I studied. Are you claustrophobic?"

Claude entered last, backing inside and pressing the down button. As he squeezed his large body into the small rectangular space, Billy was forced against Ethan, facing him.

Ethan gave her a wry grin. "Not like this, I'm not. What's your name?"

"Billy."

The elevator started to move down.

"I think *I'm* claustrophobic," Claude said dryly.

She craned her neck to look at him but couldn't fully turn around in the space without pushing further into Ethan. Since Claude's back was to her, she wouldn't be able to see his face regardless.

Still, the last thing they needed was a 250-pound man having an anxiety attack in this small space. They were fifteen stories up, and the contraption moved at a snail's pace downward.

"You've got ear pods or headphones with you?" Billy asked Claude.

"Yeah."

"Put them in and play ocean sounds or orchestral piano. Something soothing."

"Okay." He fumbled in his pockets, his movements pushing Billy more into Ethan.

With another rumble of thunder, the elevator shuddered to a stop and the light extinguished. A small glow emitted from an emergency light in one corner.

Power outage. Shit.

They weren't in any danger, but trapping one's client in an elevator on the first day of the job was not ideal.

"My apologies," she told Ethan. "I was supposed to spend the night observing you and your team only, but I couldn't let you walk into the path of unpredictability and danger on the guest elevators."

He chuckled, and she felt the rumbling of his chest against hers. "You don't control the weather. Besides, this is better than being stuck on an elevator with drunken partygoers."

Behind her, Claude seemed to settle, listening to whatever soothing sounds he'd found through his phone.

She could feel the rise and fall of Ethan's chest as they breathed the same air. Their clothes were wet, and moisture dripped from his hair, along his jaw, trailing down his neck. She had an inexplicable vision of following the trail back up with her tongue.

Compose yourself.

She raised her gaze higher, into a pair of light-emerald eyes.

Any minute now, the generator would kick in and the elevator would resume.

Any minute now.

ETHAN SHIFTED HIS WEIGHT, trying to figure out where to put his hands without inadvertently groping his new bodyguard. Damn, she smelled good. Something subtle —like fresh rainwater mixed with a faint floral fragrance —and nothing like the strong perfumes he'd endured most of the night.

He looked down at Billy—those of deep-brown eyes and smooth skin. Her lips were too close. When his eyes trailed lower, he could see the start of cleavage—smooth, pale skin caressed by the silky fabric of her dress.

He brought his gaze back to hers. "Is that a gun in your pocket, or are you just happy to see me?" he joked, hoping to get his mind off what her proximity was doing to his imagination.

"Right. Sorry." Billy's voice had an edge of huskiness. She started to move, adjusting the gun holster on the left side of her chest which was hidden beneath the shrug jacket she wore over her black dress.

He sucked in a breath and put his hands on her hips. "No, no. Don't move. I—" but it was too late.

"Oh." Her cheeks grew red. "That's not a gun."

"No, it's not." Ethan tilted his head and let the back of it rest on the wall as he stared at the ceiling of the elevator.

She cleared her throat. "I can try to move over to—"

He tightened his grip on her waist to keep her from moving and creating more friction between them. "Please don't."

She stilled.

He glanced down at Billy. Her lips were slightly parted and her pupils dilated. For a moment, he wondered if she was equally as aroused as he was, but such musings weren't helping his situation. He stared back at the ceiling, searching his mind for mundane thoughts.

Instead, images of the shooting peppered him— broken glass, a breeze through the shattered window, screams piercing the night.

He kept his grip on Billy, this time to keep him grounded from the horrible replays of the post-concert-sniper incident.

At last, the larger light overhead illuminated, and the elevator began to move.

Billy pulled her luggage behind her as she walked next to Barry through the hotel lobby. She kept her pace unhurried since her partner's osteoarthritis wouldn't appreciate her powerwalking.

Mercifully, she was out of her dress and heels and back in her standard navy-blue work suit, same as Barry. Her comfortable combat boots were noiseless on the polished marble floor.

They had arrived the day prior in DC to observe Ethan's team covertly—until it turned up close and personal for Billy. Now it was time to officially start the job.

"This will be a nice change," Barry said. "No international travel for this job. No baking in the hot sun, watching tennis matches."

Billy nodded. Their security services for women on the professional tennis circuit had been arduous. That being said, she'd seen some amazing sites across Europe she otherwise would have missed. She'd also gained a healthy respect for the intense schedule of professional athletes.

"You're quiet," Barry remarked, adjusting his waistband.

She looked at him, scanning from his worn leather shoes to his generous belly, which seemed to defy gravity, up to his small, keen eyes.

"I mean," he continued, "you've never been one for small talk, but you're especially quiet. Is it the assignment?"

She rolled her shoulders. She liked Rider Security and Investigation and her new boss and CEO, Mica Rider.

The woman was tough and savvy, but Billy felt unbalanced by the role Mica had given her.

"I've done nothing but straightforward protection since joining Rider SI," Billy explained. "I'm surprised Mica asked me to take an investigative role. It's not exactly my area of expertise."

Barry snorted. "Want to trade roles? I have to train a bunch of doughnut-eating amateurs how to be bodyguards. Besides, Mica's not having you go undercover like Ryan and Reece do—or even deep cover like Dorian does. You just need to keep your eyes and ears open—see if we can learn who the perpetrator is."

"I'll trade roles with you," she said flatly, not reminding him that she'd done undercover work last night and the result had been disastrous. Sure, they discovered weaknesses in Ethan's security team, but she'd also wound up arousing the client and herself in the process. She hadn't shared that part of the story with Barry.

"Nope." Barry shook his head. "Mine was a rhetorical question. I don't want to hang out with some degenerate rock star with a god complex. And what kind of name is Ethan Storm—certainly not the one he was born with."

They reached the check-in counter and waited in line.

"Yeah." Billy chuckled. "He probably had it changed from Ernie Boombottom or something."

"Hey, my grandmother's neighbor's name was Boombottom."

"So you once told me."

She enjoyed security, but perhaps the investigative part would spice up the job. She had zero desire to spend her time taking care of a drunk or a drug addict. Yet, according to the background information Mica had given Billy, Ethan was neither. He'd stayed sober last night on the hotel rooftop.

Of course, that didn't mean her information was infallible. Based on the tabloids, he was an unabashed playboy—every week a different Barbie doll had an arm around his shoulder. Such fraternizing could compromise their ability to protect him. The women had certainly flocked to him at the party last night.

Billy turned to Barry. "So, based on Ethan's file, who do you think is out to get him—the publicist, the ex-wife, the drummer, rogue fan, the gardener?"

Barry shrugged. "That's your job—along with Claire and Mica."

She put a hand on her hip. "You haven't read the file, have you?"

He rubbed the bald patch on his head. "I skimmed it. I don't need to read the file to protect the asset. I've been doing this for thirty years, Billy."

She couldn't argue with him. What Barry lacked in physical speed, he made up for with weapon accuracy. The former Special Forces soldier didn't look like the deadly weapon he was.

"The gardener?" Barry asked. "Does he have a gardener?"

"I have no idea. I was just seeing if you were paying attention."

They moved closer in line and were next up to check in. Billy's gaze wandered around the lobby, observing the marble floors and sparkling chandeliers.

"This is the life, Billy." Barry grinned, taking it all in beside her.

"A five-star hotel or a three-star hotel, they're all the same to me—a roof and a bed. I'm not sure what you're drooling over. You won't have time to enjoy the pool or the spa."

Billy never let herself enjoy those things when she was on the job. She'd heard of security guards getting accustomed to the lavish lifestyles of those they protected. Some went broke trying to afford to live that way when they were no longer on the job. She did, however, appreciate that the more luxurious hotels had nicer fitness centers. Those she put to good use.

"The beds are always nicer. I get to enjoy that," Barry said.

They reached the front desk and checked in. The clerk gave them key cards for two rooms connected by a shared sitting room. They would be on the same floor as Ethan Storm.

The clerk produced a small map, preparing to give them the layout of elevators, restaurants, and amenities. "Have you been to the DC Ritz-Carlton before?"

"No." Billy took the map. "But I'll manage. Thanks." She'd already memorized the layout, and she knew the service elevators at this hotel were decently sized—should she find herself stuck inside one with Ethan again.

Barry followed behind her to the elevator as she took in the mounted cameras and exit routes. The elevator was key card access only which was a nice extra layer of protection—easily penetrated for a determined person, but it separated the riffraff from real threats.

After they rode the elevator up, they walked to the end of the hallway and reached the adjoining rooms. Billy walked into her room and scrutinized the expansive space with a king-size bed, chaise lounge, big screen TV, and mini fridge. It was the size of her entire loft apartment in Atlanta—the one she called home but rarely spent more than a few days out of a month at.

She set her suitcase on the rack. It was time to tidy her post-travel appearance and meet the new client—in a more respectable manner.

Perhaps she could take a second chance to make a first impression.

3

*E*than strummed his guitar and felt the music, searching for the notes to fit his song. He jotted down an F sharp on the paper in front of him.

His assistant's familiar three brisk knocks were followed by her entering his hotel room. She wore a brown and white polka-dot dress and had her brown hair pulled back in a ponytail.

"Ethan, Ms. Billy Jean Parrish and Mr. Barry Howell from Rider Security," Alice announced.

And Investigation, Ethan thought. The last part of the company's name was key. He had security guards—good old boys he'd known since high school—but he didn't have an investigative team.

Until now.

A balding man in his late fifties with a barrel-shaped

belly, wearing a suit, stood beside Billy. Her short hair was dry now, and she wore a two-piece business suit with a slim-fitting blazer and matching slacks. The professional, clean-cut look was finished with practical-looking, polished boots. Her expression was neutral, but her keen brown eyes appeared to be absorbing everything—the hotel room, his assistant, his guitar, and his disarray of music sheets near the sofa.

"Thank you, Alice." Ethan stood and extended a hand as he held his guitar out of the way. "Billy Jean?"

She had only said her name was Billy at their last introduction. After the elevator encounter last night, she'd escorted him to his car where Pope had waited, and then she'd vanished.

"My mom was a Michael Jackson fan, though mine is spelled with a 'y.'" She smiled, her heart-shaped lips opening and brightening her face around a pert nose.

In a word—cute. But still professional. Her smile had preceded his remark on her name and faded with her mention of her mother. She'd smiled, Ethan realized, because he had addressed her first rather than her partner. He also realized he was shaking her hand too long.

He released her hand and shook Barry's as he addressed both of them. "Thank you for coming. The Rider SI team came highly recommended." He'd asked around to friends in the business, not wanting to delegate something this important to just anyone. Ethan also liked that Mica Rider had been honest and straightforward on the phone. "Based on our first interaction last night, your services are much needed."

"Any questions about what Mica explained?" Barry asked.

Ethan smiled. "She knew what I needed better than I did. I have no additional questions. She explained everything very thoroughly." He turned and walked toward his coffee machine. "Can I get you a cup of joe?"

"No, thank you," Billy replied.

"I'll take one," Barry said. "Though that fancy machine looks like it'll make everything except a simple cup of joe. Looks like you need a degree to operate it"

Ethan chuckled. "It'll make about any type of coffee you want. Thanks, Alice, I'll take it from here."

His assistant left the room.

When the door closed, Ethan said, "I prepped Alice earlier that I wanted to talk to my new temporary hires alone. She knows the basics of why you're here and will help in any way she can. As instructed by Mica, only I know your investigative role."

He glanced at Billy as he started making Barry's coffee. He could glean a lot from a person based on what they liked to drink and how they accepted someone's hospitality to make them coffee. Someone who accepted nothing was guarded—either not trusting or not trustworthy, or both.

Ethan fixed a coffee for Barry and himself, handed one cup off, then invited them to have a seat on the hotel room sofa. They sat beside each other, and Ethan sat in a cushioned chair.

"I called Mica and explained that I needed additional security after a bullet whizzed past my ear last week."

"Attempted murder," Billy broke in.

Ethan blinked at her.

"I studied the footage, Mr. Storm. We collected various video postings from social media from multiple angles. If you hadn't ducked, that would've been a head shot."

"But it hit the window." He was taller than the window. Surely, she was mistaken. He'd replayed the events in his mind and had been able to convince himself that he wasn't the target.

"The shot had a downward trajectory. The shooter was probably on the second floor of a building adjacent to the concert hall."

"The police didn't find anything." He stared at his espresso, which suddenly looked unappealing. Maybe he didn't need to add caffeine to the jolt of concern pummeling his stomach.

"Nor would they in crowded chaos," Billy said.

Barry nudged his partner in the ribs.

Billy threw a hand up. "I'm supposed to sugarcoat it for him?" she asked Barry.

Ethan set his cup down on the table beside his sheet music. "It's okay. I appreciate the honesty. I told Mica about needing additional security. I walked her through my current staff and their qualifications, adding that these are men with families to support. I don't want to replace anyone, but I also don't want anyone getting shot because they're protecting me. Mica explained that my men need security training and I need an inside pair of investigative eyes." He crossed his legs and leaned back. "So, who's who?"

Billy leaned forward. "He's the trainer. I'm the eyes."

Ethan looked into her rich brown eyes and long lashes.

Yes, she *was* the eyes.

———

AFTER AN HOUR of going over protocols in his hotel room, Billy watched Ethan walk toward the door, which seemed to be her and Barry's cue to stand. Ethan's movements were as relaxed as the stone-washed jeans he wore. She tried not to notice how his gray T-shirt hugged his torso.

Ethan swung open the door. "Alice, can you see what Barry needs to get started?"

"Barry, you'll get whatever you need to set up to meet my security. When you're ready, Alice will fetch me, and I'll introduce you to the boys."

Ethan's efficient assistant whisked Barry away, and the hotel room door closed behind them. The famous singer moved with confidence and ease as he scooped up his guitar and strummed it. Billy glimpsed his long fingers moving in smooth, rehearsed motion.

He hadn't dismissed her yet.

"So, attempted murder?" He kept his gaze down on his guitar strings.

He had short light-brown hair and a clean-shaven face. She'd seen various versions of facial hair on him in the tabloids. It didn't matter if he had a trimmed beard, a few days of stubble, or a smooth jaw, he was a handsome man with liquid, mint-green eyes.

"I'm sorry if I was too blunt. I'm a blunt person." She

wanted to do her very best on her new assignment, but her personality was what it was.

"Straight shooter. Now I know." He grinned. He strummed a brief harmony before placing a palm on the strings and abruptly stopping the music. "So, how does this investigative part work?"

"I grill you about who might want to hurt you. You regurgitate everything you already told the police, I'll prod some more, and we'll see if anything was missed."

"And if that doesn't work?"

Billy glanced at his monstrous, gleaming coffee machine. Investigative work wasn't her forte, but she also wasn't an amateur. And she wasn't alone. Claire was the Rider team's investigative bloodhound and could turn up most secrets anyone kept in electronic format. She'd been the one to give Billy a collection of video snippets of the shooting.

"I'm your spy," she said. "I need to hear and see everything transpiring around you—every concert, all of your off-stage time, and each last-minute change of plans and why. I'm by your side for all of it until the mystery is solved."

"Sounds exhausting." He lightly plucked a few strings on his guitar.

"If I need a break, Barry tags in for me."

"So, you just became my new best friend?"

"I'm nobody's friend." She didn't break eye contact when he stared at her.

He cocked his head to one side. "Ain't that a shame?"

Those vibrant green eyes had dark-silver flecks. The intensity of his stare finally caused her to shift her gaze to the window. Boats glided down the Potomac River under a sky of clearest blue.

"My priority is your protection. That means I'm nobody's friend."

"Everybody's a suspect?" he said coyly.

"Yes."

"You can't even be *my* friend?"

The harder her voice got, the lighter his became, almost to the point of teasing. And his grin had a seductive edge she suspected had been perfected from decades on stage and on camera. The tone reminded her of their elevator encounter, and the room suddenly felt ten degrees hotter.

"I especially can't be *your* friend. Until we get to the bottom of who's a threat to you, I'm an intrusive invader into your privacy. Trust me, my presence won't feel friendly."

He picked up his coffee and took a sip. "There's that bluntness again. I do trust you. I believe I like you, Billy Jean."

Her heart skittered a beat when he said her name that way, but she attributed it to the large black coffee she'd had that morning and the anticipation of taking on a new type of investigative role. He may like her now, but he'd be sick of her before this assignment was over. She wasn't here to win anyone's favoritism. She had a job to do.

Then she remembered Mica's coaching words when she'd put Billy in charge of this project: "The client's security is our number one concern, but he's still the one who keeps or discards our business. You're going to be the main interface between the client and the company, so you have to be congenial."

Congenial. The word was a foreign concept to Billy.

She considered the way Ethan's jaw had tensed when she'd said "attempted murder." She'd been in fights, been shot at, and had the training to manage all of it. He was a civilian who'd had his first brush with death.

Billy cleared her throat. "If I'm ever too blunt, let me know. I'll try to tone it down."

"I'll do that." He continued strumming a gentle melody on the guitar. "And since I'm friendly by nature, you let me know if I'm ever too friendly."

Billy suppressed a snort and replaced it with a curt nod. She was a tomboy in a suit with ten years' experience in the Marines. She never had problems with people being *too friendly*. In fact, her only friends were her work colleagues at Rider SI and a few marines she'd kept in touch with over the years.

"What's the bracelet symbolize?" Ethan asked.

Billy touched fingers to the green and gray woven fabric on her wrist. "No symbol. It's a tool called a paracord bracelet. It has seven strands of parachute-strength material. Disconnected and extended, the strands can be used for tying or securing objects, making a tent, or as fishing line."

"Survivalist's tool. So, it symbolizes your knowledge and readiness to face any survival situation."

"Yes, I suppose it does."

"When do we start your interrogation of me?" Ethan asked.

Was he flirting? No, she must have misinterpreted his

tone. Perhaps this was the "friendly by nature" part he'd referred to earlier.

"The sooner the better. You've got dinner with your agent tonight. Tomorrow morning is your interview with *Rolling Stone* magazine, so you'll already spend the day answering questions. You may not feel like it after that, but your performances at the Capital One Arena are Friday and Saturday night, so we can't wait too long."

He raised his eyebrows. "You've already memorized my schedule."

"I know the broad overview of your tour through June, but I will always know the intimate details of the next five days of your life."

"Intimate?"

His question conjured images of his body pressed against hers in the elevator. The faint sound of his wet tuxedo brushing against her black dress echoed in her ears.

Billy cleared her mind and matter-of-factly explained, "Intimate in the sense of where you spend every hour. But since you brought it up, you marked 'no intimate relationships' on your client form. If you do form relationships while on this tour, I need to know about them —preferably in advance so I can background check her or him. I realize celebrities, such as yourself, aren't accustomed to this, but this is what's safest."

Ethan chuckled. "You do cover all the bases, don't you? First of all, if there was someone, it'd be a *she*. Secondly, I don't sleep around with fans. If you read that somewhere, you have material that's fifteen years outdated or outright lies."

"I wasn't referring to you, specifically. But I've been on the protection detail of musicians and celebrities on tour."

He kept his easy demeanor. "Well, we're nothing like that around here. My crew—band and security—are all family men these days. Our excitement is video-chatting with loved ones at the end of the day."

"Understood, Mr. Storm." She felt she'd conveyed what was important: relationships were subject to investigation.

"Ethan. Not Mr. Storm. Everybody calls me Ethan."

"Ethan." Two syllables were easier than three, and if she needed to blend in at a social function, calling him the name everyone else used would be best. "Is Ethan Storm your real name or stage name?" Barry would ask her to find out, so she might as well take the initiative.

"Real name."

"If there's nothing else, I'll unpack and then meet your crew with Barry."

He nodded with an appraising look. "And then I'll see you at dinner with my agent."

4

———

$\mathcal{B}$illy and Barry sat at the hotel room conference table with the six bodyguards on Ethan's payroll.

She appreciated the round table which conveyed the team approach she and Barry liked to take when incorporating themselves into an established security team. They weren't there to seize control but to augment—like using premium gas instead of standard unleaded.

What the men wouldn't know was that Barry and Billy had also been hired to investigate the origin of the threat. Only Ethan knew their other role. And since his bodyguards knew Ethan well and might have personal reasons to dislike him, they would all be subjected to the Rider SI covert investigation.

With everyone around the table dressed in suits, they

could have been mistaken for a sales convention. Except, no one was smiling and everyone was armed.

Barry addressed the group. "Thank you all for coming. I'm Barry Howell, and this is Billy Jean Parrish. We go by Billy and Barry. Billy's background includes ten years in the Marines and seven years with the company. I served twenty years in the military, part of that with Special Forces, and I've been in private security since Maxine Rider started this company."

Barry spoke with pleasant reassurance as he kept his hands relaxed on the table, fingers linked. His mannerisms reminded Billy of Sun Tzu's *The Art of War*, which she'd read many times in the Marines. *"A leader leads by example, not by force."*

Barry continued, "I want to take a moment to review our role here, even though Ethan may have already told you. We're not here to replace anyone. When the escalated danger against Ethan resolves, you'll still be here and we'll be gone. While we're here, we'll establish new and different routines, tighter and more synchronized. One of us—Billy or I—will always be on point. You may not be accustomed taking orders from someone new, but don't think about it that way. Ethan hired us. Ethan trusts us. You're taking orders from your long-standing friend and employer. If you object to something we're doing, talk to us. We're approachable."

He glanced at Billy with a grin. "Well, I'm approachable."

Billy arched an eyebrow.

"Keep us in the loop and communicate," he continued. "The team that communicates, innovates. And if you're not satisfied with our responses, speak with Ethan."

As Barry talked, Billy assessed the reactions of Ethan's guards. They seemed tentatively receptive to Barry's words and amicable approach. No one appeared tense or hostile. No one revealed a worried expression.

She knew their backgrounds from Claire's briefing. Claude and Pope were closest to Ethan. The three of them had known each other since high school. Claude was large with broad shoulders and meaty hands. His cheeks seemed perpetually flushed. He'd played football in high school—linebacker. He'd no doubt been chosen for his size, which made for a nice crowd deterrent, but he moved slowly.

Pope, on the other hand, was leaner and faster. He'd tried his hand at race car driving, but when NASCAR didn't work out, he became Ethan's driver. An excellent choice for getaways, but Pope needed to learn new security skills in order to contribute more to the team.

The others were JJ, Scott, Harry, and Wayne. Collectively, they had a hodgepodge of experience as bouncers, kick boxers, bodybuilders, and personal trainers. Ethan had hired them over the years through word-of-mouth recommendations from friends or family members. All of them had worked for Ethan for at least five years.

They seemed like a loyal bunch, but Billy's job was to dig beneath the surface and see if anything festered.

Ethan was buttoning the top button on his white shirt when a knock sounded at his door. He tucked his shirt into his slacks. "Come in."

Pope let Meg Martin into the hotel room.

Ethan's agent wore a tailored suit and heels. Her hair was fashioned in an impeccable blonde bob. Maybe Meg could do the interview tomorrow with *Rolling Stone* magazine. She had a better face for it. Besides, the writer was going to ask Ethan all about the shooting and nothing about his songwriting or family life. Meg could answer questions about the shooting. She hadn't been there, but even though Ethan had been present, he still wasn't sure exactly what had happened. It was a single gunshot and over so fast.

Attempted murder, according to Billy. The two of them would ponder that possibility again later.

"Ethan!" Meg smiled and air-kissed his right cheek. Good thing, because her red lipstick would have taken time to scrub off.

"Thanks for coming a few minutes early. I wanted to fill you in on my new security members."

"Oh?"

Ethan began attaching his cufflinks. He'd never cared much for male jewelry, but these little silver beauties had Alyssa's initials—A.H.—on them with a diamond between the letters. They'd been a gift from her and were the only ones he ever wore.

"This is the team I hired after the shooting," he reminded her. He'd mentioned extra security to her, but perhaps he hadn't made it clear he would follow through on the hire. "They're going to give Pope, Claude, and the rest additional training." As planned, he left out the investigative role Billy was playing.

Billy wouldn't be interviewing everyone the way the police or a private detective might do, but she was there as a keen observer. Also, Mica had assured him she'd have someone researching everyone in his life from their private correspondence to their finances. It was better, Mica had explained, if his friends and colleagues didn't know Ethan was paying to have them all investigated.

"That seems like a very practical move," Meg said. "More security around our superstar can never be a bad thing."

"I need to warn you, the addition will be more intrusive. Where I go, they go."

She gave an unsure smile—at least, he thought it was a smile. The more Botox she had injected into her face, the harder it was to tell. "We'll manage. Your safety comes first."

Another knock came at the door.

"Come in," Ethan called again.

Billy entered, wearing the same slacks and white, buttoned shirt as before. Over that was a navy blazer—under which was the gun he'd felt the other night. Ethan noticed her pants were tailored and fit her small hips perfectly.

"Meg, this is Billy Parrish. Billy, Meg Martin, my agent." He liked thinking of her as Billy Jean, but since she preferred just Billy, he would make sure other people knew her as such. He'd keep the Billy Jean part for himself.

Meg extended a hand, and the women shook. Billy

was the same height as Meg with heels—so probably about five-five. Other than the tailored suit and small pearl earrings, nothing about Billy's appearance suggested expense. This was in contrast to the five rings, thick gold necklace, and thousands of dollars in plastic surgery Meg sported. Well, Ethan thought, they were women with two very different priorities and roles.

Ethan took pride in surrounding himself with successful, professional women. He wanted to send the right message to Alyssa. Her mother was a dermatologist, so Alyssa already had a great role model there, but Ethan wanted to show her that men valued women for the capable people they were.

Meg looked around Billy. "Just you?"

"Just me at the dinner table with you."

Ethan had invited her to their dinner since Billy wanted to take the measure of the people around him. He looked forward to having her there, though Billy would only discover that Meg couldn't have had any part in his attempted assassination.

"Barry, my partner, will be close by. Pope is still the driver, and Claude is at the door."

"Which door?" Meg asked tauntingly.

"Whichever one Ethan goes in and out of."

Meg smirked. "What about the bathroom door?"

"Sometimes, yes."

Meg chuckled as she looked at Ethan. "Well, your new hires are very zealous. That's good. We want Ethan well protected." She patted his arm.

Billy continued, "As his agent, you may like us less

when we have to usher him through crowds and forgo autographs."

Blunt Billy strikes again. Ethan turned away to hide his smile from Meg. He slipped on his shoes and picked up his blazer.

Meg's mouth fell open. "He can't disappoint fans."

"Transfers in and out of establishments are some of the most vulnerable moments, as Ethan's attack clearly demonstrated."

"You'll kill his career." Meg's cheeks reddened.

"Better his career than his life," Billy smoothly fired back. "But it won't be so dramatic. I've covered security duty for celebrities, a few super-fans will express their disappointment, but it won't be career-ending."

Meg had worked hard building Ethan's fan-base over the years, so he wasn't surprised she was defensive about anything threatening her diligent efforts and their livelihood. But he couldn't make a living if he wasn't alive.

Meg gave an irritated crinkle of her nose. "Mother knows best."

Ethan cringed at the derogatory tone in Meg's words.

"I've been called worse." Billy, unfazed, motioned for the door. "Shall we?"

Ethan chuckled and followed Billy out of the hotel room. Meg followed behind them. Pope, who'd been standing outside the room, pulled the door shut and brought up the rear.

Mica had provided Ethan with Billy's service record, so he knew the woman was physically tough. Now he knew petty comments from other women had no effect

on her. He liked that she could handle herself, both
mentally and physically.

BILLY SAT before the screen on the video chat in her hotel
room after Ethan and Meg's dinner. She'd changed into
shorts and a white tank top before bed.

"How did the first twenty-four hours go?" Mica asked.

"It went well. I set the expectations you and I
discussed. Ethan didn't balk at anything, but then he is a
fairly easygoing kind of guy."

"How is his agent?"

"Shallow and self-centered. Maybe even likes Ethan,
judging by her reaction to a woman protecting him. But
she doesn't have motive. If anything bad happens to
Ethan, she'll lose money."

During the car ride to the restaurant, Billy had ridden
beside Pope while Ethan and Meg sat in the back seat
and talked business. She'd listened quietly as Meg took
charge of their conversation, focusing on the tour and
coaching Ethan on aspects of his publicity and the
upcoming interview.

"What about jealousy as motive?" Mica asked as she
stirred what looked like a mug with ice cream in it.

Billy considered Meg's plastic surgery and wardrobe.
"I think she likes money too much to let emotion dictate
her actions. Claire's financial profile shows as much going
out as coming in. She runs a tight margin. What are you
grinning about?"

Mica had a million-watt smile framed in Marilyn-

Monroe-platinum hair. No one who met her for the first time would ever guess how dangerous she was. "I'm congratulating myself on picking the right person for the job. You're a regular Sherlock Holmes."

"Which one? Robert Downey Jr. or Benedict Cumberbatch?"

"Hmm." Mica licked her spoon. "If those are my only choices of the dozens of actors who've played Sherlock, then Cumberbatch, it is. You don't have the humor or speed of conversation for Downey."

"Good choice. Benedict actually let one of his bodyguards be an extra on his show once."

"I'm headed out for a walk," Barry called to her from across the sitting room of their adjoining rooms.

Billy waved goodbye to Barry over her shoulder.

Mica continued, "If I'd known we were going to have an in-depth conversation about my Sherlock analogy, I would have selected a female detective to reference."

"I used to watch *Charlie's Angels* re-runs." She also thought the comparison was more fitting since she, Claire, and Mica were investigating as a team. "I was a fan —you know before I grew up and asked myself why every episode required at least one scantily clad scene. I've worked for Rider SI for seven years, and the job has never once required a bikini," Billy said.

"I've worn the occasional seductive dress as a PI. Never a bikini. Which angel was your favorite?" Mica asked.

"Jaclyn Smith—classy, sophisticated, and glamorous."

"You are full of surprises, Billy."

"What?"

"Nothing." Mica stuck her spoon in her mug and raised her hands in mock surrender on the screen. "Check in with me again in a few days and give me another update."

"Sure thing, boss."

Mica smiled.

Billy disconnected the call.

"I didn't mean to eavesdrop."

Billy stood and spun around. Ethan stood in the sitting room separating her room from Barry's. He wore the same slacks and shirt from dinner, with the top two buttons undone.

She felt a flush creep up her neck and into her cheeks. People with money seemed to think they could waltz whereever they damn well desired.

"Barry let me in on his way out," Ethan explained.

"I have a phone if you need to reach me."

"I don't like texting—it's impersonal, when I can just walk down the hall and have a conversation. Since Barry let me inside, I didn't think I was intruding. By your reaction, I can see that I am." He tugged at one of the cufflinks he wore.

"No, it's fine." She straightened her shirt and made a mental note to close the adjoining bedroom door in the future. "What do you need to discuss?"

"The band wants to practice tomorrow afternoon. I'm hoping we can move your interview of me up to the morning, *before* my magazine interview."

"Done. Anything else?"

He shifted his weight on his feet and ran a hand through his hair. "Listen. I'm all about equality. If there were two Barrys in these rooms instead of a Barry and a Billy Jean, I would have walked over here just like this."

"I didn't interpret the intrusion as anything gender-based."

"Good." He started to leave but turned back with a perplexed look. "Why not?"

"I've seen your type in the media, I'm not it." She spoke the words matter-of-factly.

She took no offense to the preferences of men she guarded. She'd seen photographs of the women in Ethan's life—short skirts, large breasts, long hair. The elevator encounter had been nothing more than a reaction to their close proximity. She hadn't deluded herself into thinking the rock star had been specifically attracted to her.

Ethan pursed his lips in the first sign of annoyance she'd seen from him. "I would kindly appreciate if you didn't consider tabloids a reliable source of information."

His words weren't harsh, but she felt their sting, nonetheless. She was here in an investigational capacity, which meant she should be keeping an open mind. She shouldn't draw conclusions based on her own biases. Just because the majority of the celebrities she'd guarded slept with a myriad of people, it didn't mean they all did.

"Understood."

The corner of Ethan's mouth tilted up. "That's all?"

Billy was puzzled. What more did he want? Her word "understood" conveyed the semblance of an apology and the commitment to do better next time. A full-out apology wasn't necessary for so slight an offense.

"Usually I get more of a debate when I argue with women," Ethan said.

Billy cracked a smile. "This doesn't qualify as an argument. And I thought we weren't bringing gender into this."

Ethan laughed, and the sound filled her with unexpected enjoyment.

"Understood," he said with another laugh, though the word came across as more of a "touché."

"You know my tour will take us to California," he added with a mischievous glint in his eye.

"I'm aware."

"I just bring it up because I heard you lamenting about a job without the opportunity to wear a bikini."

She opened her mouth to protest.

"But to be fair," he pointed a finger at her, "if you wear one, all of the security team should probably match. You know, to avoid gender bias."

He left her standing in the hotel room with the awful mental image of Barry in a bikini.

5

illy stood in the shadows as Ethan underwent his interview with the magazine writer. The interview started off friendly enough, as the writer asked about Ethan's family and his songwriting. They talked through his upcoming music tour and how well his latest album was performing.

Billy had conducted her interview of him earlier—her holding a black coffee from the continental breakfast buffet and him with a potent-yet-frothy caffeinated beverage from his elaborate machine.

She'd avoided asking him questions about the night of the shooting because she knew he would have to rehash the memory now with the journalist, and she'd be there to listen.

A spy in the corner. A fly on the wall. A silent portrait

watching, seeing, and learning all. But she had one more layer of responsibility—to assimilate everything and use that information to discover his would-be killer.

"You had a scary night a week ago just after the New Jersey concert ended." The reporter's tone was congenial even as her hungry eyes conveyed how eager she was to sink her teeth into the delicious, dramatic details of that night.

Ethan nodded grimly. He seemed resigned to accept the fact that these types of questions would continually be asked, so he might as well address them head-on. "Someone shot out the window of my ride."

"News reports are speculating that the shot was intended for you."

"That's entirely possible. I had dropped my phone and was bending over to pick it up when the shot was fired."

"That must've been terrifying."

"At the time it was chaos and confusion. In the moments afterward, as we drove away, I grew concerned not knowing if one of my fans or one of my staff had been shot. It wasn't until word came in that no one was injured when I realized the danger to myself."

"Your daughter, Alyssa, must've been frightened for you."

"She was the first person I called. Fortunately, I reached her by phone before the media did and before she saw any of the video replays on television. I was able to let her know I was okay before she knew to worry."

Billy felt a strange pressure in her chest. She didn't think the raw emotion from Ethan was staged or acting.

He wasn't in tears or even close to tears, but he had been shaken by events. Well, she was here now. Her job was to ensure he never had to face anything like that again.

"Can you tell us who you think is behind the shooting?"

"I have no idea. I know the police are looking into it. I have faith the people investigating will uncover the truth."

Billy assessed his statement. They were actually two entirely different sentences. The police were looking into the shooting. But the people he was referring to were his investigative team, Rider SI.

My investigation, Billy thought.

But not hers alone. Claire was meticulously searching through suspects' internet secrets, and Billy would continually discuss her findings with Mica, using her as a sounding board to speculate about potentially guilty parties.

"You have a lot of fans rooting for you and praying for your safety." The reporter smiled.

"Yes, they've been extremely supportive. I've received letters, emails, tweets, and even flowers."

"It seems the threat of danger isn't keeping your fans away, as ticket and music sales spiked after the incident."

"Did they? I haven't heard any updated numbers from my agent yet, but I'm appreciative of everyone's support."

"No plans to cancel any shows due to the attack?"

"The shows will go on." He turned and looked directly at the reporter. "The perpetrator will be caught."

Mica knocked on Claire's door before nudging it open. The small office contained three large computer monitors overcrowding a desk under a ceiling of small, glowing LED lights. Mica wondered on many occasions if this constituted a fire hazard.

Claire sat on a yoga ball while wearing ear pods, bobbing her head to music, and typing on her computer. Her purple locks swayed.

When she noticed Mica, Claire took out her ear buds and turned toward her. "Hey, update time?"

"Yeah, what've you got?" Mica asked.

Claire pulled up a spreadsheet and enlarged it to fill her center screen. "I have columns of people within Ethan's sphere of influence separated: family, close friends, friends, social media friends, fans, coworkers, and enemies."

"Enemies? Tell me about this column."

"These are anyone who's ever sent him hate mail or posted hate comments on social media. Honestly, when I run financial backgrounds on these people, no one appears to have the financial fluency to hire a sniper."

"That's why they're mostly grayed-out?" Mica asked.

"Correct."

"Tell me about the other colors."

"Yellows might have motive, meaning I've found evidence of conflict with Ethan. People in blue have the financial capacity to hire a hit."

"And yellow and blue make green," Mica deduced.

"Yup, green is motive and money."

Mica scrutinized the screen. "Not many. Looks like the ex-wife qualifies."

"Money, but weak motive. You could argue Tamika has motive by virtue of being the ex-wife, but Billy says she and Ethan are amicable, according to Billy's interview of him."

"Her only red flag is being the ex-wife?"

"That and a hefty insurance claim," Claire said.

"Ah. Money. Is there anything in her financial profile to suggest she needs a lump sum?"

"No. She makes good money as a dermatologist, is financially responsible, and gets child support from Ethan, which she puts away in savings. He pays on time."

"Okay. We're off to a good start. Keep digging. Send me your report on all the yellows, blues, and greens, and I'll comb through them."

"You got it."

"How's Billy doing?"

Claire stretched on her ball. "Actually, really good. She's straightforward and analytical. I'm hoping we help her crack the case. I think it will give her the confidence boost she needs to take more of a lead role on future cases."

BILLY FOLLOWED Ethan into the rehearsal room to meet his band. He'd had Alice rent a small soundproof conference room at the hotel for practice space.

"Here's the gang. Gang, this is Billy." Ethan said as he pointed, "Dan is lead guitar."

Dan gave a two-finger salute as he tuned his instrument. "Howdy."

He had a thin build and graying hair with a matching mustache. His look combined with his casual greeting had her likening him to Sam Elliot, the actor. He wore jeans and a Guns-n-Roses T-shirt.

"This is Edgar. He's on bass," Ethan said.

Edgar was adjusting his amp, and Billy took in the sight of the broad-shouldered black man folded over, fine-tuning a piece of equipment, and dressed in brown corduroy overalls. He grunted his greeting.

"He's not much for words. You get used to it," Ethan added. "And this is Niko. Drummer and new guy."

Niko tossed his hands up in the air, which shook the mangy brown locks running over his face. "Dude, I've been with the band for fifteen months now. You're still introducing me as *the new guy*."

Niko was the youngest looking—and sounding—of the group. He sat behind his drum set, tapping his foot on the floor and looking as if he was waiting on the others. His blue jeans consisted of more holes than material, and his T-shirt read, "Save the Whales."

"Why a new drummer?" Billy asked.

Dan crinkled his nose. "We had to get rid of the last one, but we don't talk about him."

Edgar grunted something that sounded maybe like a "nope." It could have been any one syllable word really, but it definitely sounded negative whereas his noise of greeting to Billy had been more cordial.

Niko shrugged as if nobody had told him the story of the last drummer either.

Billy needed the details of that story. It could be a motive for murder.

. . .

AFTER INTRODUCTIONS, Ethan watched Billy leave.

Standing close to her, he'd been able to smell the fresh, clean, floral scent of her, like gardenias. He'd smelled it on the elevator as well. She wore the same suit she always wore, but he couldn't help picture her in the tank top and shorts he'd seen the other night. He liked that look even more than the black dress.

He knew his interest in her would pass. The fleeting attraction was simply the product of not having dated in a while. Loneliness created urges he wouldn't otherwise have—and for his bodyguard, no less. Also contributing was their constant proximity; except he worked closely with other women and never considered becoming romantically involved with them.

Well, he'd have to resign himself to simply enjoy Billy's conversation and company while riding out his attraction until it faded.

Ethan picked up his guitar, ready for rehearsal, and said sarcastically, "Thanks, guys. Real warm welcome."

"We were polite," Niko protested, flipping hair out of his eyes.

Edgar grunted in agreement.

Dan arched an eyebrow. "She's your bodyguard, right? Not your girlfriend. What'd you want us to say?"

"I don't know. Something friendly."

"She's cute," Niko added. "Is she single?"

"She's off-limits," Ethan said with surprising haste.

Dan's other eyebrow raised to level with the first.

"Not like that," Ethan countered. "She's my body-guard. Nobody dates any of my bodyguards."

Edgar grunted.

Ethan frowned at the bass guitarist. "Whose side are you on?"

"Easy, dude," Niko tapped his drumsticks together. "Off-limits. We understand." He'd spoken the last two words as if Ethan had marked his territory.

"What's her story, anyway?" Dan asked.

"Marine. She's been in private security a while now."

Dan whistled. "So, she's a badass. Despite her cuteness, she does carry that I-can-kick-your-ass-seven-ways-to-Sunday look about her."

"Another good reason for her to be off-limits," Ethan said. "I don't need any of you showing up with broken fingers before a concert."

Edgar grunted his agreement as he sat up and picked up his guitar.

"She'd take a bullet for you?" Niko asked.

Ethan looked down at his strings and lowered his voice. "Yeah, that's her job. And Barry's, and Pope's, and Claude's and the lot. But it's not going to come that." He almost added that Billy and her team were going to find the shooter before he stopped himself. He wasn't supposed to tell anyone Rider SI's "other" role on his protection detail.

His band members silently watched him as he strummed his guitar, not making eye contact.

"Can we practice now?" Ethan snapped.

"Sure thing, boss," Dan said.

BILLY CIRCLED the perimeter at the cafe on 7th Street where Ethan and Meg were inside having a late lunch with the owner of a video gaming company. The area was too crowded for Billy's comfort, but at least they'd agreed to eat indoors instead of on the street.

Billy pulled out her buzzing phone. Blocked caller. "Hello?"

"How are you, Billy?" Her old boss Maxine's gravelly voice emitted from the device.

Billy smiled at the familiar sound. "Damn good to hear from you. How's retirement?" She wouldn't use names or speak of Maxine's retirement home in Antigua since the former CEO of Rider SI had enemies and phone calls could be compromised.

"Life is good," Maxine answered, then added, "Your first investigative role."

"Mica told you?"

"She likes to bounce ideas off me. I thought her assigning you a new role was a good idea."

"I was concerned at first about doing a good job. I still am a bit. But I'm looking forward to it." So far, she'd met Ethan's assistant, agent, and band. With each day of her investigation—each encounter with a member of Ethan's inner-circle—she would learn more and unwrap the layers around him to uncover the source of danger.

"Keep your eyes and ears open. You'll do great. Besides, it's a team effort."

Billy grinned to herself as she recalled her *Charlie's*

Angels comparison. Except, she also had to guard Ethan which limited how much investigating she could do.

Sirens sounded and Billy snapped her gaze toward the street. A police car passed the restaurant on its way to some other destination.

"That's all I got," Maxine said. "You take care."

"Thanks."

Maxine clicked off.

Billy shook her head in amusement. A pep talk from Maxine Rider. Billy had to admit it felt good to hear the older woman's voice. Her spirits lifted as she contemplated how Maxine had both taken the time to call and believed she would do a good job.

If her old boss only knew Billy had been having inappropriately romantic thoughts about the man she was hired to protect.

6

———

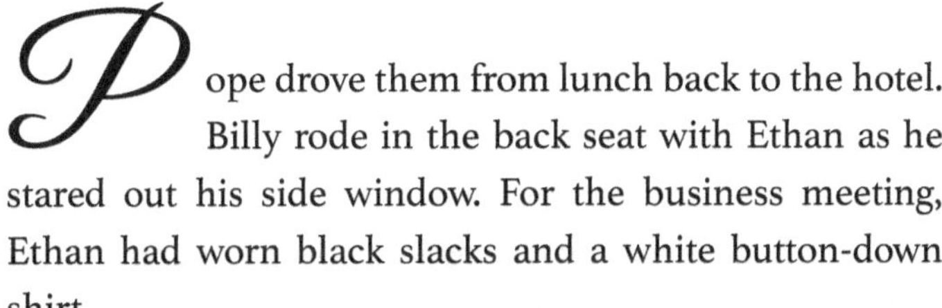

Pope drove them from lunch back to the hotel. Billy rode in the back seat with Ethan as he stared out his side window. For the business meeting, Ethan had worn black slacks and a white button-down shirt.

The car was silent. Billy was accustomed to silence, even comfortable with it. She didn't feel the need to pollute the air with small talk, which wasn't her role here anyway.

But she did wonder what Ethan was thinking about—the interview, the gaming company, his next performance, his next hit song? She didn't usually wonder what her clients were thinking. Why now? Why Ethan? Perhaps it was normal to have these thoughts when one was getting to know a client through careful investigation.

"So, Billy Jean, you know all about my life. What's your story?"

She'd fielded this question many times from clients. Most people were just being polite or filling what they perceived to be an uncomfortable silence. Most had neither the interest nor the time for her full story.

"I grew up in West Virginia. Joined the Marines at eighteen and did ten years of service. I earned my degree through AMU, the military college, and have been on the Rider team ever since." Billy congratulated herself on a flawless performance of her well-rehearsed speech.

"West Virginia. Coal-mining territory."

"My dad was a coal miner." She'd hated it. Hated the smell—the stench mixed with cigarette smoke and a nightcap of whiskey. She'd go to school smelling like a stale cigarette marinated in a lump of coal.

"You don't have an accent."

"Thank you." She'd worked hard to wash away any resemblance of the hillbilly accent her father and brothers had. She was nothing like the mean-spirited lot of them. Hugh, her congenial younger brother, was the exception.

Ethan smiled. "That bad, huh?"

"I grew up with two older brothers—two bullies just as mean as my father." She glanced at Ethan whose strong green eyes coaxed words from her. "They did everything from stealing my ballet slippers to cutting my hair to slipping hot sauce into my soup."

Childhood had been a lesson in survival. And her mother had been no help. Billy learned early on that complaining or tattling only earned her a lecture about gratitude, which was almost as intolerable as the bullying she'd endured.

What did she have to be upset about, her mother would ask. Billy had three meals and a roof over her head —that was more than people in India had. *And eat your lima beans, girl. Don't you know there are starving children in Ethiopia?* Could her mother have even pointed out Ethiopia on a map?

"Rough crowd. Are they the reason you joined the military so young?" Ethan asked.

"It was my way out of West Virginia, away from the mines, and to see the world." She'd met Maxine Rider in the Marines and the two of them had instantly connected through their coal-mining-family background.

"Maybe those brothers toughened you up in preparation for the Marines."

She should have responded with "maybe"—a noncommittal single word to signal the end of the conversation. Instead, Billy divulged, "They crushed every interest I ever had—music, ballet, dance. There was nothing left but to run away. The only way to run away when you don't have money is to enlist. I don't regret it. My military experience paved the way for me to earn the job I have today."

He looked at her with soft green eyes through dark lashes. "How many lives have you saved?"

She considered the question. "I don't know exactly. Sometimes you don't know which decision in the heat of the moment saved a life and which didn't matter. I've never lost a client."

"Ever been shot?"

When Pope pulled up to the curb, Billy and Ethan exited the car and walked inside the hotel. On the elevator, they were alone. Memories of their bodies pressed together had heat radiating through her core. Would she ever be able to ride an elevator without thinking of him?

She pushed the images aside and returned to their conversation. "Shot at, but never shot."

"Does it get easier?"

She knew he was asking more about himself this time.

Congenial, she reminded herself, though she was finding Ethan easy to converse with.

"It gets *different.* Each time, I have more experience and training time so my emotional reaction is more controlled." When he frowned, she added, "That doesn't mean I don't still shake after an attack or replay events in my mind about which bullet was closer."

When the elevator doors opened, Billy pursed her lips. She needed to stop opening up to this man before he started to wonder about her emotional stability.

"Thanks for the encouragement." The sincerity in Ethan's voice gave her an unexpected jolt of satisfaction.

For a moment, she feared he was considering hugging her, but they kept walking down the hall until they reached Claude outside Ethan's hotel room.

ETHAN GREETED CLAUDE with a pat on the shoulder.

"Room's secure," Claude told Billy. He turned to Ethan. "You have company."

Giddy joy instantly spread through Ethan. "Alyssa?"

"Yes, sir."

Ethan burst into the room, his arms wide.

Alyssa—all four feet or her—leapt into her father's arms. "Daddy!"

Alyssa giggled as he swung her in a circle and her gorgeous head of tight curls flowed out in all directions like a mane. Her dark-caramel skin was warm and soft to his touch.

"I missed you!" Ethan cried. "Maybe we can go out for ice cream." He paused, then looked toward Billy for confirmation.

Billy shot him a look as she fixed herself a glass of water.

"Or order it in," he amended.

"Who's your friend?" His small, but opinionated, eight-year-old in a cute purple dress gave Billy a disapproving once-over.

He noted Alyssa's suspicious tone at the presence of a woman in her father's hotel room. Billy didn't look offended. He suppressed an amused smile.

"This," he began, sitting on the couch and pulling his daughter into his lap, "is my new bodyguard." He boasted as if Billy was a vintage guitar he'd just purchased, but the sight of her barely suppressed grin gave him a small thrill.

Alyssa's eyes went wide in astonishment as her mouth turned from a frown to a smile. "Whoa. No way. You got a *girl* bodyguard? That's so cool."

Unseen by his daughter, Ethan winked at Billy. The normally impassive woman revealed a moment of uncharacteristic flushing. Was her discomfort from the wink or the overall excess attention? Ethan wasn't sure.

Alyssa wriggled out of his grasp and walked over to Billy. "I'm Alyssa. Alyssa Hardy. I use my mom's remarried name so people can't easily find me because my dad is popular. One day, when I'm a stage performer, I'll be Alyssa Storm."

"I'm Billy." She looked as though she was unsure if she should shake hands or wave. She opted for a causal fist-bump.

Ethan took it as a sign that Billy probably liked kids, she just didn't have much experience around them.

"Billy *Jean*," Ethan corrected, wriggling his eyebrows at Alyssa as he picked up his guitar.

"Really? That's amazeballs." Alyssa turned back to him with a wide smile.

Amazeballs? Billy mouthed to Ethan.

He grinned and began strumming his strings to the Michael Jackson song. Alyssa, on cue, began singing "Billie Jean."

Then Ethan took over the chorus, changing the lyrics:

> *"Billy Jean is not my friend*
> *She's just a guard to keep me out of the sun*
> *She says I can't have fun*
> *I can't dance on the ground spin around."*

Alyssa broke into rhythmic dancing, and the music duo finally had Billy laughing.

When they stopped their playfulness, Billy cleared

her throat. "You know she's not a good person in that song."

Ethan set the guitar down. "What do you think, Alyssa, is our Billy Jean a beauty queen? I was thinking Charlize Theron."

He thought of the actress's tough look in *The Italian Job* and *Atomic Blonde,* though Alyssa hadn't seen those movies.

"Yes! Cool under pressure and put together like her role in *Hancock* with Will Smith. Go like this," Alyssa told Billy as she tilted her head to one side and gave a movie star smile.

"No." Billy sipped her water.

"See," Ethan said, loving the way he and his daughter made Billy squirm beneath the surface even as she tried not to betray her mixed discomfort and enjoyment of their banter, "not my friend. Billy Jean warned me."

Alyssa laughed. "She's still cool. I guess she's a bodyguard, so she's not supposed to have fun." She turned her attention back to Billy. "Have you ever been shot?"

Billy blinked at Ethan, who chuckled. "Like father—like daughter."

"Do you carry a gun?" the girl asked.

"Yes."

"Can I see it?"

"No."

BILLY WALKED TOWARD THE DOOR, shaking her head at Alyssa's question, yet unable to completely suppress a smile. If she hung out with the pair of them much longer, she might just start to have fun.

Before she could open the door to leave and let them enjoy their evening together, two brisk knocks were followed by a woman entering. She wore a cream-colored dress that stopped just above her knees, revealing slender, ebony legs. Her black hair was long and straight, accentuating her strong cheekbones.

"Dr. Hardy." Billy stopped and stiffened, military style.

"Mom, this is Dad's new bodyguard! He hired a *girl*." Alyssa bounced on her toes.

"So, I see." She handed off a large paper bag of food to Ethan. "I'm Tamika." She extended a hand to Billy and they shook. "I've been telling Ethan he needs *real* bodyguards, not a handful of overweight high school buddies. What's your background?"

"Marines followed by protection for the past seven years."

"Really, you don't look old enough for all of that."

"I'm thirty-five." Billy was not a woman who cared about hiding her age.

"Fascinating, I wouldn't have guessed I was only a few years older than you. You have excellent skin condition."

"I'll take that as a complement, coming from a dermatologist." What else could she say? Billy didn't want to talk about exfoliating products with another woman. That was way out of her comfort zone.

At a loss for conversation, she was ready to go back to being a portrait on the wall. Except, she was also supposed to be investigating. No way she could ask

Tamika questions about enemies and who might take a shot at Ethan in front of Alyssa, though. She'd have to wait for another opportunity.

A tall black man with bright eyes followed behind Tamika, carrying a second bag of food.

"This is my husband, Moody," Tamika said.

"Pleasure." He shook with his free hand.

Alyssa gave each of them a hug before Ethan and Moody began unloading the bag of take out from P.F. Chang's.

"I was just leaving. Enjoy your family dinner," Billy said.

"Oh, but you're fresh company," Tamika said with a mischievous twinkle in her eye. "Your presence will make for new conversation topics. Please, stay."

If Ethan was a third wheel (fourth wheel?) here, that would make Billy—what?—the spare tire? No thanks. She looked to Ethan for support, since he could dismiss her.

He gave a sly grin. "Usually Claude joins us. It'll be a nice change of pace to have you."

Billy ground her teeth together. She didn't need any more awkward moments. She pulled open the hotel room door. "Claude, I've been requested to stay for dinner. You can take the rest of the night off."

"But P.F. Chang's is my favorite," he protested. At her look, he slunk away.

Billy closed the door and swung the fin lock secure. She sat at the table covered in take-out boxes, with Ethan on one side and Moody on the other. Alyssa sat between Ethan and Tamika. Billy tried to recall the last time she'd had a group meal with people other than the Rider team. She couldn't. She'd been to many galas and functions, always on duty, guarding the people at the table but not seated there herself.

She took a conservative portion of food and braced herself to be social. She needed to use the opportunity to listen and learn. Investigative work.

"Ethan, how is the gaming negotiation going?" Moody asked.

Ethan swallowed a bite of his beef with broccoli. "So far, so good."

Tamika looked at Billy. "Ethan won't brag because he's not like that, but this contract is huge. A virtual reality dance game is considering his songs as one of their party packs."

Ethan nodded. "If I win the contract, I get a percentage every time someone downloads my music pack to play on the game."

"I've played the game," Alyssa said. "It's way cool. I'm the one who told Dad he should do it. Then he told Meg, and she's been trying to seal the deal."

"That's exciting," Billy agreed, genuinely happy for him. "I'm not surprised, though, your dad has awesome songs."

"You've listened to my songs?" Ethan blinked at her.

Billy pushed rice around on her plate. "Sure. Me and ten million other Americans." She knew his stats from Claire's data. Billy was certainly not going to confess that she downloaded one of his albums onto her phone after their elevator introduction.

His voice was, well, *amazeballs*. Sexy, gritty, hard, soft, hopeful, sorrowful—he had the full range of emotions on display in the songs on his albums.

"Billy, what do you do when you're not guarding people?" Moody asked.

"I like boxing—for exercise. Just on a bag, not against anyone." She chewed a bite of sweet pork and swallowed.

"Billy the boxer," Alyssa said, making it sound far more glamorous than Billy knew it was.

"Anything else?" Moody asked.

"I don't get a lot of downtime. But my last assignment on the tennis tour enabled me to visit places I'd never been to. I made a hobby of sightseeing and reading the history of the cities we traveled through."

"Like where?" Alyssa asked.

"Like gorgeous churches built hundreds of years ago and still standing."

"Whoa. Have you seen Notre-Dame?"

"I did, before the fire damaged it. And this other neat church in Alsace. They couldn't finish the second tower because it would collapse the entire structure."

Alyssa frowned. "Well, that's just poor planning."

Everyone laughed.

"Mom and Moody and I are going to Paris next year," Alyssa said.

Billy glanced at Ethan who appeared unperturbed at this vacation announcement that didn't include him.

"You'll have a great time," Billy told Alyssa. "I'm sure you'll see the usual attractions—and don't forget the chocolate tour. But I also recommend *Musée de l'Armée*. There are a ton of military weapons. And Napoleon's tomb sits in *Église Du Dôme* there."

"Do you speak French?"

"Je parle un peu de François. A little."

Alyssa bounced excitedly in her seat. "Moody has never traveled outside of the US."

"What do you do for work?" Billy asked him. She knew the answer, but it was her turn to ask a question in the congenial rally of casual conversation.

"I'm a lawyer. Mostly estate planning and trusts. Tamika and I met when she came to my office for a consultation. As far as I'm concerned, it was love at first sight." He reached and squeezed her hand.

Ethan smiled, as though genuinely happy for both of them. Billy was baffled. She couldn't picture her parents happy at the dinner table much less *divorced* and happy.

Alyssa made playful gagging noises.

"What about you, Billy?" Tamika asked.

"Me?"

"Married? Dating? Single?"

Around the table, all eyes fell on her. She took a sip of water. For a moment, she wished she was back overseas, hunting insurgents. She was trained for fighting, not group interrogations about her love life—or lack of one. But she'd never go back into the military; for all the valuable training she learned and friendships she'd forged, there had been too much loss and too much frustration at bureaucratic red tape.

"Single."

"Always single?" Tamika probed, her tone friendly.

Billy rolled her shoulders. "Never married. I've dated off and on, but my lifestyle isn't conducive to long-term relationships. I travel a lot with the job."

"I'm sure Mr. Right is out there," Moody said.

Billy nodded. Maybe he was. Her lifestyle excuse was wearing thin over time, especially as other Rider team members found matches and made relationships work. Mason had married tennis star Aurora Meridian and organized his rotation detail around another tennis player in order to remain near Aurora on tour. Now that they had a child, he kept his work stateside.

Ryan had married a physician who moved to live with him in Atlanta, where Rider SI maintained their base of operation. He and his wife, Jenna, coordinated their schedules so their time off coincided.

Mica's relationship also gave Billy a beacon of hope. Although Mica didn't travel much for work now that she ran Rider SI, she was a strong, independent woman, like Billy. Mica was a savvy street fighter with the scars to prove it. And yet, she'd found her equal in a man not intimidated by her physical and mental strength. In fact, David seemed enamored of Mica's many talents. Talents, in Billy's experience, that had men excusing themselves early in her relationships.

If all of these people with careers similar to her own had found their match, maybe she could, too.

7

Despite the brisk April breeze in Fort Dupont Park, Ethan's bodyguards bent over, gasping for air. Although they wore shorts and T-shirts for the exercise, they were all sweating after Billy's drills.

Billy surveyed her work with pride. She'd taken the five of them—Pope, Claude, JJ, Scott, and Harry—to the park for training. Barry and Wayne stayed back at the hotel with Ethan, who was practicing with his band.

Barry had been coaching the men on tactical defense, but Billy wanted a day of her own hands-on training. The session would also allow her to become better acquainted with the bodyguards and further solidify whether they belonged in the "suspect" or "not-a-suspect" column of her investigation.

She analyzed each of their defensive strengths while

they trained. Using a football to represent Ethan, they performed different scenarios. Pope had good reflexes, but he needed more sparring practice; his motions weren't deliberate enough in close quarters. Claude was slow, but his size made him good for moving the football a few yards against a crowd. JJ was small and fast; he could take an inexperienced opponent in a one-on-one fight, which made him ideal for dealing with the threat while Claude got the football to safety. Scott and Harry were willing to get their hands dirty and weren't afraid of a scuffle, but they needed some serious cardio in their training.

Billy took the men through their paces and a dozen different scenarios. What if Ethan was attacked on stage? Rogue fan versus armed assailant. What if Ethan was attacked backstage? What if they were en-route to the car? What if he was shopping with Alyssa at the mall (JJ was the shortest, so he played Alyssa)? What if Ethan was at a crowded restaurant on a date?

"Ethan, date?" Pope scoffed, catching his breath.

"He's a celebrity, of course he goes on dates," Billy said. She looked around at the blank stares from the men. "When was the last time he went on a date?"

Claude rubbed his head, Pope his chin, and the other men shrugged.

"Back in the day, under the influence, he slept around. Not sure you'd call them dates," Pope said. When Harry smacked him in the arm, he added, defensively, "What? It's not a secret. Hell, he wrote it in his memoir."

"He has a memoir?" Why didn't she know this?

"Yeah. So, anyway, he's been low-key since Alyssa was born and hasn't dated much."

Claude added, "The tabloids always manage to make it look like Ethan does. Some woman cozies up to him for a picture and suddenly wedding bells are ringing in the near future."

"That's the way the world is when you're an eligible bachelor," JJ said.

"Are you saying he hasn't dated anyone since his divorce and Alyssa's birth?" Billy asked.

Harry snapped his fingers. "There was that one broad … Sue or Susie something."

"Suzanne," Pope said.

"Yeah, Suzanne. But she didn't like it when she had to share time with Alyssa, and you know Ethan only gets a few days here and there with his daughter when he's on the road."

Claude nodded grimly. "Suzanne had to go."

"She kind of looked down on us, too," Pope added. "As if we were a bunch of morons."

Suzanne. Billy made a mental note to have Claire run a background check and see if Suzanne left with any hard feelings that would have manifested in an attempted assassination later.

"I don't see morons," Billy said. "I see loyal men who want to keep their friend safe. But Ethan wants you all to stay safe as well. Tell me about your body protection."

"Kevlar's too hot," Claude said almost immediately.

"It's also bulky," Pope added. "And fans get scared when security starts looking like soldiers going into battle."

Billy pulled a leg behind her and stretched. "Okay. Bullet-resistant clothing then. There are long-sleeve jackets for cold weather and sleeveless for hot weather, which you can wear a button-down shirt over. At my company, we're each fitted with a bullet-resistant suit."

The process was arduous—getting a background check and personal sizing for a suit—but such was the price of safety.

"The suit you wear around Ethan is bulletproof?" JJ asked.

"Bullet-resistant. Nothing is bulletproof. Except, maybe a tank. But the suit has an NIJ Level IIa rating."

"Speak English," JJ said.

"National Institute of Justice Level IIa rating means it can protect you from a .38, .40, and .45 caliber gun as well as a 9mm, and even some .357 Magnum rounds. And by protect, I mean you won't die. You're still going to suffer. For a higher-powered gun—say .44 Magnum—you need a IIIA."

"How much does your suit cost?" Claude asked.

"Eight thousand."

Pope let out a low whistle.

"The point is that each of you needs bullet-resistant clothing, and Ethan wouldn't hesitate to buy something that might save your life."

AFTER THE TRAINING, Billy showered and changed back into her suit. She entered in the guest office suite of the hotel and went to work.

The room had several desks set up with Wi-Fi where people could connect their laptops in a quiet space and work. Ethan was rehearsing in a different part of the hotel now under the supervision of Barry and Claude.

When Billy heard footsteps approaching, she quickly removed the USB from the computer, pocketed it, and set the laptop back to screensaver mode. She'd already planted spyware on Meg's laptop, and now Alice's was complete.

As the door swung open, Billy leaned back and put her boots up on the desk.

Alice entered and started. "Oh. What are doing here?"

"Waiting on you." The statement was partially true. In addition to installing the spyware for Claire to access Alice's computer, Billy wanted to talk with Ethan's assistant one-on-one.

Alice set her coffee and purse down beside her laptop at a different desk. She wore a dress with bold sunflowers, practical pumps, and her brown hair loose to her shoulders.

"Thank you for taking the time to find a new venue for the autograph event," Billy said.

"Sure. We have to keep Ethan safe. If anything ever happened to him ..." her voice trailed.

Billy knew Alice hadn't been there the night of the shooting, but footage had played on the news often enough she'd probably seen it. Watching her boss's brush with mortality must have rattled her.

"Scary stuff." Billy tried to offer empathy.

Alice took a shaky breath without making eye contact.

"Yeah." She took a prescription bottle from her purse, popped a pill, and swallowed it down with coffee.

The motion was so rehearsed that Billy suspected Alice didn't even realize she'd done it front of her. She sat quietly, watching the assistant.

"Oh." Alice smiled nervously. "I have a heart condition."

Billy nodded, though she knew it wasn't a heart condition. According to Claire, Alice took benzodiazepines for anxiety. Being medicated for a disorder wasn't a crime and was certainly understandable in a high-stress job, working for a celebrity and taking orders from someone like Meg.

But the absentmindedness with which Alice took her sedatives suggested they may have become a problem for her. The woman hadn't tried any other relaxation techniques first before self-medicating, and those pills could represent an addiction. Addicts posed a security threat.

"Meg doesn't like me," Billy said. She couldn't care less about Meg's opinion of her, but the topic seemed like a good segue to get Alice's opinion of the woman.

Alice snorted and swiveled in her chair to look at Billy. "Meg doesn't like anyone."

"She likes Ethan."

"She likes Ethan's money," Alice corrected.

"Have they ever been romantically involved?" Billy plucked a pen off the desk and twirled it in her fingers, trying to appear casual—which was hard to pull off wearing a bullet-resistant suit, combat boots, a holstered 9mm, and a knife hidden in her boot.

She suspected she wasn't very convincing, but Alice's medicine seemed to kick in and she relaxed.

"God, no. Meg is so not his type. He likes the girl-next-door look."

Billy cocked her head to one side as she assessed Alice's look—definitely girl next door. She always wore dresses and fixed her hair conservatively. But the woman was twelve years younger than Ethan.

Claire hadn't found evidence of the two of them involved, and Ethan gave no indication of such. Billy couldn't think of a way to ask Alice without sounding like she was romantically interested in him or investigating his personal life.

Billy set down the pen and stood. "I'll let you get back to work."

"Keep Ethan safe."

"I intend to."

TWO DAYS LATER, Billy waited in Ethan's hotel room. He stood near the window, rubbing the callouses on his hands together. He'd asked her to his room but hadn't yet told her the purpose of his summons. The light from the window shone on one side of his face. He wore jeans and a T-shirt. His brow furrowed and relaxed, furrowed and relaxed.

"I've gone over the schematics of The Anthem," she said. Ethan's next concert was tomorrow night, so it wasn't difficult to deduce the source of his worry. She added,

"We've been working with your team. They're more prepared now. We'll get you in and out safely."

Over the last two days, she had read part of his memoir. He'd written about nervousness before shows; one of the reasons he'd liked drinking was to take the edge off. That was no longer an option. Today, however, she suspected his concern was because of what danger might surface rather than a fear of sufficient crowd-pleasing.

She'd never been so enthralled with a client until Ethan. She tried to tell herself her interest had nothing to do with the attraction she felt for him, which was merely the product of their close proximity on the elevator.

The simple recollection of him so close to her with his fingertips pressed into her hips weakened her knees. But such a physiological response didn't mean she'd act on it. She was here to do a job. Just as she'd been trained in the Marines to react differently to fear from most people, so too could she act differently to attraction.

After the elevator incident, she'd escorted Ethan safely out of the hotel. She had transferred care of him to Barry, and left to dry herself from the rainwater. They'd never discussed what had happened on the elevator. And she would never mention it—even if she perhaps fantasized about events unfolding differently with just the two of them in that confined space.

Ethan continued to stare out the window.

Billy took a step closer. "I'll be there every step of the way. You and your crew are going to be fine."

He looked at her with blazing green eyes. "Thank you. But I feel like a coward for worrying so much."

She shook her head. "Do you remember the scene in your memoir when you were in bar fight and felt fearless?"

"You read my memoir?"

"Partially, but I'll finish it. Anyway, what did you have to fear back then? It was you against one man, face-to-face. A hitman is a different animal. And you're a different person now. You have Alyssa to think about, and your band and bodyguards. During your *Rolling Stone* interview, the first people you mentioned being worried about after the sniper shot was everybody else. If I'm right, your current fear is about putting everyone around you in danger."

He ran a hand through his hair. "Yeah, you're right."

"Worrying about the safety of others makes you a decent human being—not a coward. If it's any consolation, an assassin who shoots the wrong person tarnishes his or her reputation. So far, you're the only one targeted, and I'm not going to let anything happen to you."

"Weirdly, that is some consolation." A slight grin lifted one corner of his mouth. "You have some unusual methods of giving reassurance in your conversations."

She chuckled. "So I've been told."

He moved toward her, slowly but deliberately. Stopping close but without touching her, he said, "Billy Jean, I want—"

A knock sounded at the door, followed by someone entering.

Billy slid a large step back from Ethan.

"Oh," Alice stepped inside, "I didn't mean to interrupt."

Ethan tucked his hands in his pockets. "You weren't. We were reviewing the security protocols for tomorrow's concert."

"Oh, okay. Um. Atlanta is next, and the hotel has to move your room, so you won't have the view you requested." She wrung her hands together.

"That's fine. You made sure they moved Billy and Barry near my room?"

"I'll take care of it."

As Alice and Ethan continued conversing, Billy slipped out of the room. She leaned back against the wall when the door shut, heart thumping in her chest to the beat of Ethan's rock song, "Yours Tonight:" *Begging you to stay / Break my heart when you pull away.*

8

On a late Friday night, Ethan's concert was coming to an end. Billy made her way to the stage exit. She had memorized the schematics of the sixty-million-dollar, fifty-seven-thousand-square-foot venue in DC. It had three floors and over a dozen exits. She knew them all. Importantly, back doors for immediate exits were plentiful and out of access for the general admission floor.

Metal detectors and bag inspection up front gave the security team some measure of reassurance. In addition to Ethan's team, onsite security included venue staff and local police officers.

She walked the halls, music blaring in the background, but she wasn't here to enjoy it. At the last half-hour mark, she checked in with each team member via their earpiece communication device. All good.

She walked beside the stage where Ethan was singing his final song, "Natural Love."

> *Talk is cheap*
> *Love is steep*
> *But your natural love*
> *my heart will keep.*

Ethan wore black pants and a purple silk V-neck shirt. Dan and Edgar stood several paces behind him, playing their guitars. Niko caressed his drums. A guest performer played on a grand piano. She noticed Ethan usually brought in a keyboardist or pianist and sometimes played it himself.

His voice was stunning, though she preferred listening to him practice in the absence of a noisy crowd. He could vacillate his tone between a working-man's vibe and high class with a range from sultry to sorrowful. His voice was smooth without an accent, not rugged like Bruce Springsteen but seductive like Michael Bublé or Dan Reynolds.

Emotion was deeply embedded in Ethan's tone, and he could make his audience feel heartache or loss, happiness or elation. Every word was sung with perfection. His rock 'n' roll was main-stream America mixed with a touch of hip-hop, blues, disco, and harder rock depending on the mood and content of the song.

From his memoir, Billy knew Ethan had learned guitar and piano growing up and played the clubs of the

California coast. He'd learned to play a wide range of music because musicians played what the fans desired if they wanted to keep playing.

Only once he'd proven his ability on stage by performing popular songs, had he earned the right to play songs of his own creation. The audience became receptive to something new once taste buds were first satisfied by familiar songs. As he developed and promoted his own music, he'd finally earned the recognition to open for other bands. Finally, and through the support of his agent and his band, Ethan had been offered his own record deal.

Billy understood this long, stepwise process was often the key to success. She'd only earned a spot on the Rider team because she first had military experience in the Marines. Now that she had seven years of experience in private security, she was taking the next step to investigation.

She looked out into the crowd—so many adoring fans. And 99.9 percent of them were harmless. But someone out there meant Ethan harm.

When the song finished and the lights dimmed, the audience cheered ecstatically. As the lights beamed brighter, Ethan waved, bowed, and pressed his hands together in gratitude. The clapping continued, and, one by one, he had the crowd praise each of his band members.

Billy waited for him at the bottom of the steps along with Claude. Pope was at the car. Barry was keeping the direct path to the backdoor open. The other men were stationed along points of Ethan's exit routes—the main route and the two contingency routes.

The concert wasn't the risky part, leaving the building was. A dozen things could go wrong during the exit. Much to Meg's dismay, Billy had ordered the cancellation and refund of all backstage passes. That eliminated at least some of the wild cards from dressing rooms and performer exits.

Ethan left the mic and guitar on stage and stepped lightly down the stairs, his face beaming.

Billy jolted slightly. Damn, he was a fine-looking specimen of a man.

Ethan gave Claude a sweaty bear hug before turning to Billy and hugging her, too. She stifled her surprise and took the hug right into an escort. They had to make one high-risk stop before she could get him safely into the car.

They passed JJ on the way up the stairs and entered the private suite, where Meg schmoozed with high-paying fans and investors. The decor in the suite probably cost more than Billy's salary—swiveling leather chairs, black upholstered wall coverings, and a marble wet bar. Everything looked posh, with a gold-and-black theme and bathed in soft ambient lighting.

Claude remained near the stairs as Billy watched the crowd for sudden movements. Ethan socialized, making his rounds throughout the room, talking to acquaintances and meeting new people. Meg stayed at his side and paraded him around like a show pony, but Ethan had a way of adding his own personal touch—asking about wives, husbands, kids, and recent travels. He thanked everyone for coming.

Billy marveled silently at his charisma. He made socializing—a task she found stressful and arduous—look effortless.

While Ethan was talking to a group of men and women, Meg walked over to Billy. "You see how he needs this, right? You see how important it is that he still spends time with fans?"

"I never argued the point, ma'am." Billy knew the southern-style address would grate on Meg's nerves. "I'm just the temporary hired help to keep him safe, and it's my job to present the best ways to do that."

AFTER AN HOUR OF SOCIALIZING, Ethan was ready to wind down for the night. Billy positioned herself back at his side. All night, she'd been watching him. She was his personal angel—just the sight of her had a calming effect on him.

There was a tiff between her and Meg, but Billy seemed to manage her without needing Ethan's help. He enjoyed the way Meg's haughtiness rolled off Billy like water off a duck's back. The tighter Meg wound herself, the calmer Billy became. Meg could be catty to other women, but she'd been instrumental to Ethan's fame. Because of those contributions, he tried to overlook some of her personality flaws.

Ethan said his goodbyes to his friends and acquaintances, and Billy led him through hallways and out the back door, with Claude bringing up the rear. Barry and Wayne had cleared the path to the car where Pope waited in the driver's seat.

When they climbed in the back and Claude closed the door, Ethan finally relaxed. Everything had unfolded as smoothly as Billy had promised.

"That was your first concert since New Jersey. You okay?" Billy asked.

"I'm okay." He nodded. He touched her hand and squeezed. "Thank you."

When she looked at him, he hoped she would see the gratitude in his eyes so she could feel it as much as hear it.

"Of course." She swallowed and turned to look out the window.

He grinned. She was unflappable during an entire protection detail and indifferent to Meg's squawking. But a touch and a look from him had her cheeks flushing and her body language torn between attraction and denial.

Even though he stared, she didn't turn back to face him. She also didn't let go of his hand.

"You should call Alyssa and let her know you're okay."

He smiled and kissed the back of Billy's hand before letting go and withdrawing his phone from his pocket.

Someday he hoped she would stare back at him like she had on the elevator.

AFTER A WEEK of observation and asking questions, Billy gained an understanding of the people cycling in and out of Ethan's circle. The band traveled in a van—with all of the performance equipment that wouldn't have been practical for plane rides. Ethan stayed in the bus, and the security team alternated riding in the bus and the Tahoe.

Alice flew ahead of the musicians and security to ensure room and venue reservations were properly in place.

Meg didn't travel with the band. She had other clients she managed. She usually flew in on a broom—er—plane to check on Ethan before the concert and stay until the after-party.

Alyssa visited one weekend a month. Her mother and stepfather only joined if Ethan was within driving distance of DC and they could make a family trip out of the excursion.

Ethan and the band had arrived in Atlanta yesterday, and today Ethan rehearsed at a music studio with a group of stage dancers.

When Billy took her lunch break, she stepped outside and returned a call to her younger brother. Hugh had called earlier and left a message for her to call him back.

"Hi, Billy." He sounded tired.

Was it the thought of talking to her or taking care of his three children that had him fatigued?

"Hugh, how are you?"

"I'm good. How are you?"

"Fine. How are the kids?"

"Everyone's good, Billy. How's your work? I glimpsed you on TV the other night. You're guarding that singer Ethan Storm, right?"

"Yeah." She was guarding him, invading his privacy,

investigating his friends, and ogling his body. She cleared her throat. "Do you like his music?" Could she get Hugh and his family tickets to a concert? She'd never considered getting tickets to a client's events, but Ethan was congenial and family-oriented; he might agree.

"Of course. Who doesn't like his music?"

Who doesn't like him? It was hard to imagine anyone taking a shot at him. So far, she and the Rider team had uncovered no one they could pin a hired hit on.

She remembered the feel of that brief, zealous hug after his performance. He smelled like leather, oak, and sweat—exactly how she would expect him to smell after a night of passion under the sheets. And if his lips felt that good on her hand, imagine if...

Get a grip, Billy.

"Look," Hugh's tone dipped low, "Mom told me you stopped by the house."

Billy's fervor from thinking of Ethan instantly cooled. "Yeah? She tell you the warm welcome I got, or how she didn't come visit me at my motel room later?"

Hugh sighed. "Nobody fights anymore except during or after your visits," he said meekly.

Swell, he was going to lay the blame on her. "I guess it's a good thing I don't visit very often. Everyone can conveniently forget the past and never have to feel an ounce of remorse. Besides, Ed can't fight anyone with the shape he's in, and Mac's too slow to catch a turtle."

"Dad's dying."

Billy ran a hand through her hair. Suddenly, she wished she were at the boxing gym instead of on the job. "Yeah, I could see that." Even if she hadn't visited, she knew from the medical bills she paid that her father's condition was deteriorating.

"So, maybe you should be reconciling rather than picking fights," Hugh suggested.

Be grateful, Billy. Wasn't that the message she'd always received? Don't complain. Like she didn't have a right to her own feelings. She wasn't allowed to feel angry or hurt at the injustice of it all.

"Our chance at reconciliation disappeared the day I enlisted." She hadn't come home until her ten years was up. By that time, her father had started showing the early stages of dementia. She'd come home battle-hardened and ready to face her fears only to find a shadow of the demon she'd once known. So, she'd unleashed pent-up anger at Mac and Art.

Now who is the bully, Billy?

To this day, the words still knifed her.

"I'll keep my distance," she said to Hugh on the phone. "Any other messages you wanted to deliver?"

"Billy," Hugh's pleading tone suggested she was somehow being unmanageable or overreacting. Another sigh. "You can visit *me* any time."

"Thanks." She clicked off the phone. She visited Hugh once a year, enough to see her nieces and nephews as they grew up and have an awkward conversation with her younger brother as they tried to avoid talking about the past.

Billy pocketed her phone and walked back inside the studio. She watched Ethan practice his choreographed dance to "Burning Flame."

Your love is a wonder
Your lips whisper my name
Bodies close, feel the raging thunder
Light my burning flame
My body's yours to plunder

Flanked by a dozen dancers, he moved with ease around them—hips swaying and shoes sliding on the smooth surface as he sang.

The man had moves.

She'd be blind not to notice. She glanced around the studio and observed other women watching Ethan. She was sure their mouths watered as they stared in various forms of the same trance. Meg and Alice were among them.

Billy glanced back at the dancers swirling around the singer and grinned as she recalled the disagreement she'd overheard. Meg had expressed displeasure with the dancers' outfits—they were too conservative in her opinion. People wanted to see more cleavage and thigh real estate. Ethan had plainly stated he had a daughter and wouldn't use women as sex symbols. He'd ended the conversation even as Meg's expression had conveyed her disapproval.

Their disagreement had been heated, but nothing of their interaction suggested motive for murder. Meg wanted sexier because sex sells, and Ethan had put his foot down.

Just one more reason personal thoughts of him were getting harder to shake.

9

———

After the rehearsal, Ethan was out of costume and back in his preferred jeans and cotton shirt. He took a silent ride in the Tahoe back to the hotel. Outside, a bright spring sun shone down on the Atlanta freeway.

Ethan followed Billy to his hotel room with Barry beside to him, while Pope and Claude parked the car. Billy swiped the key card and entered first in order to perform Ethan's room inspection. Ethan dutifully waited by the entrance.

"Billy Jean, won't you stay a moment?" Ethan asked when she was done with her security sweep.

She remained in his hotel room after Barry left.

"Please, have a seat." He grabbed two cranberry-apple juices from the fridge and handed her one as she sat down. "We've only worked together about a week, but I can tell something is bothering you. It's not easy since you're very emotionally controlled. I hope I'm not over-stepping my bounds, pointing it out to you."

"Are you worried about your protection detail?" Billy asked.

She hadn't denied something bothered her which gave Ethan the satisfaction of knowing his detection skills were accurate. But what did that say about him? He was tuned into Billy's presence near him and all the subtleties of her body language.

"Not at all," he began. "I think your house could be burning down and you wouldn't let it affect your job. I just—" Hell, why had he brought it up? "I hope you have someone you can talk to. If not, I'm a pretty good listener."

She gave a forced smile. "I'm fine. Family always gets under your skin in a way no one else can. No one's house is burning down, I assure you." She stood with the unopened drink in her hand. "Was there anything else?"

He shook his head. She was on emotional lockdown tighter than Fort Knox. Was this defense mechanism learned in the military or from the family who got under her skin?

"We're going to be friends before all of this is over, Billy Jean," he called to her as she reached the door. "Mark my words."

At his playful tone, she glanced back at him. She looked like she had no idea how to respond.

He grinned. Good. She wasn't so unflappable that he couldn't throw her off balance. Perhaps that was the key to developing a friendship with her—unbalancing that careful emotional control.

He couldn't pinpoint why he wanted to be friends—maybe because he was friends with all of his bodyguards; maybe because she'd thrown down the gauntlet on day one, when she'd declared they would never be friends. Or maybe it was because he wanted to uncover the softer side of her. He suspected a passionate woman lay beneath all that tightly bottled self-control.

Billy hesitated at the door, turned, and sat back down. "In compliance with my promise to be intrusive and not a friend, we need to discuss your schedule."

He frowned. She seemed to revert to formal speech when his congenial nature threatened to make her open up to him. It was as though she was throwing up an invisible forcefield.

She continued, "I've reviewed the stops in each town where your concerts are being held. You've scheduled an abundance of extracurricular activities, which makes keeping you safe more challenging."

"You want me to hide out in a hotel room? That's not going to happen."

"Many of the activities you have planned are in public places. Uncontrollable places, which can have uncontrollable outcomes."

She delivered her message as if rehearsed—as if she'd told this to celebrities ad nauseam and had no real expectation that he'd yield to her cautious advice.

He leaned back on the couch and crossed his legs. "There are five things I absolutely must do in every city where I tour." He used his fingers to tick them off. "First, I go to the nearest children's hospital—or farther away if I've already been to the nearest one. There, I stay long enough to chat and sing three songs. Second, I go to a gospel church and enjoy lively, uplifting music. Third, I find a new tourist attraction to explore. Fourth is partaking of some local restaurant with a local dish. The fifth and last thing is the concert. Not every activity is in that order, but the concert is always last. Those activities are nonnegotiable, anything else that you feel is superfluous, we can discuss."

Billy shook her head. "Why? I mean, why those activities? Surely they don't bolster sales much."

He grinned. "Yes, much to the chagrin of Meg, they probably don't do much for concert sales. The children's hospital is part of giving back to the community. Those kids can't go to a concert. They can't be exposed to God-knows-what in a crowd of people and that's even if their family could afford a ticket when they have medical bills to worry about. So, I bring the music to them, and we all feel good about it.

"The church is about keeping my faith. I'd forgotten it once—buried it under gallons of alcohol and self-loathing. But going back to a church of singing, praising, and praying people reminds me of my gift and where it came from. Even if you're not a religious person, you will feel moved by the faith and joy of the people in a gospel church."

"Gospel seems an interesting choice, since you're from California."

"Tamika grew up in the South. I met her after a concert in Atlanta. She took me to church with her, and I was instantly in love—with her and gospel music. This was back when she was finishing college. We made it our thing—go to a gospel church whenever we had a weekend together."

"I've seen church choirs performing in some of your concert videos."

"Yes, I have a few songs that lend themselves to having a choir for the live performance. It enhances the experience." He leveled his gaze at her. "You've watched my concerts?"

"Of course. I need to understand the layout—distance from the crowd to the stage and what exit routes will be most expedient while you're on stage since you have choreographed places you stand depending upon where you are in the song."

"Right." All in the name of his protection detail. He concealed his disappointment that she hadn't watched his concerts to see *him*. But the notion was a ridiculous anyway, since she saw him every day.

Billy nodded as she stood. "Okay. Five things at every location, and we'll negotiate the rest. I appreciate you taking the time to explain it to me."

He bobbed his head and picked up his guitar. Billy left, and when the door closed behind her, he strummed the melody to the Temptations' "My Girl."

THE NEXT MORNING, Billy arrived at Ethan's hotel door, carrying a cup of coffee—coffee that had arrived to her via room service that morning with a note.

Try this one. Black. Nothing fancy.
But it's an Ecuadorian blend.
— Ethan

His persistence to connect with her on a personal level had her smiling. He truly had to be friends with someone who worked for him.

Barry was waiting outside Ethan's door. "Meg is talking with him."

"That's my cue to be intrusive." Billy smiled, sliding her key card in the door.

She wanted to be present for discussions with people in Ethan's inner circle. And if she was intruding on a personal moment, then she'd know Ethan hadn't been truthful about the absence of a relationship in his life, which could affect the investigation.

"It's done, Meg. Everyone's safety is more important." Ethan's voice was tight as Billy entered the room.

"Morning, Billy Jean. Shall we?" He hefted his guitar and walked past her.

She was to escort him to practice with his band downstairs in a rented hotel conference room.

"Um, Billy, a moment?" Meg held a finger in the air like a teacher in a classroom vying for her students' attention.

"I go where he goes." Billy turned to leave, but Meg placed a hand on her forearm. Billy leveled her gaze at the woman in what Claire had once dubbed the "I-can-kill-you-with-my-bare-hands" look.

Meg quickly removed her hand.

Billy *could* kill her with her bare hands, but the irony

of Claire's terminology was that Billy had never killed anyone in hand-to-hand combat. She'd been in gunfights overseas in the Marine Corp but never up close with the enemy. The fistfights and knife fights she'd been in were during her protection details with Rider SI and had never ended in death. Pain usually sufficiently deterred people from further violence before it escalated to the point of homicide.

"I'll catch up you to," Billy called to Barry.

She let the door close.

Meg's face tightened once they were alone. "Look. You are going to suffocate Ethan's career."

Billy crossed her arms. "What are you talking about?"

"You canceled his autographing next week."

"Not canceled. Alice is looking into another location. I'm moving it because it was in a park with a dozen vantage points for a sniper."

Meg scoffed. "Next, you'll be canceling the children's hospital performance."

"No. The hospital is badge access only with controlled entry and exit points. I don't have a problem with that."

Meg tossed her head back. "The sound of you! As if you lord over Ethan's domain."

Billy blinked, surprised but not in the least offended. Was this about more than Ethan's safety? Was Meg jealous? Billy was certain another woman had never been jealous of her, and certainly Meg had no cause to be now.

Billy softened her voice and lowered her arms to her side. *Congenial*, she reminded herself. "I'm just doing my job. I only have my client's safety in mind at all times."

Rather than take the peace offering, Meg glared at her

with distain. "The only danger he's in is you destroying his career!"

"I beg to differ. He was shot at with a high-power rifle."

As Meg's temper flared, Billy became calmer.

"And the wedding? You canceled his RSVP."

"The Beaufort wedding?" Billy shook her head. "Not a controlled environment. Besides, he can attend the man's fourth wedding, which, by Jimmy Beaufort's marriage record, should take place in about eighteen months."

The agent shook her head. "There's no getting through to you is there?"

"The feeling's mutual."

Meg's lips puckered in displeasure.

Billy resisted the urge to warn her that making faces like that would put some of those wrinkles back she'd paid so much to have stretched.

"Now look here—"

Billy straightened into her soldier stand of attention and stared past the woman. "Ma'am, if you would like to file a complaint with my office, you are welcome to do so. Right now, I need to get back to work." She knew the "ma'am" would take Meg right over the edge, but diplomacy wasn't Billy's strength, and congeniality had already failed.

"I'll do that," Meg called to her backside as Billy left the room.

Ethan attended a business lunch the next day with Wayne, Scott, and Barry on protection duty. During that time, Billy wandered to the hotel pool where the band relaxed.

"Billy, to what do we owe the pleasure?" Dan raised his glass of soda her direction.

Edgar floated on his back in the pool, eyes closed. Niko sat near the bar, flirting with a woman in a bikini.

Billy sat down in a chair beside Dan, who lounged under the sun.

"We've made a few changes to Ethan's schedule. I wanted to get the band's beat on things."

"Band's beat. I see what you did there." The corner of Dan's mustache twitched. "You've come to the right person."

She squinted under the sun as she glanced at the other band members. "I figure Edgar would give me a series of grunts and Niko would say 'everything is cool.'"

"True. True. I can speak for the group and confidently say we're in favor of anything that keeps Ethan safe." He sipped his soda. "Ethan made a good life for all of us. When he started self-imploding, we thought it was the end of the line. No more band. We disbanded while he focused on sobriety and songwriting."

She sat back and kept quiet to let Dan continue. Being mostly a quiet observer so far hadn't unearthed the danger to Ethan. Perhaps she could gently probe his band as any concerned employee might do without raising suspicion about an investigation.

"When he called a meeting and said he wanted to go back on tour, we were thrilled. A few years had passed, but our fan base was still there. Ethan's only requirement was that we didn't put any pressure on him with alcohol or drugs."

"Everybody agreed?" she asked.

Dan shrugged. "We lost the keyboardist, but he was too alpha anyway. A band can only have one team leader, and that's Ethan."

"Was the keyboardist angry?"

"Sure, but he signed somewhere else and started touring in Europe. The split was good for him."

"But the previous drummer rejoined the team when Ethan brought the band back together?" Billy asked.

"Sure did. He didn't quite understand that wild parties were a thing of the past. After he and Ethan butted heads a few times, Ethan gave him the boot."

"How bad was the break? Bad enough the drummer would pay somebody to take a shot at Ethan?"

Dan waved his hand as he finished his soda. "No, the guy was a hot head, but I doubt he did it." Dan stroked his mustache. "Hot heads get their own retaliation. The person who hires a hit is cold and calculating. Dispassionate."

"Who in Ethan's life fits that profile?"

Dan shrugged. "No clue."

10

Billy sat with Ethan and Alyssa in the back seat while Pope drove and Claude rode shotgun. Alyssa had flown in from DC for the weekend to spend time with her father. Ethan had insisted he go with the group to pick her up from the airport.

Alyssa wore pink polka-dot leggings and a T-shirt that said, "I'm too sassy for my shirt," in glittering silver script.

Ethan instructed Pope to pull up to a strip mall, and he parked in front of a nail salon with a flashing neon sign.

"What are you doing?" Billy asked.

Alyssa's face lit up. "Pedicures!"

Billy scrambled to get out of the car before the little girl could climb over her. Her eyes scanned the parking lot. It was practically deserted, but Billy detested unscheduled stops.

"No customers inside," Claude said as he looked through the shop window.

Billy stood beside the car and surveyed the area. Ethan joined her and placed a hand on her shoulder, silencing her plans to protest.

Billy spun to Pope, who was climbing out of the driver seat. "Sweep the rear entrance. Claude, you're watching the front." She texted Barry, who was back at the hotel, to let him know of the detour.

As they entered the nail salon, Alyssa skipped over to the wall of nail polishes. With eyes sparkling in excitement, she looked at the rainbow of colors.

"Two pedicures, please," Ethan told the clerk at the desk.

Billy didn't hide her surprise.

"What? A guy can't get a pedicure?" he asked her.

"It's fine. It's just—"

"What? Not very masculine?" He laughed. "You should see the things I've done in the name of love—tea parties, dining with dolls, and, yes, pedicures and even manicures. If this is Alyssa's idea of quality time, then I'm in."

Billy grinned. Damn, he was an amazing father.

Ethan slid off his shoes and rolled up his pant legs as the attendant started the hot water in the foot basin.

"You should join us." He motioned to a third, vacant seat.

"Um, no."

"Ever had one?"

"No. I grew up defending myself from two older brothers. There was no such thing as pampering in our household."

"You're missing out."

"I'm on the job."

"And your employer is telling you to relax and get a pedicure. Nobody is going to ambush us at a nail salon."

"Is this because I'm a woman?" She crossed her arms. "You wouldn't make the same offer to a male bodyguard."

He stopped rolling his pant leg up midway and gave her a lazy-lidded stare of incredulity. He pulled out his phone and put it on speaker so she could hear. After a single ring he said, "Yo, Pope?"

"Boss."

"Join us for a pedicure?"

There was a hesitant pause. "I'm good, thanks."

Billy narrowed her eyes at Ethan.

Ethan gave a victory smile as he disconnected the call.

"Join us!" Alyssa cried. "If you do, you can pick the group activity we do tomorrow."

Billy cocked her head to one side, considering the offer. She looked at Ethan.

"Fair is fair," he conceded.

"Okay," Billy relented.

Two minutes later, she sunk her feet into warm, effervescent water as her seat mechanically massaged her back. She'd placed her suit jacket behind the chair along with her gun, but both were easily within reach. Her pant legs were rolled up to the knees.

Ethan wriggled his eyes at her. "Nice, huh?"

"Wow. This feels amazing." The message chair

groaned as if it was trying to separate thick braids of rope in the muscles in her back. Had she been carrying around so much tension?

From her seat on the other side of her dad, Alyssa looked over at Billy. "What color did you pick?"

"No color."

"You have to have a color, silly."

"Clear."

"*Bor-ring.*" Alyssa faked a yawn.

Billy laughed.

The little girl held up the polish she'd chosen and shook it in the air. "Bubblegum pink."

"If I were to wear nail polish, which I don't, it would not be something called *bubblegum.*"

"I picture you as more of a lipstick red," Ethan said.

Billy tried to discern his meaning. Was he saying she was attractive? Seductive? Or that she had the potential to be those things with something as simple as applying nail polish?

She tried to remember the last time she'd felt feminine and attractive. Sometimes on days off, she'd wear a dress and go to a bar. Most of the men weren't looking for attractive; they were looking for someone palatable enough to pass for a one-night stand—and, well, so was she.

On the job, she caught no one's attention. Men rarely noticed a bodyguard in a suit with no makeup. Ethan noticed. But was he attracted to her—or was his nature as a performer to be charming and charismatic to everyone, especially someone of the opposite sex? The more time she spent with him, the harder it was to tell. She would never attempt to find out which was true. She could get one-night stands when she wanted them, but they wouldn't be with a client.

"*Pleeeeease*, pick a color," Alyssa pleaded.

"How about if you pick a color for me—not bubblegum."

Alyssa gave her dad a conspiratorial grin and dashed over to the nail polish shelves.

THE NEXT DAY, Billy crouched behind the barrier, gun in hand. The enemy was so close she could practically hear his nasal breathing.

Beside her, Billy's partner mimicked her every move. The rookie grinned at her. Billy grunted and shook her head. The rookie had potential, but she needed to stay focused. She adjusted her goggles.

Neutralize the threat.

"Ready?" Billy asked.

They had reviewed their offensive attack, but it would only succeed if they stuck to the plan.

"Come out with your hands up!" a gruff voice demanded. This was followed by the dull *thunk* of bullets hitting the barrier wall.

"Now!" Billy prompted in a harsh whisper.

As Billy darted out from the blue foam wall, Alyssa scurried out from her hiding spot to emerge from the other side.

Billy ducked and rolled in her fitted exercise clothes as Pope fired a Nerf bullet at her. The shot missed, and she came up beside the round yellow foam cylinder Claude was hiding behind. She made a direct shot to his chest as he protested, shocked by her speed.

She crouched, hiding behind Claude's large body as Pope fired again.

"Hey!" Claude snapped when the foam bullet struck him in the temple.

"Oh, friendly fire," Billy chided. "You should talk to your partner about that."

"I got Daddy! I got Daddy!" Alyssa cried triumphantly.

The timing of the distraction was perfect. Pope turned and prepared to take aim at the exposed little girl, who tap-danced her victory.

Billy rose, aimed, and fired. The bullet struck Pope in the upper back before bouncing harmlessly to the floor.

"Oh man." Pope dropped his hands to his side.

"Woo-hoo!" Alyssa crowed.

Billy chuckled as Ethan got to his feet, sporting a goofy grin.

"Do the thing! Do the thing! You promised," Alyssa prodded Billy.

Amused, Billy tilted her Nerf gun muzzle up and blew away imaginary smoke.

Alyssa smiled, her face glowing with delight.

"Five to zero, Billy Jean." Ethan gave her an admiring look, which made the gymnasium seem suddenly warm, like the inside of an MRAP tactical vehicle. Except that a mine-resistant, ambush-protected vehicle would feel less sweltering than the heat from Ethan's eyes. "We tried every combination, and you're always on the winning team."

"You wouldn't have confidence in my role protecting you if I didn't win every gun fight."

Claude stood and adjusted his sweatpants. "We haven't tried Billy alone. Four against one."

"Wouldn't matter," Pope grumbled.

"Another!" Alyssa demanded.

Since Billy's first victory—her and Pope against Ethan, Alyssa, and Claude—Alyssa had insisted on being on Billy's team.

Ethan gave an apologetic shake of his head. "No. I think we've all been beat down enough for one afternoon."

Alyssa whined her protest.

"How about Bones steak for dinner," he offered.

"Yes!" Alyssa agreed.

AFTER ALYSSA RETURNED HOME to her mother for the week, Ethan worked on songwriting in his hotel room. He let the emotions of missing his daughter wash over him. Emotions—good or bad, elation or despair and the spectrum in between—were the coffee-bean foundation of his espresso songs. His job was to finely grind those emotions and add the right amount of foam to create rich lyrics with a delicious melody.

After the Atlanta concert, Ethan wouldn't see Alyssa for a few weeks. He wanted more time with her but didn't want to fly her all over the country. He would only achieve his goal if he traveled less. As he approached forty, he was ready cut back. If he got the virtual reality dance game contract, he could afford to travel less so he could spend more time with his daughter.

Life had given him her as a gift, and he wouldn't take it for granted. He finally felt like he had direction as he captained his own ship. When he'd been a young musician, he'd played his heart out for nights on end, dreaming of performing for huge audiences and sweeping people away in the emotion of his music. When his tireless efforts paid off, he didn't know how to handle the pressure of fame.

Alcohol had blunted his imposter syndrome and kept him from facing his fears. His addiction also caused him to identify as some type of rebel loner, and he'd isolated himself from any lasting relationships except those of his band. Once he'd achieved sobriety for a length of time, he'd been able to take a long look at what he wanted in life. And he wanted what others had—family, solidarity, partnership. He wanted to provide for his family but also spend quality time with Alyssa.

He looked down at his notebook where he'd scribbled lyrics.

> *Your Charlize Theron smile*
> *Your simple lifestyle*
> *Your lipstick-red nails*
> *Your attention to details*

Apparently, he was thinking of another female in his life. Billy had been adorable at pedicures, and even allowed herself to have fun at the Nerf fight. He could easily imagine weekends with the three of them enjoying life—hiking, zip-lining, local fairs, laser tag.

But Billy was a temporary addition to his world. She'd leave after she finished her investigation. Still, there was no harm in indulging in a fantasy which would never happen and compose a song about such a fantasy while he was at it.

BILLY HAD two days off in Atlanta and planned to spend the time tidying her apartment, checking mail, and paying bills. As lead investigator, she was uncomfortable taking any days off, but company policy dictated breaks in any work schedule, and she understood the importance of mental downtime.

Since her apartment was as clean as she'd left it, the mail was mostly junk, and she'd paid all her bills electronically, her assigned tasks took her all of one hour.

She paced her floor. She had no desire to spend the two days off in isolation, lounging around her house in her underwear—well, maybe one day like that.

Pulling her phone out of her pocket, she called Claire.

"Hey, how are things going? Any vacation plans?" Claire asked.

Of course, Claire knew Billy's exact travel plans. She probably also knew Billy was standing in her apartment.

Hmm. Claire probably also knew how Ethan was doing from Barry's reports. Whoa. Where did that come from? Since when had Billy ever spent a moment of her free time wondering how a client was doing?

"No vacation plans," Billy replied. "And most people call two days off a weekend, not a vacation."

"When's the last time you took an actual vacation?" Claire asked.

Billy thought about the question. During her protective detail within the tennis circuit, she'd had a few days here and there to go sightseeing in different countries they'd toured. None of those were long enough to be considered immersive, getaway vacations—true recreational escapes from everyday life.

"Wow," Claire interjected. "Judging by the really long pause, it's been a while. There's more to life than the job, Billy."

An image of Ethan's green eyes and seductive smile crept into Billy's mind—probably because of Claire's reference to "the job" and not because he represented a tempting "more to life" something.

"I called to see if you want to go boxing," Billy said.

"I boxed yesterday."

"Real boxing," Billy countered. "Not your virtual reality ring fights."

"Yeah, okay. When?"

"One hour."

"Okay, but not that place that smells like cat litter."

"It's affordable."

THE GYM a few blocks from Billy's apartment complex smelled like cat litter because it had once been a kennel.

The subsequent owners gutted the place, but the smell lingered, even after they installed weights, a rink, a quarter-mile perimeter running track, and a series of punching bags.

Billy waited for Claire outside the gym because she knew her friend wouldn't want to walk in past a dozen sweaty men on the machines to get to the back corner where the punching bags hung. She and Claire were both introverts but with different quirks. Billy could be in a crowd and contentedly observe or ignore everyone without socializing. Claire preferred to avoid gatherings altogether but opened up completely to a few close friends.

Claire arrived dressed in tight yoga pants and a fitted T-shirt. Her hair was cut into a smooth bob with a purple sheen, which gleamed under sunlight. She was going to get more than a few stares, as pretty as she was, but she was happily married to an actor who intermittently consulted for Rider SI.

They walked to the back of the gym, where Billy began wrapping Claire's hands and pulling gloves on her.

"How is the job going?" Claire asked.

"Good. Great, actually."

"Because?"

"I like the investigative component, and Ethan is actually a nice guy—you know, for a celebrity. His security team was accepting of us. His daughter is adorable." She thought about her now red toenails but decided to omit divulging that detail to Claire.

"And good music," Claire added, but her tone held a hint of mischievousness.

"Yes. Good music." Billy finished the last glove, eyeing Claire suspiciously.

Claire bumped her gloves together as she bounced on her toes. "I noticed you downloaded his songs onto your phone."

Company phone, Billy thought. Claire had seen the downloads even though Billy had bought them on her dime with her own music account.

"*All* of his songs." Claire leveled her gaze at Billy.

Billy shrugged. "His music is good. Some of them have a perfect boxing beat."

"Uh-huh. And the others?"

"I like them. What are you insinuating?"

"You have a crush."

"Of course I have a crush. Half of the women in America have a crush on Ethan Storm. Now, punch," Billy commanded.

Claire turned toward the punching bag and began her assault. "But you're not like half of the women in America."

"I'm still a woman. Concentrate. You're not turning your hips."

"How bad is the crush?" Claire asked.

Billy held the punching bag still for her. "I don't understand the question. Crushes have some type of ranking scale?"

"Sure." She punched between every few words. "One for mildly endearing and ten for you'll cry and gorge on chocolate chip cookie dough ice cream when you're no longer with him."

Billy shook her head. "Sometimes I'm not sure you

and I even speak the same language. When the job is done, it's done. I can admire a man and his talents from two feet or two thousand miles."

"And you'll have his music wherever you go."

"That's right."

"And his memoir." Claire grinned and wriggled her eyebrows before punching the bag again.

"How the hell did you know I read Ethan's memoir?"

"Barry told me."

"It's for research. You're dropping your shoulder. You need to focus."

"This is harder than my VR boxing. The gloves are heavy, and making actual physical contact with something is jarring."

"Okay, my turn."

Claire had riled her enough; Billy needed to punch something.

11

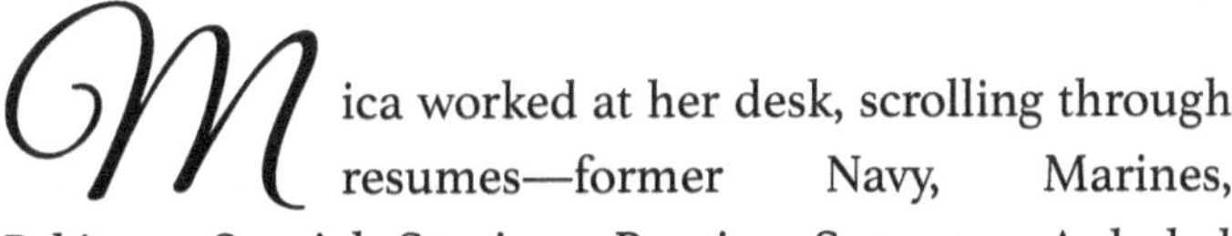

Mica worked at her desk, scrolling through resumes—former Navy, Marines, Pakistan Special Services, Russian Spetsnaz. A lethal bunch, but what of their moral character?

With the growth of Rider SI business, she needed to hire more but didn't merely need soldiers who could pull triggers. She needed critical thinkers who were fierce under pressure. She needed the offspring of one of these heavy weights and an astrophysicist.

Somehow Maxine had found perfect fits—Ryan and Dorian especially. Now Billy was proving to be more than just a shield. If Mica was going to fulfill her plan to bolster the investigative side of the company, she needed smart hires.

Claire had provided her with additional information

on each of the applicants. Several had degrees. Several also had mental health issues—anxiety, depression, and bipolar personalities often manifesting as drug or alcohol addiction, or PTSD dulled with drug or alcohol addiction. Others had criminal records. Mica wasn't wholly opposed to someone if they'd made mistakes early in life —but some of the applicants had been arrested within the past five years. She needed level-headed and even-tempered candidates.

Her doorbell rang, disrupting her thoughts. She hopped out of chair and opened the front door to see her father on the porch. He rarely took breaks from his body shop to drop by her house unannounced.

"Dad, what a pleasant surprise." She greeted him with a hug as he entered her house.

"Hey, baby girl." He wore blue jeans and a T-shirt with grease stains.

"I wished you'd told me you were coming; I could have ordered in lunch for us," she said.

"Nah. I just dropped by to see my favorite daughter and favorite grandchild."

"Only daughter." She swatted at him playfully. "And your *only* grandchild won't be making a guest appearance for many more months."

"I brought this." He handed her a baby-blue paper bag.

She peeked inside as she led him to her home office. "Ah. Another Braves onesie. You're going to spoil this child."

"Have a seat." She gestured to the chair opposite her desk as she walked back to her chair and sat.

Her father plopped down and leaned back. "How is the applicant hunt coming?"

"Awful. I brought in five to interview. Two had no people skills. Two asked me out on a date—when you cannot possibly miss seeing my wedding ring. And one left early because he said he couldn't work for a woman."

"I may be able to help."

"Really?" She leaned forward. Her father was retired military so he might have contacts he could reach out to.

"Yes, but have an open mind."

Her hopes deflated slightly.

"I was having beers with a buddy of mine from the service, real stand-up guy, who tells me this unbelievable story about his son. So, during college, his son, Lee, has a breakdown and gets diagnosed with schizophrenia. Lee jets off to South America where he goes off the grid. Then he resurfaces in the US for a year, and then he's gone again. His dad even hires an investigator, but Lee has vanished. After twenty years, he's thinking his son is dead and gone. The end.

"But a few years ago, two boys, about eighteen show up and tell my friend they're his grandsons. They've got this wild story about how their dad dragged them all over South America on this whole *Rise of the Terminator* premise. Like they had to be prepared for the apocalypse."

"This man, Lee, raised his sons that way? That's awful."

"Yes, up until they were sixteen. Then, he brings them back to the States where he has a heart attack and dies. Both boys go into foster care."

"This is a terrible story," Mica said.

"But my buddy checked it out. It's all true. He couldn't find Lee in South America because they were using their mother's name—Alonso. But they're actually US citizens since Lee brought the woman back to the States to deliver. Anyway, my friend paid for their college. They got stellar grades all four years."

"I guess that makes for a happy ending." Mica tried to remember how her conversation with her father had started, because he always had a purpose to his stories.

"Not quite. They're educated, smart as whips, and bilingual, but they can't get decent jobs because of juvie records from the few years it took them to adjust to, you know, learning there isn't an apocalypse coming—or at least learning that most people don't live their lives that way."

"Can't get jobs?" She threaded her fingers together on top of the desk. "You're not going to suggest I hire a couple of kids—"

"Not kids. They're twenty-two. They have degrees and high marks."

"If you want them employed, hire them for your shop."

"I don't need any more help at the body shop. But you need help here."

"With that kind of unstable background, I won't know what I'm getting."

He crossed his arms. "Name one employee of Rider SI with a normal childhood."

Mica pursed her lips. "I need people with defensive and offensive training—and weapons training."

"They survived South America off the grid with a father who taught them how to stay alive under the guise that the end of the world was near. They have all of that training."

Mica scowled at her father's ridiculous proposal. "I'll agree to meet them only."

SINCE ATLANTA WAS Rider SI base of operations, Ethan had decided to invite Mica and the rest of the Rider team out to dinner. After his concert at the Cobb Energy Performing Art Center in two days, he'd be on the road to New Orleans.

He had briefly met Mica when she'd video-conferenced with him to talk about the sniper attack in New Jersey and reviewed what her company could do for him if he hired them. After witnessing what a great job Billy and Barry did over the course of several weeks, Ethan wanted to show his appreciation with a dinner.

He opened the invitation to all of the Rider team and spouses, but most of them, understandably, were working. Billy and Barry, of course, would be there. Mica was coming and bringing her husband, David, an ER physician in downtown Atlanta. Claire would be there with her husband, Drake, who apparently did some sort of consulting for the Rider team.

Ethan had insisted Billy pick the dining location. In keeping with his rules about the cities he visited, it had to be authentic and he wanted it to be somewhere she'd been before and enjoyed.

As they approached Buford Highway Chinatown food court, Billy seemed more stiff than usual.

"This place looks great. And it's low profile. We won't have any problems with security." His words didn't seem to put her at ease. "What's troubling you, Billy Jean?"

"The ambience isn't really celebrity-caliber."

"Are you worried you're not going to impress me?" He smiled. "If that's the case, I'm flattered it bothers you so much. I wasn't always famous, you know. I played in dive bars and ate fast food. I didn't ask you for a fancy restaurant. I asked you for an authentic place you like."

Billy finally relaxed as they walked into the bustling Chinese food court and toward Hong Kong BBQ.

Ethan recognized Mica's blonde hair immediately and approached the tables the Rider team had pushed together to fit everyone. After introductions were exchanged, David and Drake left the table and went to the counter to place orders. The two men seemed like good friends, chatting about the NBA playoffs as they walked away.

"This is so exciting." Claire brimmed with a joy that matched her vibrant purple hair.

"I'd tell you she was this excited about the pork and duck, but she's actually a big fan of yours," Billy said.

"I appreciate fans. And I'm glad to hear it, since I had Alice reserve a suite at the Atlanta concert in case the Rider team could attend."

"That's fantastic!" Claire practically squealed.

Billy smiled, obviously enjoying her coworker's enthusiasm. Ethan got the sense they were all very much like a family. Billy had tender relationships with these people, perhaps filling a void her own family couldn't provide for her. Ethan liked them all the more because of it.

When David and Drake returned to the table, Claire blurted out Ethan's invitation to the concert.

"That's very generous. I'd love to go. Your music is wonderful," Drake said as he took his seat.

David smiled as he placed a hand on Mica's shoulder and squeezed. "I don't know when it is or if I'm working, but I'll be sure to swap shifts so we can go."

"So, you all know all about me since you've been investigating every aspect of my life. Tell me about yourselves," Ethan said, helping distribute waters and sodas on the table.

Claire went first. "Drake is an actor and does voiceovers and audio ads. And he rescued me after a kidnapping. But that's a whole other story."

Ethan raised his eyebrows. "I'd like to hear that story sometime."

Drake smiled, something bright and worthy of Hollywood. He stole a kiss on Claire's cheek.

"Since we're bragging on each other," Billy said, "Claire and the Rider team brought down a criminal mastermind. Claire is genius when it comes to computers. If you have secrets you don't want others to know about, don't put them in electronic format."

Ethan sipped his soda. "I only hire the best." He turned to David. "And how did you come to be involved in this medley of talent?"

"I'm here to patch up the mishaps," said the ER physician. "Not really. But I'm only half-kidding. Mica and I knew each other in high school and reconnected when she showed up half-dead in my emergency room. After that, I wriggled my way into her life and vowed never to let go."

Ethan glanced at Billy, who appeared relaxed around her friends.

"Billy tells us you were able to spend some time with your daughter recently," Mica said to Ethan.

"We had a great time with her. Billy took us to Nerf gunfighting and absolutely destroyed all of us. It was a blast."

Billy chuckled. "It was fun."

"Fun?" He scoffed playfully. "My own daughter chose you over me so she could be on the winning team."

Billy shrugged. "When you're popular," she said in mocking wistfulness.

Mica and David exchanged looks as though interpreting Ethan's exchange with Billy as something flirtatious. It had been. And the attraction he felt for Billy only intensified as they spent time together. He'd thought it would be more fleeting. Yet, what could he do about it?

If he respected her and her job, not a damn thing.

AFTER DINNER, Billy drove them back to the hotel, with Ethan and Barry in the backseat.

"That was delicious," Ethan said.

"Sure was." In the rearview mirror, Billy saw Barry rub his gravid belly. He probably was only twenty percent body fat, but it had all congregated in one location.

Billy loved the food, but the night had been made memorable by the friends who'd gathered. She didn't think so many of the Rider team had been together outside of work since Claire's wedding. Ethan seemed to fit right in. He had the rare talent of molding himself to fit any social situation.

"I enjoyed the Rider team's company," Ethan added, as if reading her thoughts.

"They enjoyed you," Barry said, oblivious to the way Ethan glanced in the mirror to see if Billy would interact with him.

But she pretended she didn't see his face as she drove and tried to process her enjoyment of the night.

Barry continued, "They're going to be talking about the concert every day leading up to it and likely for years after."

Billy pulled up to the hotel's curb and passed the car off to valet as Barry and Ethan got out. Once inside, the three of them entered the elevator.

"You got this? I need an antacid." Barry asked, peeling away from them when the elevator stopped.

"Yeah," Billy affirmed.

She walked Ethan to his suite and unlocked his door. He stepped just inside and waited for her to do a sweep of his room.

As she went through her routine, Billy thought about the Nerf gunfight. She couldn't remember the last time she'd cut loose and just had fun. She'd had relaxing times off the job but not goofy girl fun.

And Ethan had been such a supportive father, letting

Alyssa dictate the teams and not caring if he won or lost, as long as his daughter had fun.

Billy thought of her father. If he'd ever had a playful bone in his body, she'd never seen it. He'd allowed himself to be embittered by the hardships in life. Joy was a foreign concept to him. He self-medicated with alcohol and cigarettes.

"You okay?" Ethan asked.

Billy turned her gaze from the window to look at Ethan. "I'm fine."

She tried to recall if a client had ever asked about her well-being. After a moment, she realized Ethan was still watching her, waiting for more of a response.

"I had fun the other day with Alyssa. A lot of fun. My childhood was ... not a happy one." She hesitated, not wanting to bare her inner turmoil to Ethan, but he had a way of coaxing information out of her. "You're a great father."

"I have my moments." He was standing in front of the door, looking as though he didn't want the night or the conversation to end.

Billy shook her head. "It's more than that. You let Alyssa express herself—happy, sad, mad, frustrated."

He shrugged. "Sure. She's a kid, she needs to learn how to process her emotions."

He made it sound impossibly simple. He wasn't giving himself enough credit as a parent.

"Okay. For instance, if I had complained to my mom the way Alyssa complained to you during the car ride about how Tamika woke her up too early for the trip here, I'd have gotten a lecture about being grateful my parents had taken the time to take me on a trip. I'd have been told about all the other children across the world whose families can't afford toilets, much less travel plans. You ... you just listened. With empathy." She sat down heavily on the couch in his room.

His brow furrowed. "You can't teach a child using a perspective they can't comprehend. I'd rather Alyssa sees I validate her feelings and carries that example forward to her interactions with others. Life experiences will show her that small things, like waking up early, aren't so important that they're worth complaining about. But me saying such a thing directly doesn't change her perspective."

"You probably never told her to finish her vegetables because there are starving children in Ethiopia."

"That's just absurd. Your mother said that? It makes no sense." He sat beside her on the sofa and turned slightly toward her.

Billy chuckled. "I called home once. And only once. I was in bootcamp, physically and mentally exhausted and wanting to hear a friendly voice. I called my mom and told her I missed her and training was hard. 'You knew what you signed up for,' was her reply. She wasn't bitter. The tone wasn't ugly. It was just another way of telling me it wasn't okay to feel what I felt.

"I didn't know the Marines would be as hard as it turned out to be. You have a vision in your head when you make a life-changing commitment, but no one truly knows what they're 'signing up for' with every decision."

Ethan slipped his hand into hers. Warmth radiated

up her arm, and she couldn't find the strength to pull away from him.

She continued speaking. "I was so hurt on the call, I felt like telling her she knew what she was signing up for when she married my father—even though I'm sure she had no idea he was an abusive bastard." Billy sniffed and took a shaky breath to compose herself. She never fell apart like this, yet Ethan had a way of not making her feel self-conscious.

"No disrespect to your mother, but what did all of that 'tough love' do for you? Instead of teaching you to be happy and grateful, you learned how not to empathize with others. You learned to distance yourself. And you learned to feel guilty. Guilt when you succeed—because pride is frowned upon. Guilt when you fail—because self-pity is frowned upon. You have emotions no one ever taught you how to handle in a healthy fashion."

"Music star *and* counselor?" Billy asked.

"When you get sober and write a memoir, you analyze a whole lot of emotions. I was also so terrified of screwing up Alyssa because of my sordid past that I read a lot of parenting books. People say it takes a village to raise a child—it actually takes about seventeen different manuals."

Billy chuckled softly.

"Come here. I'm not passing up the opportunity to hug it out." He tugged her jacket sleeve—insistent but not forceful. "Come on. You'll feel better."

She leaned into him.

The embrace felt good. Too good.

12

———

The day after the dinner with Ethan, Mica decided to work on arranging the nursery. She and David had chosen sage-green coloring and a jungle theme. They opted not to learn the gender of the baby until after it was born. David had painted the room, and together they had assembled the crib. Now, Mica hung curtains printed with elephant and giraffe figures.

"Need a hand?" David appeared in the doorway and leaned against the frame.

"Thanks, but I'm almost done."

"Claire called."

"Anything urgent?"

"Just an update on the Storm file. She said it could wait. How's the case coming?"

Mica liked that David took an interest in the Rider

company and her active case files. Like his medical patients' information, her clients were confidential, so she was cautious with how much information she shared. However, someone as high-profile is Ethan Storm was in the media all the time and her security-detail coverage was no secret. Now that the men had met over dinner, she felt she could divulge a few details.

"Slow progress." She fitted the curtain over the rod sliding the fabric on inch by inch. "We ruled out a lot of people—his band, his crew, his ex-wife, his ex-girlfriend. We ruled in no one."

"That's still progress. I remind impatient patients of that all the time. When they get frustrated while they're going through testing and we don't have a diagnosis yet, I expound on all of the life-threatening things we've ruled out. Peace of mind goes with that knowledge."

"You're saying I should be grateful for all the people it's not?"

"Even if you don't feel that way, if the client is ever frustrated by what he or she perceives to be a slow pace, remind them of the reassurances your tremendous hard work has brought to the case so far."

She took two steps up the stool, raised the curtain rod, and set it on the braces. From the corner of her eye she noticed David's slight twitching and straightening.

"Relax, doctor. I'm a foot and a half off the ground. I won't fall just because I have a little extra weight around the belly."

"You don't actually. You're barely even showing yet."

"I can feel the difference. Baby's there and so are the hormones. Nausea has been hitting me hard this week."

"There's medication you can take for that," David said.

"Sure, and the side effects are constipation. Who wants to trade one problem for another? No thanks."

"How is Billy doing in her new role?"

"She's doing great. I think she's a natural. She's got a good analytical head. And she's done well planting a little spyware for Claire. I made the right call putting her on as on-site investigator."

David walked up to Mica and kissed her on the lips. "I know you'll find your bad guy. Maybe it's time to think outside the box."

"How so?"

"I don't know. But when I can't figure out a diagnosis, I try to think outside the box. Or phone a friend."

Phone a friend. Think outside the box.

Mica considered the suggestions. Maybe what she actually needed to do was phone an enemy.

"The Atlanta concert went well," Billy said.

She and Barry walked the rest-stop trail around picnic tables, as they stretched their legs. They'd stopped somewhere in Mississippi on their way to New Orleans.

"I think we've whipped Claude, Pope, and the rest of the gang into shape," Barry added.

"There are a few little things that still need work—some attention to small details."

"Like what?"

"Like, one of the hallways had a rolling tray tower

parked in it. Somebody can hide behind one of those or tip it over as a barrier. And I found one of the exit doors propped open so a venue caterer employee could smoke out back. These were subtle but still chinks in our armor."

"Won't be long until they won't need us anymore."

"Perhaps. We'll continue through a few more shows at least. More if we haven't found the perpetrator."

Once the threat was uncovered, Rider SI's work of protecting Ethan Storm would be done. Since they hadn't found the person after weeks of digging and two concerts had passed, they were resigned to waiting for the perpetrator to make an error in order to find him or her.

Billy hadn't spoken to Ethan much since their entirely too cathartic moment of close proximity on his hotel room couch. She'd felt better, lighter somehow, as though the sludge of resentment she'd been lugging around like a dead weight had started to melt. Fortunately, she'd composed herself and left Ethan's room that night with the sort of farewell she'd have given a friend. She'd proven to herself she could enter and exit his embrace without a loss of self-control.

"It was nice of Ethan to invite the Rider team to the Atlanta concert," Barry said.

"He's a thoughtful guy." She wondered briefly if her voice held a little too much admiration. "I didn't get to see much of Mica, David, Claire, or Drake since I was on duty, but I briefly stopped by their concert suite when Ethan went there to say hi."

"Is Claire making any progress?" Barry asked.

Billy rolled her shoulders to stretch them. Long days

of travel made her stiff, but the travel time gave them planning time—time to review schematics of the next concert venue, time to review security weaknesses at the next hotel, and more.

"We have a lot of rule-outs. I'm still homing in on Meg. I don't allow her to be alone in a room with Ethan if I can be there. Something about her feels off, and it isn't just the impressive boob job."

Barry snorted. "It's amazing those things don't tip her forward."

"Yeah, especially in the heels she wears. Anyway, I don't know what her motive could be. If anything happens to Ethan, she's out a lot of money, but everything about her is fake, including her concern for his safety. And that raises a red flag."

IN NEW ORLEANS, the week before his concert, Ethan was staying true to his schedule. He was spending a morning at the famed Café du Monde for beignets and coffee. He'd already been to the children's hospital, and his gospel church visit was next on the agenda.

The restaurant in the French Quarter was a security nightmare, according to Billy, with its flowing foot traffic and open seating. Billy sat with him at the small table watching their surroundings as Barry and Claude patrolled the perimeter.

"Relax, Billy Jean," Ethan said. "Have a beignet. This is an iconic café. Serving the city since 1862." He wore dark sunglasses, and so far hadn't been recognized by any fans.

He pushed the plate of beignets toward her. "Try one."

She lifted a piece and took a bite, careful to use a napkin to avoid getting powdered sugar on her dark suit. She washed the pastry down with a sip of the *cafe au lait* he'd ordered for her.

"Wow. That's delicious. You'd like Les Deux Magots in Paris. It has a similar feel—larger menu but similar ambiance." Her face lit up at the memory of the place she'd been.

Ethan enjoyed the way her eyes sparkled in rare moments of relaxation. He liked that he could evoke those moments. He even liked to think few men could loosen Billy's armor the way he could, but perhaps that was his ego fooling him.

Yet, he felt fairly certain after their time together in Atlanta last week—Alyssa, Chinatown, and discussing her childhood—she might go so far as to call him a friend. He wouldn't push, though, as tempting as it was.

She took another bite of beignet and sip of coffee before replacing the cup in the saucer and launching into an update on the topic of her investigation and the training of his men.

He leaned back in his seat. "Billy Jean, I like that you're thorough, and I wholeheartedly trust you with the security details—and with my life. But when I have a few peaceful moments at a café to relax, I don't want to spend precious time talking about my safety."

"Understood."

He grinned. "Because I'd hate to have to swap you back out for Claude. He'll fill the silence with talk of football, not death threats."

"I can talk about football."

Intriguing. She didn't want to be replaced at his mealtime. She certainly didn't have to sit beside him to protect him. And she could have replied with her standard reminder statement that she wasn't here to be his buddy. Instead, she'd offered to be accommodating.

Maybe she was enjoying their proximity as much as he did.

MICA WALKED through security at the US Penitentiary in Atlanta. She wore black slacks and a mint green blouse. She was glad Lucius Titan had approved her visitation request, but perhaps not surprised. She'd had to play a waiting game of paperwork and background checks, but she was finally going to meet face-to-face with the criminal.

Since Billy stalled in finding the culprit in proximity to Ethan and Claire had stalled in her electronic investigation, Mica was resorting to more extreme measures. Billy needed to remain in her role revolving around the rock star, and Mica wasn't willing to compromise any of her team's safety by having them meet with the conniving criminal. She came here alone, knowing that if the interaction went poorly, she might have added another bull's-eye to her back.

Lucius was seated in a wheelchair on the other side of

a table. He wore a khaki inmate jumper and a smug look. His dark eyes matched his dark hair, which was impeccably cut and combed. His skin was pale under the fluorescent lights, but his strong features were handsome.

The sinister mastermind gestured to the empty chair as if he owned the place. Mica glanced at the guard near the door leading to the prison. The chair, made of metal, felt hard and cold when she sat.

"Mica McMillan. Except it's Mica Rider now, and you've taken over Maxine's business." His eyes twinkled as he smiled—surprisingly without a diabolical gleam, but something untrustworthy still lurked.

Or perhaps Mica was projecting her own distrust; Lucius was a killer—among a list of other atrocities. He should have been in a maximum-security prison, but his lackey, AJ, had taken most of the fall for his hired hits. As such, Lucius had been convicted of trafficking women even though he was guilty of so much more.

"Thank you for agreeing to see me." She might as well start politely, even as the sight of him made her skin crawl.

"Who would turn you away? You're a blonde knockout. I'll be the envy of inmates for a month. But you're also part of the team who bested me."

Maxine Rider and her team had executed an elaborate sting to incriminate Lucius in his crimes and facilitate indictment.

"You attacked one of our own," Mica calmly stated, reminding him of the reason they'd worked against him. Lucius had kidnapped Claire and sealed his own fate.

"I underestimated all of you. That was my mistake. I

assure you, Maxine has already visited to threaten her wrath should I misstep. How is Max these days?"

Mica narrowed her eyes. She sensed nothing of anger or bitterness in Lucius's tone. She'd expected to be met with threats of retribution.

"Maxine is doing well. Retirement suits her."

Lucius gave a tsk. "I'm sure she won't be idle for long. But you didn't come to discuss your mother-in-law. What can I do for the lovely, lethal Mica Rider?"

"There's a contract on one of my clients. Shooter missed, which means he or she might try again. I need a list of possible names."

Without being able to find the hitman—or hitwoman —by first figuring out who hired him or her, Mica's next approach was to work backward.

There was a chance this sniper for hire could have belonged to Lucius or one of his associates. He'd been known to lease killers for hire. Alternatively, he could make inquiries to discover the person's identity.

"MO?" Lucius asked.

"Hawk on perch. With a 0.300 Win-Mag."

The .300 Winchester Magnum ammunition didn't narrow down the type of assailant, since hunters, military, and law enforcement all used them. The bullets had proven long-range reliability.

Lucius rubbed his chin. "Range?"

"One thousand yards. Favorable weather conditions."

"Who's the target?" Lucius asked.

Mica pursed her lips.

Lucius raised his hands in mock surrender. "Mica,

what can I do from in here?" He looked around the prison's visitation room.

She suspected he still had the power to exact his will outside these walls.

He continued, "Let me help. It'll be a nice distraction. It beats Sunday night football bets. I can help you better if you tell me the mark."

Mica hesitated. She needed answers and believed Lucius would be able to deliver information. But at what cost?

"Ethan Storm." She braced herself for what bargain Lucius would try to strike.

He smiled, though without much warmth. "That wasn't so hard. And kudos for getting such a high-profile client. Give me a few days, maybe weeks with how glacial time moves in here, to make some inquiries. If I have something of value, I'll let you know."

Mica stood. "How will you deliver the information to me?" She needed to know if one of Lucius's men would be in touch via phone or email.

His smile widened, this time reaching his dark eyes. "I'll deliver the information when you come back here and visit me again."

Sh-sugar, she thought.

She took her barely contained dismay with her as she turned and left.

13

———————

illy stood outside the church, listening to the uplifting sound of the music. Singing praise carried on the air. Inside, Ethan and the band enjoyed the service. Outside, she, Claude, and Barry and stood guard. Pope had stayed in the car.

Belden's "Build on the Rock" rang through the air, even though the church doors were closed:

> *On visions of earthly treasure;*
> *Some build on the waves of sin and strife,*
> *Of fame, and worldly pleasure.*
> *We'll build on the Rock*

Listening to the music, she felt a pang in her chest, thinking of Kara—one of the soldiers who'd been in

Billy's platoon. Before she could ponder the sensation further, Ethan and the band emerged from the church.

"I'm going to stretch my legs," he told his friends. "I'll see you tomorrow for practice."

Dan, Edgar, and Niko walked toward their van in the parking lot as Ethan strolled toward Billy.

He nodded at her as he slipped on his sunglasses. "Walk with me?"

"Of course." She walked beside him on the sidewalk, with Claude in the lead and Barry behind them.

"The music sounded beautiful," she said.

"Yeah, it was."

"It reminded me of someone. A friend from the Marines." Kara had dark skin, a warm smile, and a great sense of humor. She'd been a dear friend. "She liked to listen to gospel." Billy took a shaky breath. "I buried my sister-in-arms ten years ago, and somehow I'd forgotten her taste in music or the way she sometimes hummed 'Amazing Grace' before lights out."

Ethan put an arm around her, squeezed, and let go again.

"Kara died a soldier," Billy said.

"But she lives on in the melody of the music she loved," Ethan told her.

Billy smiled at the imagery as the sorrow seeped out of her. The pain of a comrade never completely faded, and it incessantly warred with the guilt that she'd survived when others hadn't. But the pain had eased over time, and Billy had tried to let the pleasant memories take root and blossom over the wicked ones.

"I have a sad-happy memory, too."

"Oh?"

"One of the sick kids I played for in DC passed away," Ethan said.

"I'm sorry."

"Her parents sent me a very nice email last night about how the few hours I'd spent there and the songs I'd shared brightened her world."

"You gave her a gift."

They walked on the sidewalk under oak trees with dangling Spanish moss and passed tall magnolias with their waxy green leaves and thick white flowers.

"Yeah, I'm glad she had that to take with her. I still hate she didn't survive, but her parents said my music reminds them of her happiness. I'm glad her parents told me. I just have to process it a bit more."

Billy glanced down at Ethan's hand. She wanted to hold it, feel the strength and warmth and give him some of her own. But she rarely made such compassionate gestures, and the distance looked like too large a gap to cross.

"You're a good listener, Billy Jean. I appreciate you."

***

THE NEXT DAY, Billy roamed the perimeter of the photo shoot with Scott and Wayne. Pope and Claude had the day off while Barry watched the entry and JJ was on wheels.

The shoot took place on a Spanish ship replica—a floating museum parked on the Mississippi river, which Ethan had rented for a half day.

Ethan and the band wore all black against the backdrop of dark wood and blue sky. Ethan looked casual in a black T-shirt snug on his biceps. Niko wore a button-down shirt with the sleeves ripped off to reveal frayed edges and tattooed arms. His long hair was down and straight along his shoulders. Dan wore a black leather jacket over his black T-shirt, both of which contrasted nicely with his gray mustache. Edgar wore black overalls.

The group cut up through the shoot—teasing each other about their expressions or comparing notes on embarrassing moments in parenthood.

Billy meandered on the periphery but was drawn below deck at the sound of hushed but hostile voices.

"You treat him like a monopoly piece you move around the board." Alice's voice was a harsh contrast to her usual docile tune.

"Oh, grow up. His career is soaring because of me," Meg shot back with her usual condescending tone.

Since the stairs creaked with her descent, Billy announced her arrival when she reached the room in which they stood. "Everybody okay?"

Meg stood with crossed arms, towering over Alice. She wore a black skirt suit, which looked as menacing as her expression compared to Alice's white dress with blue lilies and wide-eyed worry.

"We're fine," Meg snapped. She gave Alice one last glare before storming past Billy and out of the room.

Alice sniffed and hugged herself.

Billy entered the room with bunk beds on one side and period clothing on display on the other. "You want to talk about it?"

"No. I hate Meg. She's so manipulative, and Ethan doesn't even see it." She wiped at her eyes.

Billy slipped her hands into her pockets. "He seems to trust her."

"Wouldn't be the first mistake he's made."

"The drinking?"

Alice shrugged. "Tamika."

Billy considered Alice's answer. Was Tamika a mistake? Ethan didn't think so. They'd discovered they had different expectations, but Ethan had explained in his memoir that he'd do it all again for the outcome of having Alyssa.

Billy gave Alice a long moment to elaborate but she didn't.

"She has her own life now with Moody. It all worked out," Billy said.

Alice snorted a disagreement but didn't explain her behavior.

"You've worked with Ethan for how long now?" Billy wanted to get Alice to open up to her. If she did, maybe she could learn something valuable about Meg.

"I was hired when he restarted the band ... sober."

"If you're worried Meg doesn't have Ethan's best interest at heart, talk to him. He's very approachable."

Alice shot her a look and closed her body language even further. Billy tried to decipher what that meant.

"No." She shook her head. "No, I can't bother him." She walked around Billy and up the narrow, wooden stairs. "I have to get back to work."

The travel from New Orleans to Dallas was as uneventful as the New Orleans concert, and now the Dallas concert was a few days away.

Ethan worked on songs alone the morning of his birthday. He took calls from Alyssa and Tamika, and no one else. Fresh flowers, shimmering metallic balloons, and colorful gifts decorated his hotel room. Gifts ranged from cologne, to chocolate, to bottles of wine.

A knock sounded at his door, followed by the electronic click of his door unlocking.

Billy entered, short brown bangs swooshing across her forehead. She had a cup of coffee in one hand—the Columbian blend he'd sent her that morning—and a navy-blue box in the other.

He glanced around at the clutter of gifts and music sheets around his room, but nothing could be done about it. "What's up?"

"Happy birthday."

"Thank you."

She cleared her throat before thrusting the small box toward him.

"Oh. Thanks." He accepted it.

Since she continued to stand, unmoving, he took the cue to open the gift. He lifted the lid to see a guitar pick— black with white skull and crossbones.

He picked it up and inspected the smooth surface. "Very cool."

"You said in your memoir that you have a commemorative guitar pick for every year sober. Now you have one for surviving a hit."

His eyebrows lifted.

"It's silly. I'm sorry. Probably too dark or twisted."

She started to reach for the pick, but he jerked his hand away from her. "I like it. And my surprise is not because I think it's morose. My surprise is because you finished my memoir."

"Yeah, well. Intrusive. Remember?"

He grinned. Not intrusive. She tried to downplay it, but she had many other ways of dispassionately researching him. The fact that she'd read his memoir felt personal—intimate—when she already spent so much time with him.

She walked over to his collection of gifts and picked up a bottle of wine to read the label. "Somebody thought this was a nice gift for you?"

"I take no offense at the alcohol—people either don't know or don't care that I'm a recovering alcoholic." The temptation to unleash that side of himself died a long time ago. "I'll regift the booze—usually to Wayne and JJ and the band, who have the loyalty to have sworn off drinking in my presence." He'd fired the drummer preceding Niko, who'd showed up high to practice one day.

He turned the pick over in his fingers. "Forty years old."

"Forty years young," Billy corrected him.

He smiled. He certainly didn't feel old. He kept in shape, ate healthy, and kept to his routine.

"And so much fame by forty," she added.

"I've come a long way from dive bars and cheap liquor. But I always worked hard. Sure, discovery by a record label that had the channels to promote my music had been a bit of fortuitous timing, but serendipity wouldn't have happened without the preceding hard work of practice, music writing, and building a fan base on social media."

"'Those who are victorious plan effectively and change decisively.'"

"Exactly. Who said that?"

"Sun Tzu. *The Art of War* was my reading staple during my military tours."

"I like that one. I'm a fan of, 'Chance favors the prepared mind, and opportunity favors the bold.' Louis Pasteur."

"I wish I had the opportunity to gift wrap a closed investigation as a birthday present." Billy ran her fingers along the petals of a lily from one of his bouquets.

Ethan leaned back on the couch. "Oh, I don't know. Then you'd leave—your work here would be done. It would be a shame to lose you after we're finally friends. And on my birthday no less."

She smiled but didn't look up from the flowers. She also didn't deny his classification of them as friends.

When she turned to face him, she looked radiant framed in orange, pink, and white flowers with the morning sun streaming through the window to her right, casting a glow along her skin. "You don't have any activities outside your room until this evening, but if you need a break for lunch or a walk, the team is here for you."

"Thanks." He glanced at his watch and back up. "Let's go to the gym at ten."

"I'll be back for you." She walked to the door, coffee in hand, and left.

Ethan stared at the door as it closed. What would be a fantastic birthday gift? Unwrapping that carefully constructed shell around Billy and finding out what desires lay beneath it.

As BILLY LEFT Ethan's hotel room, her phone buzzed.

"How is the investigation going?" Maxine asked.

"Slow. Claire has been doing her usual digging, but the perpetrator's steps have been well covered."

Billy had been in touch with either Claire or Mica every few days, aware that the investigation was a joint effort. Still, she'd felt her role had been too passive of late.

"Sometimes these things take time. Whoever is responsible will mess up, and Rider SI will be in place this time to catch the perp."

Another pep talk. Billy grinned. She liked this new side of Maxine—not lonely and overworked.

"Yes, we're in place should another threat occur." She let herself back into her hotel room where she planned to review the schematics again for Ethan's birthday venue tonight.

"In the meantime, you get to listen to good music."

An image of Ethan appeared in Billy's mind. Full lips, strong jaw, intense eyes that had their own gravitational force, pulling her gaze toward them. She'd wanted to linger longer in his hotel room and had felt a small thrill when he'd suggested the gym.

"How are things with your Russian man?"

Maxine let out a grunt. "We are really good, Billy. And

I don't think in seven years of working together you ever once asked me about my personal life."

Crap. Maxine was right. Billy knew about Maxine's past—from a rough first marriage to a grown child angry with her and the years it took to reconnect—through bits and pieces Maxine had talked about only when whiskey had loosened her tongue. But Billy had never asked her outright. Until now.

"What's his name?"

"I don't—"

"You can't bullshit me, Billy. You wouldn't ask about my man unless you were thinking about one of your own."

"It's a ridiculous crush."

"Billy, you are one of the most level-headed people I know. You are also distrusting, skeptical, and critical. If there's someone you are romantically interested in, I'm sure it's more than a crush."

It's a dream, Billy thought. *It isn't real.*

"It doesn't matter. We live in different worlds."

"Would you have said that about me and Vlad not so long ago?" Maxine asked. "I sure as hell did."

"Yeah, I guess so."

"You're really not going to tell me his name?" Maxine asked.

"I'm really not."

The older woman sighed. "Well, we wouldn't be having this discussion at all if he wasn't someone important to you. I hope you give your feelings a chance. Don't shut him out because of some absurd notion the two of you are incompatible before finding out if there's any truth to such a statement."

"Yeah, will do."

"Now, get back to work."

Billy smiled into the phone. "Sure thing."

14

The crowded party had Billy on high alert. Blue balloons decorated one corner with the number "40."

At least she knew no one was armed—except Ethan's bodyguards. The swanky Dallas nightclub required everyone to go through metal detectors first. They catered to the needs of celebrities.

Yet, if Billy wanted to hurt someone, she knew a dozen ways that didn't require a type of weapon that would set off a metal detector. So far, the only threats to her client were the many women who flocked to him to steal a kiss to his cheek, a hug, or a selfie.

Billy suspected the gathering was more Meg's doing as a publicity stunt than the type of birthday party Ethan would have designed for himself.

At the bar, one woman ordered Ethan a drink as another greeted him with an arm over his shoulder. Ethan accepted the drink, and Claude flawlessly exchanged the alcoholic beverage for a club soda. The men had keeping temptation away from their friend down to an art. Ethan had given them high praise in his memoir for their role in his achieving and maintaining sobriety.

Ethan smiled and socialized, looking dapper dressed in all black with his silver cufflinks.

Meg approached in a low-cut red dress that hugged her curves. She shooed the ogling women away from Ethan.

Leaning in, she gave him an air kiss to the cheek. "Let's dance, darling. I've had a few drinks, and I need a trustworthy dance partner." She tossed an arm around his shoulder.

Billy suppressed an eye roll. In her many years protecting celebrities, she'd mastered the art of an internal eye roll.

Ethan would dance with Meg, not because he was attracted to her but because he was a decent man who didn't embarrass an inebriated, desperate woman.

Billy followed them, intending to hover dutifully at the edge of the dance floor.

Meg cackled. "Really? Is your guard dog going to dance with us? That's not the type of threesome I'd enjoy."

"Meg," Ethan warned in a cautionary tone Billy had never heard him use.

She laughed. "Joking. I'm just joking." Still, she

plucked the club soda from Ethan's hand and passed it dismissively to Billy as though she was a waitress rather than his bodyguard.

Meg's petty dismissal didn't offend her. Billy wasn't a threat to any of Ethan's relationships, and she wouldn't trade lifestyles with Meg for a millisecond. Ethan wasn't romantically interested in Meg any more than then rest of the women pining for his attention. His priority was Alyssa.

Billy downed the club soda as she surveyed the room while keeping an eye on Ethan and Meg dancing. Ice clinked in the empty glass.

Why did these women fall over themselves to be close to him? He was attractive, sure, but they knew nothing of his personality. Did they only want the claim to have slept with him?

That was a shame.

He was actually quite a catch—not that any of them knew that. He was a compassionate and caring father. He wrote moving songs about love and loss with lyrics and melody poured from his heart and soul. And he had an amazing body. She replayed the elevator encounter, except this time they were alone ... and naked. She envisioned raking fingernails down his back.

Whoa. Where had that fantasy come from?

Billy sucked in a breath as her gaze slid from Ethan on the dance floor to the empty glass in her hand. When she looked back up, the room swayed slightly.

"*Shit.* Barry, I'm compromised," she spoke into her ear com.

"What? What's wrong?"

"Something was in my drink. I think I've been roofied." The colorful disco lights blurred around her. She blinked and shook her head, but her hazy, haloed vision didn't clear.

"Somebody roofied *you*?" Barry asked.

The incredulity in his voice irked her. "Not me, specifically. I drank Ethan's club soda."

"Why the hell—? Never mind. Let's get you out of here." His voice moved from his com to directly beside Billy but still sounded oddly distant.

She always marveled at how fast Barry could move when the situation necessitated urgency.

"Pope, Claude," Barry snapped, "I'm taking Billy out. She's been compromised. You got this?"

"We got this."

"I'm keeping my coms on. You keep me updated."

"We will."

Barry's meaty hand closed around Billy's forearm as she focused on staying upright.

As Ethan danced with Meg, he caught sight of a commotion around Billy. Barry had her by the arm as he barked something to Pope and Claude.

Ethan dropped his hands from Meg's. "Excuse me."

"But the song isn't over," Meg protested.

Ethan barely heard her complaints as he tried to discern Billy's distress. She didn't look well. Her usual focused expression looked distant, and her cheeks were flushed.

"Is Billy Jean okay?" Ethan asked Barry when he reached Billy's side.

"She's okay. I'm taking her back to the hotel."

Ethan followed them, walking beside Billy. "What happened?"

She looked up at him beneath dark lashes. "You're one to ask." She spoke in a teasing tone Ethan had never heard from her.

Barry pushed through the crowd.

"What do you mean?" Ethan asked her.

"I'll explain later," Barry said.

They reached the outside of the club. JJ pulled up to the curb, and Claude and Pope flanked Ethan and Billy, guarding their rear as Barry's keen eyes watched for danger ahead. Ethan took over supporting Billy.

"You smell good. Damn good," Billy said.

Ethan chuckled.

She breathed deeply. "Just to be clear. I've been drugged. This is not me swooning. I don't swoon."

Ethan looked down at her and smiled. "I'd never accuse you of such an egregious act."

They climbed into the rented limousine—Billy, Claude, and Barry in the back with Ethan. Pope sat up front with JJ.

Billy leaned into Ethan, snuggling against him.

Barry looked mortified. "I'll take her."

"It's okay." Ethan didn't mind her slight figure against him. In fact, she smelled good too—fresh gardenias. "Tell me what happened?"

Barry held up one of the club's glasses. The drink in it

was gone and only ice remained. "She drank from this glass, and now she's ... well, like this."

Billy ran a hand along her chest and began fidgeting with her buttons. Ethan took hold of her hand to keep her from undoing them.

"It's so hot," she complained breathlessly. "I think the drink was spiked with Rohypnol."

"The date-rape drug?" Ethan looked at Billy's attire.

She was attractive, but there were a lot of more seductively dressed women who could have been easier targets. And he'd be damned if somebody was going to get away with a stunt like this at his private birthday party. Someone he knew—someone he considered a friend—was responsible.

Then he remembered Meg taking the drink from his hand and passing it off to Billy. "Claude gave me that club soda."

"Bingo," Billy slurred.

Claude's eyes went wide. "Ethan, I didn't—"

"No, no. I would never think that of you." Ethan started to raise his hand to calm Claude, but as soon as he did, Billy reached up and fondled the hair at the base of his neck. He took her hand again.

"Sorry," Billy said. She turned to look at Claude with overly intent focus as she smacked her lips together. "Who else touched the glass?"

"Just me and the bartender," Claude answered.

"Which *bastenser*?" she slurred.

"We'll look into it, Billy." Barry said. "First, let's get you checked out."

"I don't need me to get you checked out," Billy

jumbled the words. "I've had benzos before. This is it. This is them. I just need to sleep it off with Ethan. No, no. That was supposed to be—sorry, Ethan, I'm not very professional right now."

"It's okay, Billy. You were drugged, and apparently with sedatives targeted at me."

Barry seemed to visibly relax, as though he thought Ethan would blame his partner for her actions right now.

She leaned into Ethan again as they exited the car at the hotel valet curb. Ethan, Barry, and Claude escorted her up to her room—all while she alternated between cussing at the situation and apologizing to Ethan.

"*Chunk*," Billy snapped, looking at Claude through narrowed eyes. "You need to retrace your steps with that drink. Think of anyone who came in contact with it." She put her hand to her head as if dizzy.

"We'll handle it, Billy," Barry said again, worry in his voice.

Ethan wondered if Barry had ever seen his partner vulnerable like this. Billy was always unflappable. Under the influence, she was loopy but in an adorable way.

Inside her hotel room, Ethan eased her onto the bed. "I'll stay with her."

"No," Billy and Barry said in unison.

"Look," Ethan said sternly to Barry, "you need to get back and investigate while the trail's still hot—or whatever the terminology is—which means your protective team on me is down people. You can't take another person out to watch Billy. I'll watch her, and the rest of the team watches me. Hell, I'm responsible for somebody roofying her anyway."

Barry's expression hardened as the soft light of the room reflected off his balding, sweating head. "You're not responsible for Billy stepping between you and harm. That's her job. And you insult her by suggesting anything else. But you do make a point about staffing shortages. I'll take *Chunk* back with me," he made the same *Goonies* movie reference Billy had, "and we'll see who he recognizes. Everyone else will stay here."

"Good. But let's move Billy to my room. There's a sofa I can sleep on in there."

In her small room, Ethan would have to lie next to her in the bed if he wanted to get some shut-eye, and such proximity seemed like a bad idea with her tipsy. When Ethan turned back to Billy, her eyes were closed, and he wondered if she'd passed out. Right.

He bent and scooped her up into his arms. "Grab her bag and get the door, will you?"

Barry scurried to do both with Claude leading the way to Ethan's hotel room.

In a few minutes, Ethan was alone with Billy as Barry and Claude went back to the club. Pope and JJ guarded Ethan's door. Ethan fixed Billy a glass of ice water while she fumbled to remove her shoes and socks.

As he handed her the water, he grinned at the sight of her painted toenails.

She accepted the glass but looked at it with disappointment. "What, no *mocha-cappo-express-horchata-latte*?" she teased.

"If you want coffee, I'll make you coffee." He sat beside her on the couch.

She took large gulps of water. "I want ... many things."

He kept silent, giving her the opportunity to elaborate on what those "many things" might entail. She stared at him with something like hungry desire, but she blinked and it was gone.

"What do you want?" she asked.

He slid off his boots and leaned back on the couch. "To settle down. To stop the tours or at least shorten them. To spend more time with Alyssa. Your turn."

"Hmm. Settle down." The way she said the words, Ethan couldn't tell if she was thinking about what he wanted or saying what she wanted.

"You want to settle down, too?" he asked.

"Yeah. Yeah, I'd like that. I'm on tour too, you know. All the time."

"You certainly are."

"But I stay in the shadows. I like the shadows."

"You look good in the light, Billy Jean." He pursed his mouth shut. Was he coming on to her?

He had no business flirting with his bodyguard, especially under these circumstances. But if he was going to let her know how he felt about her, perhaps it would be easiest when her guard was down.

"So do you." She climbed closer so that she loomed over him. Hungry eyes roamed his face and mouth.

He wanted her to kiss him; she didn't have to go far to reach his lips. He held back, not wanting to make the first move for several reasons. Since she worked for him, he was in position of power and wouldn't misuse it. Secondly, she was under the influence, and he wouldn't take advantage of her.

Why did he want her so much? He'd turned down so

many willing women over the years for all sorts of reasons: they wanted to be with a rock star as their claim to the fame; they wanted the fortune or the attention. None of them asked what he wanted. None of them cared about Alyssa. Billy was a woman uninterested in his wealth or prestige and who cared about his daughter.

And she was off-limits. He had said it himself.

Heat radiated from her body and her eyes. Spine-tingling excitement coursed through him as he waited for her to press those succulent lips to his.

She shook her head and pushed herself back. "Shit. I want to keep my job."

"I want you to keep your job." He swallowed, part relieved, part disappointed.

Billy surprised him when she advanced again, this time kissing him deeply and passionately. Her motions were without hesitation or reservation. He placed his hands on her hips, enjoying their sensual exploration of each other's mouths. His mind wandered to where this could escalate—discarded clothing, skin on skin, bodies entwined. The couch. The bed. The wall. Maybe even the elevator.

He broke the kiss and slid away from her. When he stood, she stared at him in disbelief.

He tried to pull himself together. "Not like this. I want you, Billy Jean. But it's going to be when you're sober. It's going to be when you let your guard down, *willingly*. We'll talk about this tomorrow."

He walked into the bathroom, closed the door, and turned on the cold water in the shower.

15

As soon as she woke the next morning, Billy sneaked back into her room. She cleaned, dressed, and went to the lobby to grab a cup of coffee. Plain. Black. Coffee.

She'd received no room service coffee this morning—not surprising given her behavior last night.

"Walk of shame?" Barry approached as she filled a paper cup.

"Only if I'd gotten laid. Since I didn't, there is no shame." She blew steam off the surface of her beverage.

Not for lack of trying, she thought. She didn't like not being in control, and last night she'd clearly lost control. Disinhibited, her inner desires had revealed themselves —to both herself and Ethan.

"You haven't lost your sense of humor. Are you okay?" Barry asked.

Fortunately, Ethan had shoved away from her last night after she'd jumped him like a cat in heat. He'd looked shocked as he'd composed himself. He'd said something, but her heart was pounding so loudly she'd only heard part of what he said. *"We'll talk about this tomorrow."*

She sipped the coffee. "Better now. As long as Ethan doesn't kick me off the team for kissing him."

Barry choked on his coffee. "You're shitting me."

Billy shrugged. "It was accident. Sort of."

"You kissed the client, and it was sort of an accident?" He gaped at her.

"He's an attractive man, and I'd had the equivalent of four martinis on an empty stomach. So, yeah, an accident."

"Is he upset?" Barry asked.

Billy remembered the way Ethan had kissed her back. Many things were fuzzy in her recollection of last night's events, but that kiss wasn't one of them. If Ethan was upset over the kiss, it would be at his own reaction to it. Since he immediately and effectively squelched the sparks between them, he had nothing to be upset about.

"I don't see why he would be. It was one kiss. I did a lot more than that with Johan."

"On the tennis circuit?" Barry rubbed his neck. "Yeah, but he was a client's friend, not the client."

"Anyway, I don't think he's upset."

"You should apologize. And probably tell Mica."

Billy walked back toward the elevators, coffee in hand. "I'll tell Mica," she assured Barry.

But apologize to Ethan?

She pushed the button for the elevator. How could she lie? She wasn't sorry for kissing him. It was a damn fine kiss. She was sorry it hadn't lasted longer.

She needed a night of carelessness. Of stress relief. But not with a client. She'd been holding down the steady jobs over the past year with Barry while the rest of the Rider team had been dealing with a ferocious enemy —Lucius Titan. After some harrowing events, everyone was safe now, and the scumbag who'd caused so much grief was in jail. Billy had had the buildup of angst for the danger her team had been exposed to and defeated but without a sense of a release for herself.

Now, with that kiss burned into her mind, along with Ethan's fingertips on her hips, tension would mount again. She'd have to find an outlet. She wasn't worried about kissing Ethan again; she wouldn't be taking any more Rohypnol, and she had the good sense otherwise to keep her hands—and mouth—to herself ... no matter how sweet those mint-green eyes looked when crinkled with a smile.

When Billy reached her room, she called Mica for a video chat. As she waited for Mica to answer, she drank more coffee. Judging by the way she kept thinking about Ethan, her brain was still foggy. She needed to clear it for the workday ahead.

"Billy, good to see you. Barry told me what happened last night. Are you okay?"

"No worse for wear."

"Barry sent me a list of people who would've been close to the drink. Claire's running the names, but I don't think there's anyone listed we haven't already looked into—Claude, Alice, Meg, and all of the band members."

Billy blew out her cheeks. "The spiked drink may not even be related to the shooting. Those are very different methods of attack, the latter of which isn't lethal."

"Unless the plan was to sedate him and then kill him."

"Then the responsible party would have foolishly overlooked his security team."

"Speaking of his security team, I have to bench you for today, Billy."

Billy opened her mouth to protest but just as quickly saw the logic of Mica's decision and closed her lips together.

She ran a hand through her hair. "Shit. Yeah, okay. I get it." She couldn't risk sluggish reaction time if another attack happened. She certainly wouldn't want to be responsible for compromising Ethan's safety because she went back to work less than twenty-four hours after drinking sedatives.

"I'll use the time to go back over person of interest files." She finished the last drops of coffee and made a three-point shot into the trash with the empty cup.

"I kissed Ethan," Billy blurted out.

Mica leaned closer to the screen. "I don't think I heard you correctly."

"I kissed the client. I blame the Rohypnol. One kiss, nothing more."

"As your boss, I need to know if there will be any professional fallout from this."

"No. I think he recognized I wasn't myself."

"And is this going to impact your ability to work with him?"

Billy shot Mica a look to convey how ludicrous her question was.

"It's a logical question—at least for a *normal* person. Do you even have a romantic bone in your body?" Mica asked.

"I'm no anatomy expert, but I don't think bones are the part of the body where romance resides."

"Cute."

"Are we done here?" Billy asked.

"No. As your friend, I have to know—how was the kiss?"

Billy thought about coming back with "a lady never kisses and tells," but she was no proper lady. "Amazing."

Mica's eyebrows shot up.

Billy continued, "If the kiss is any prelude to what intimacy is like with Ethan, no wonder women fall at his feet."

"So, he kissed you back?" Mica leaned closer to the screen.

"For a minute. At least until he remembered he was making out with the hired help."

"Hey," Mica snapped, "he'd be lucky to have the hired help. And if he can't see that then he's not worth it."

"Worth what? Mica, it was one kiss. The end."

"Sometimes the first kiss is just the beginning."

Billy chuckled with a shake of her head.

"What?" Mica asked.

"If Maxine was still in charge, this conversation wouldn't be happening."

Mica cleared her throat and scowled. "Don't let it happen again," she said gruffly, mimicking the former CEO of Rider SI. "Is that better?"

"Much better." Billy grinned and disconnected the call.

ETHAN WOKE and checked his entry room. He was disappointed but not surprised to see that Billy had left.

After his shower last night, he'd returned to find her asleep on the couch. Since he hadn't trusted himself to take his hands off of her if he touched her again, he'd left her on the sofa and pulled the blanket from his bed over her.

After he dressed for the day—casual jeans and a T-shirt—he invited Pope inside his room for coffee.

"How's the family?" Ethan made them both a cappuccino. He smiled, thinking of Billy's jab at his taste in frothy coffees last night.

"Eh, good. The kids had fun on spring break."

"And Misty?"

"I think she's ready for summer."

Ethan recalled that Pope's wife was a high school algebra teacher. He handed Pope the coffee, and the men sat on opposite ends of the couch.

"Helluva night last night," Pope said.

"I hope Barry figures out who roofied my drink."

Ethan shifted in his seat as he changed the subject. "We've been friends a long time, Pope. You've seen me at my worst. Do you think I've pulled myself together enough so I'm relationship material again?"

"God, Ethan. You've been sober almost ten years. Tamika remarried. You could, too."

"Whoa. Nobody's saying marriage. I'm talking about dating."

"Yeah, you should date again." Pope stared down at his drink for a hesitant moment. "But you can do better than *her*."

Ethan felt a defense flare. Billy was a damn fine woman. "What do you mean?" He fought to keep his tone even.

"Well, it just seems like Meg's a bit of gold digger. And too flashy for you."

Ethan barked out a laugh.

Pope looked startled. "I thought. I mean ... she was dancing with you last night. And that red dress didn't cover up much."

"Meg had a little too much to drink is all. She and I have known each other a long time. It's not like that."

"Who then?"

Without knowing if Billy was genuinely romantically interested in him, Ethan didn't want to volunteer information. He also wouldn't want to do anything to undermine her authority with his crew. "Just hypothetically thinking about dating again."

"Good. You should. But be careful. There are women out there who'll want to take advantage of your money and status. I read somewhere that the celebrity couple divorce rate is double that of the general population."

"Sound advice." Again, Ethan was thinking of dating, not marriage.

Regardless, he knew a woman who spent most of her days not ten feet from him and wasn't swept away by his fame. Hell, she was barely impressed by it. But he wanted to see if she was as interested in him as he was in her and if their chemistry from last night was more than artificially-induced attraction.

At Ethan's long deliberation, Pope said, "Are you sure you don't have someone in mind?"

Ethan grinned. "Maybe I do."

A knock came at the door.

Ethan hopped to his feet and practically skipped to the door in anticipation of seeing Billy again. The memory of their kiss rose to the forefront of his mind. It'd been sensual and hungry. And—

Before he could open the door, a voice spoke from the other side. "Barry here."

Ethan concealed his disappointment and opened the door to let Barry inside the room. "Good morning, Barry. How's Billy's hangover?"

"She's feeling better and taking the day off."

"Makes sense," Ethan said a little too quickly.

Did it make sense? Was she avoiding him after their kiss—their heated kiss, which he had every intention of trying to replicate? Unless she didn't want to. He wouldn't push, but he wasn't above nudging her.

Barry eyed him with keen interest, making Ethan

wonder if Billy had told him what transpired between them.

"Company protocol," Barry said. "If personnel are injured on the job or physically compromised in any way there's a minimum twenty-four hours off the security detail."

So, she wasn't avoiding him—she was on mandatory leave. Ethan could accept that and wait patiently to see her again.

"Okay." Ethan rubbed his hands together. "Let's get Alice in here and go over today's schedule."

16

Two days after his birthday party, Ethan spent the morning peering over spreadsheets in his room. Tracking income and expenses was a part of his job he took seriously since achieving sobriety. He had a family and future planning to budget for if he wanted to scale back the touring.

Usually when he reconciled the budget, his mind wandered—mostly to song lyrics. Not today. Today his mind wandered to the scrumptious kiss with Billy.

They hadn't talked about it, but she was back on duty. Billy was an open book. An open book encased in iron bars—you could see it but not touch it. She was easy to read with her integrity and impeccable work ethic, but she kept herself emotionally inaccessible.

He'd expect nothing less given the level of professionalism, discretion, and dedication her job took. But then they'd kissed. He was already attracted to her and had no problem respecting her boundaries. Until he knew how she kissed. No holding back. And he'd bet the next level of intimacy with Billy would be just as intense.

But his attraction to her extended beyond the physical. She was a calming force and practical for discussing ideas, yet the sprinkle of subtle humor she added was a key ingredient to her appeal.

A knock at his door was followed by the metallic click of the electronic key unlocking.

Billy entered the room carrying a brown paper bag. "Barry bought frittatas." She set the bag down on the table and turned to leave.

"No good morning? No pleasantries?"

Billy gave an uncertain glance around the room. "Good morning."

"Stay and relax a minute." He inspected the contents of the bag. The smell of egg and roasted vegetables wafted toward him.

Billy walked over to the window and tugged a small gap in the sheer curtain closed.

"I feel like *relax* is a foreign concept for you. Do you want one of these?" He gestured to the frittata bag.

"No thanks. And I'm not here to relax. When I'm around you, I'm on the job. I don't relax on the job."

"Unless you have Rohypnol in your system." He picked up his guitar and sat back on the small sofa. He needed to keep busy if he was going to have this conversation while keeping his hands off Billy. He smiled at her.

He couldn't tell if her cheeks flushed or if that was just the sunlight through the window.

"Yes. I was a little *too* relaxed after that," she said.

"Wasn't all bad." He plucked lightly on his guitar in the semblance of casualness even as he held his breath waiting for her reply.

In a restless pace, she walked over to his desk where his finance program was open then back to the window—not directly in front of it, but cautiously to the side.

"Paying bills?"

Deflection? That was her response? Was she avoiding discussing the kiss because she was embarrassed or because she'd liked it too much?

"I review all my own finances. Not because I find the subject matter riveting but because I can't be swindled if I know my own income and expenses. Meg and Alice run the account to pay vendors, hotels, and travel expenses, but they're on a fixed budget they can't exceed."

"You know Pope and Claude's salaries are above the national average for minimally-trained bodyguards."

"Thanks to you and Barry, they're now well-trained bodyguards for when you leave."

For the briefest moment, Billy looked sad at the mention of an end to their relationship—uh, *business partnership*.

"But, yes, I do pay them very well. They put up with my crap for a long time."

"The alcohol?" she asked.

He grunted. "Yeah, the alcohol. They kept me together when I was self-destructing. I stayed in bars way too late, and they never left me, even when I was a drunk asshole to them. I never got into drugs, and I think that's because they secretly steered me clear—flushing samples people gave as gifts and tossing people out of parties if they brought drugs."

Billy sat on the chair opposite the sofa. "You're candid about it all."

He gauged the distance between them—too far. But since he was talking about his sordid past, any hope of recreating that kiss would have to be postponed. This wasn't the conversation he'd planned to have, but he wanted her to know all of him.

"I'm honest about my past, and not proud of it. It hangs over all future relationships."

"Tamika left you because of your drinking?"

"Ah, well, that's a little different. I stopped drinking with Tamika's help, and I owe her for the part she played in my recovery. But we mutually agreed to divorce because we had very different ideas of what a relationship together would look like. She thought I would give up the tours, and I thought she'd tour with me. In reality, touring is my livelihood, and she wanted to go to medical school. As you can see, we stayed friends."

"Then why is the alcohol still a concern with future relationships? You've been sober so long." She leaned forward, engaged in the conversation.

"When you're a celebrity, most women have the expectation of a social life. I don't do much of that anymore."

Billy shrugged. "So, find someone who supports your way of life."

He chuckled. "Oh, it's so simple is it? Someone who is

supportive of my career, doesn't want a nightlife, and will love and respect Alyssa."

"Completely doable. The last part is easy. Alyssa's adorable. You shouldn't worry about anyone liking her. Now, the traveling lifestyle might be harder to accommodate."

"Speaking from experience?"

Billy arched an eyebrow. "We're talking about you. I'm not in the market for a long-term relationship."

Ethan could have talked about how this was his last major tour—taking lifestyle accommodation out of the equation—but he liked the opportunity to learn more about Billy. He felt like they were putting feelers out on what the other was looking for—testing their compatibility without openly acknowledging they were comparing themselves against what the other wanted.

"Why?" he asked.

"My lifestyle isn't conducive to long-term relationships."

"Hmm. So, no one at Rider SI is married?" He knew Mica and Claire were, so he suspected he had Billy cornered.

"Yes." Her chuckle had a slightly defeated tone. "Most of them are."

"Ah, so you simply need to find someone who supports your way of life. Piece of cake."

She narrowed her eyes and gave him a wry grin. "Yeah, piece of cake."

Ethan set his guitar down and leaned toward her. "Billy Jean, about the other night—the kiss—"

A knock on the door was followed by Alice entering.

Ethan pushed to his feet—he was going to need to rethink his open-door policy.

"Ethan, the choir for the next performance had to cancel. Seems a case of norovirus struck at a church picnic. I have a list of other church choirs we can try."

He watched Billy slip out the door, catching the last glance she shot him from over her shoulder—a brief open-lipped look of longing. It vanished so fast he wondered if he'd imagined it.

THE NEXT DAY, Billy savored a bite of beef brisket as she glanced around at the panic tables. The warm Texas sun beamed above them.

"Edgar, you picked a damn fine place," Claude said, his hands and face smeared with BBQ sauce from his hickory-smoked ribs.

Edgar grunted something akin to "you're welcome" as he chomped on garlic buttered toast.

"I second that." Barry licked his fingers before saluting Edgar with his Diet Coke.

"Delicious," Billy agreed.

People bustled around them in various lines for the food trucks, drink refills, or shuffling to find an open table.

Beside her, Ethan nudged her elbow. "Relax, Billy Jean. Nobody knows about our little impromptu lunch. We're not going to be targeted at a food truck stand. Besides, Wayne and JJ have the perimeter, right? You've been training everyone." He took a bite of pulled pork.

"Everyone is well trained," she agreed.

What else could she say? That she was layering on the bodyguard affect because it helped distract her from thinking about how they were all crammed together at this picnic table, and Ethan's thigh was pressed against hers? Even over the scent of sweet molasses, slow-roasted beef and pork, and vinegar in the coleslaw, she could smell Ethan's delectable aftershave.

She added, "You could still be recognized, and then we'd have to rush you out of here."

He turned his head slightly to look at her. "I'm sure you'd manage."

Was he flirting? What was that crazy, constantly amused curve of his lips?

"It could get messy," she said flatly, staring into his liquid eyes.

He licked his lips, drawing her gaze back to his mouth. Lowering his voice beneath the hum of conversation at the table, he said, "Part of me thinks you might like a little messy."

She swallowed.

Ugh. Must be the Texas heat making the afternoon so unbearably hot. She resisted the urge to tug at her shirt collar and betray the slightest surrender to his sultry innuendo.

Instead, she plucked a pickle from her plate and— without breaking eye contact—crunched a noisy bite.

Ethan released a low, silky laugh which danced along Billy's spine and caught the attention of Dan, who was sitting across from them. His gaze flickered between the two of them as if in quiet appraisal.

Did Dan find her worthy of Ethan? She wondered. She didn't normally care about people's opinions of her. Ethan's mattered. Apparently, his best friend's opinion also mattered to her.

She knew her worth on and off the battlefield. But romantic relationships? What value could she bring to one of those?

MICA RETURNED to the state penitentiary to visit Lucius Titan again. He was a vile creature slithering out of his lair to speak with her. She loathed needing this man for information, but she wasn't above seeking help for clients, even from bottom-dwellers like him.

She was dressed conservatively in a peach-colored blouse and blue jeans, but that didn't keep Lucius from blatantly admiring the view. His greedy eyes only heightened her first-trimester nausea.

"You have information for me?" she asked, standing opposite the table from where he sat.

He gestured for her to take a seat. "Now, now," he chided playfully. "That's not how this works, Mica. You are required to sit and be civil. Why so grumpy? You didn't lose a client, did you?"

She pulled out the chair before speaking in a flat, fast monotone. "I'm hoping for rain today. My garden needs watering. Did you see that new reality TV show? It is appalling what people will do for attention and fame."

He gave her a lazy smile. "My company never stooped

to investigative work—security and protection were my forte."

"And trafficking and money laundering."

He shrugged. "Allegedly."

"I got your email to see you about the information I requested." At least, she'd received a message from someone claiming to work for Lucius who told her to visit him again. "Do you know who hired the sniper or not?" Mica asked.

"No."

Ugh! She wanted to punch him in the throat for wasting her time. She started to stand.

"But I know who the sniper is."

Mica abruptly returned to her seat.

Lucius gave a feral smile like a poker player about to lay down three of a kind and claim the pot.

"And his name is?"

"No, no. Again, that's not how this works. We share. You want my information, I receive something of value from you."

Mica gritted her teeth. Information came at a price with a man like Lucius. She didn't want to be boxed into a corner doing any dirty work for him.

As an idea came to mind, she leaned back and crossed her arms. "Fine. I tell you who's expanding in the drug world, and you tell me the name of the sniper."

His eye twitched at her unexpected news. "Very well."

"Lautaro Fernandez."

Lucius licked his lips. "Is that so?"

"He's Argentinian based, but he's bringing US gangs

into his fold. He's the new up-and-coming boss in US organized crime."

Lucius's lips betrayed a sour twist as he digested the bit of news.

"Quentin Hawkins is your sniper. Former UK Special Forces."

Mica blanched. Special Forces. That meant he'd have formidable fighting skills—ones she didn't want anyone on her team to have to face.

Lucius casually continued, "He's been a killer for hire for, oh, years now. He has an impeccable reputation. Word on the street is he's never failed to make his kill."

Mica felt her throat constrict. He'd missed Ethan, which meant Quentin's next attack was only a matter of time. And yet, weeks had passed without another attempt. She'd like to claim the sheer power of Ethan's new bodyguard team had kept evil at bay, but in reality, Billy and Barry could only do so much against a covert sniper attack. The celebrity's schedule was public, so Quentin could strike where Ethan was next expected to tour at any moment.

Why hadn't he attacked again already? What was the assassin waiting for?

Lucius gave her a feral smile. "Why Mica, sniper got your tongue?"

17

illy sat at the bar nursing a scotch. The Dallas concert went well. Six weeks on the job and there had been no further threats after the roofie. Six weeks on the job and they still hadn't identified the culprit. Was this a reflection of her amateur investigative skills?

While Ethan and his crew drove west, Billy had flown ahead to San Francisco. Part of her wanted to scope out the hotels and venues, and part of her wanted to distance herself from Ethan. A few days without being close to him would help her refocus.

Ethan had arrived in San Francisco a few hours ago, but Billy left Barry in charge of the protection detail. She hoped one more night well spent would rid her of her desire for Ethan.

When she had downtime from the job, she usually went to one of three places—a bar, a gym, or the gun range. Tonight, she'd chosen an Irish pub on Mission Street a couple of blocks from the hotel. A few drinks and a one-night stand would get Ethan Storm out of her head.

But the scotch tasted terrible, and the music was drowned out by conversations from people near her. She compared every man she saw to Ethan. None of them had his liquid green eyes or charming smile. She didn't want groping hands from a drunk man smelling like cheap liquor.

What she wanted was—well, *shit*. She couldn't have what she wanted so why was she wasting time feeling sorry for herself?

"Well, hey there gorgeous." A man in khakis and a blue button-down shirt slid onto the barstool beside her.

Was she gorgeous? She wore jeans, a purple shirt with a V neck, and a splash of mascara. Gorgeous was a stretch. She'd always been a bit of a tomboy. And she had older brothers who'd teased her, convincing her throughout her teen years that she was unattractive.

Men she'd dated in her twenties and thirties usually found her "cute" and "adorable." She didn't date them for long as those terms weren't what she'd wanted to hear as a soldier. Maybe she'd been a little too harsh in her rejection. Cute wasn't so bad, though the term didn't describe a beauty queen like Charlize Theron, her look-alike, according to Ethan.

Damn, now she was thinking of Ethan again while this tool beside her rambled on about his day at the office.

"I'm not drunk. I'm just intoxicated by you." He blinked lazily. "Tell me about yourself." He placed a hand on her knee.

On instinct, she grasped his wrist and twisted, peeling his sweaty palm off her leg as he gasped and squealed.

"I guess I'm here tonight to teach you about touching women who haven't given you permission to touch them."

As she stood and torqued his wrist further, he bent over to ease the pain.

"Okay. Okay, let me go. Let me go." His face twisted in a grimace.

When she released him, he stumbled away from her.

He stood, rubbing his wrist and glaring at her. "Crazy *bitch*."

She pulled cash out of her phone case, paid the bartender, and slipped the phone back in the pocket of her blue jeans.

Billy left the bar, intending to walk down to take in a view of the bay. She should've chosen the gun range. It would have done more to relieve the tension she felt. And clearly her mood wasn't conducive to meeting men.

A few steps into her walk, she spotted a tail. A shaggy-haired, bearded man in baggy jeans kept pace behind her. Not subtle, but maybe Shaggy was doing this intentionally to invoke fear.

She'd been jumped by street thugs before—Russian mafia to be more specific—and she'd suffered the concussion to prove it. Once they'd gotten the drop on her, she'd vowed no one would ever do that to her again.

She was grateful she'd only had a few sips of scotch

and her mind was clear. Now she needed to make a judgement call. If she turned right at the intersection, she'd reach a more population-dense area of nightlife in the Mission District.

Safety in numbers.

If she turned left, the darker, more desolate block meant she would leave the public zone and enter a shadier part of town.

No one would come to the rescue there. She smirked. No one would come to Shaggy's rescue.

Maybe she'd get that boxing practice in after all.

The stalker had been waiting outside the bar for her. Was this because he'd marked her when she went in, or because someone hired him to tail her alone at night? Street thugs looked for easy prey. Billy might have been a woman alone, but she never carried herself with any semblance of fear or insecurity to suggest she was an easy mark.

A hired hit then.

But by who? Someone after Ethan or someone from her own past?

If she got Shaggy alone, she could coax information out of him. Intuition told her to take that gamble.

But, at the intersection, a different man in baggy pants —this one was Hispanic with a chain drooping from his belt up to his back pocket—approached from her right. His hard gaze fixed on her conveyed he was a threat, too.

She turned left.

A coordinated strike.

Her heart thudded in her chest as the stakes suddenly rose. How many more were there? Were they armed?

A flash of movement caught her attention from a side alley. Light glinted from something metallic.

Instinctively, she ducked.

An aluminum baseball bat zipped through the air, and she felt a breeze swish by as she barely missed the blow to her head.

She moved into her attacker's space, giving him no room to swing the bat again.

Upper cut.

Upper cut.

Jab.

Billy punched in three quick strikes—two to his abdomen followed by one to his jaw. The other attackers were close, so she needed to injure this one immediately.

Shaggy's fist came at her face.

She pivoted, but not before his knuckles made contact. The pain in her jaw brought her to one knee, and she used the momentum to roll out of reach. Her vision blurred, and her eyes watered.

When she came back to her feet, she assessed her predicament—three attackers. Shaggy, Chain Link, and Bat Man. On the bright side, no one seemed to have a gun.

Hmm, neither did she. She wasn't on duty, so she hadn't carried it with her.

Bat Man, face beet red with anger, swung the weapon again.

Billy moved in, bringing two hands crashing down on his forearms followed by her right elbow up into his nose. He grunted and stumbled back, one hand reaching for his bloodied proboscis.

Billy twisted the bat out of his hands, ducked as Shaggy came at her with another punch, and swung the bat into the bald man's left knee. She hadn't had time to take a full swing, but she'd hit her mark.

He screamed and fell, clutching his leg.

The third attacker—Chain Link—lashed out a kick to Billy's side. She gasped on impact and fell to the concrete sidewalk.

When he came at her with his chain, she used the opening to jab the tip of the bat into his groin.

He crumpled to the ground with a groan.

Clutching her side, Billy pushed to her feet with the help of the baseball bat. "Anybody who doesn't empty their pockets right now is getting a bat to the face."

Bat Man lurched to his feet and took off running down the sidewalk.

Billy was in no condition to give chase, and she still had two men left she could interrogate.

"Pockets," she demanded, pointing the bat back and forth at them. "You have a message for me?" She figured they'd accosted her for a reason.

As they emptied their pockets, Shaggy said in a strained voice, "We were supposed to fuck you up and tell you to leave Ethan alone."

"Well, you accomplished half of your objective—you told me to leave Ethan alone. I hope you got paid half up front." Without taking her eyes off the men, she pulled her phone out of her pocket and called her partner.

Barry answered on the second ring. "I thought you were enjoying a night off?"

"Ethan's safe?" Billy asked. She hoped the attack on her wasn't part of some larger, synchronized hit on Ethan.

"He's fine. What's going on?"

"Keep him on lockdown. I need you to come help me interrogate two assholes who mistook me for a piñata. I'm marking my location and sending it to your phone. In the alley."

"Alley? What is this, London again?"

"Well, unlike London, these guys didn't get the drop on me. Mostly." She rotated her aching jaw. Then, she unhooked her paracord bracelet and pulled out one of the cords, intending to tie up her attackers.

"You okay?"

"Yeah, just get here before I decide to beat them to a pulp for the hell of it."

BILLY WALKED the hall to Ethan's room. Despite icing, her jaw and ribs still hurt. She wore sunglasses to cover the fatigue under her eyes. She and Barry had talked to her attackers until two a.m. The men didn't know who hired them. Everything had been done through covert channels—conscription, information, contract, and payment.

Perfect, she grumbled inwardly, another attack and still no answers. Fortunately, Mica hadn't benched her for the twenty-four-hour period this time.

As she approached Ethan's hotel room, Claude stood outside like a giant boulder.

"You get into a fight?" He put his hands on his hips.

Well, that answered her question as to whether or not the bruise on her face was obvious.

"Hope the other guy looks worse." Claude snorted.

"All three of them do." She knocked once before letting herself into Ethan's room with her key card.

Claude, mouth open in a disbelieving gape, followed her inside and closed the door.

"Hey, Claude, I can't decide on the green or blue." Ethan walked out of his bedroom in pants and no shirt. He held a blue shirt in one hand and a forest-green option in the other.

Billy kept her composure despite a sudden case of dry mouth. She'd seen shirtless men. This was just another shirtless man. Her hormones disagreed with her.

She glanced at her watch. "You need to be at the studio in thirty minutes. We should leave."

"Billy Jean, what happened to your face?"

She pulled off her sunglasses for all the good they were doing her. "I'm fine. We need to leave. You have an appointment."

Ethan walked closer, surveying her jaw. "Someone hit you."

Her eyes darted to Claude and back.

Ethan's jaw tightened. "Claude, can you give us minute?"

Claude's shoulders sagged, and he lumbered out of the room. When Claude was gone and the door was closed, Ethan tossed his shirts on the chaise lounge.

He extended a hand and touched fingers to her bruised jaw. "You're okay?"

Warmth spread through her at his touch. "It's been a

long night. I could use one of your fancy coffees."

He grinned. "You got it." After walking to his deluxe coffee maker, he began cranking several knobs. He added hot water to the finely ground beans then frothed the milk, creating microfoam.

She diverted her eyes from the defined muscles of his bare back.

"You were in a fight?"

"Three assholes. It was an ambush."

"Is this my fault? I mean is it related to the work you're doing for me? I thought a night off literally meant you weren't working." He focused on the coffee and didn't turn around as he talked.

"It started off as a night off. No, it is not your fault. We don't have enough evidence yet to determine if I was targeted by the same person who targeted you. Rider SI also has enemies." The attackers had specifically told her to leave Ethan alone, but she wanted to avoid making him feel more responsible than he already did. None of this was his fault even if it turned out to be related to him. "We're investigating the source of the attack."

Billy had bagged the men's IDs and phones and given them to Barry who would send them via FedEx to Claire. The techy would know how to hack their phones and access relevant information.

Ethan turned around to face her, eyes filled with worry as he added the foamed milk to her beverage. He handed her the steaming cup of coffee.

She stared at the art on the surface—a lovely looking flower. She took a sip and had to suppress a moan of delight. "I think this is the best coffee I've ever had." She wasn't sure how much having a shirtless man—more specifically, a shirtless Ethan—prepare the beverage for her played a role in her declaration.

"It's a cappuccino."

Too close. Why was he standing so close?

He looked at her, concern still evident in his expression. "You sure you're okay?"

"You should wear the green one. It accentuates your eyes." Her words surprised her. She tugged at her shirt collar. Maybe the hot coffee was raising the temperature in the room.

She swallowed and took a step back. "We need to leave now if you're going to arrive on time."

Ethan ran a hand through his hair. "Yeah, okay." He picked up the green shirt, pulled it on, and buttoned it up.

Billy slipped her sunglasses on and drank more coffee. It still tasted delicious, even with Ethan dressed.

"I want to know as soon as you do who did this to you," he said.

"I'll keep you informed."

He nodded resolutely, then grinned as he picked up his sports coat.

Did he know? He must have seen the effect he had on her.

She was losing this battle with her will. She'd blamed it on the roofie last time. This time she'd have to blame it on sleep deprivation.

As she followed him out of the room, she took a deep breath to strengthen her resolve to keep things professional with Ethan.

18

———————

$\mathcal{M}$ica was using the office gym to do Tai Chi on an exercise mat.

Claire entered and hesitated. "You want me to come back?"

"No. I want a status update. Thanks."

Claire flopped on the ground and began stretching. "I have exhausted every avenue—friends, family, acquaintances, fans, reporters, band members, bodyguards. Those with motive haven't forked out any funds to hire a hit. Billy put spyware on a few peoples' computers for me. I'm monitoring those, but nothing has surfaced so far. Billy has done everything she could do from her location. She told me she feels like a failure, having not solved the case yet."

"Sometimes, these things take time. Aurora's case took time. Jenna's we solved in days."

"That's what I told Billy," Claire said. "She's no more a failure than the rest of us. It's not like my hard work has revealed the perpetrator either."

"What about the attack on Billy? Related or unrelated?"

"It's got to be related to Ethan, but I haven't found the person who ordered the attack," Claire said. "I ran backgrounds on all of those men. They work for a West Coast gang called *Los Leones Rojos*."

"The Red Lions?" Mica crouched and came up slowly, moving in rhythmic motions.

"Yes. And fun fact: Los Leones Rojos were recently acquired by Lautaro Fernandez."

"His name keeps coming up. Not a good sign. Why is that a fun fact?" Mica asked.

"Oh, right. The incident with Lautaro predated your employment at Rider SI. So, the story is that Lautaro Fernandez ambushed Vladimir Pronin—on his own territory in Moscow, no less—at the behest of Lucius. Maxine was visiting at the time—before she and Vlad became a couple. Maxine was there with Ryan and Reece on behalf of a client. Our team was caught in the crossfire, but we probably also saved Vladimir's life during the showdown." Claire bent over to touch her toes. "Then Maxine, who takes crap from no one, retaliated by launching a Hellfire missile into one of Lautaro's manufacturing plants."

"I recall Maxine briefing me on the story. So could the attack on Billy be this guy's retaliation for the Hellfire?"

"I don't think so." Claire's purple hair danced when she shook her head. "It was a few years ago, and Maxine never took public credit. Lucius deduced it was Maxine, but I still think Lautaro Fernandez would have acted sooner if he wanted to retaliate."

Mica moved her arms through a fluid motion as she exhaled. "You're probably right. And a street hit on one of Rider's team doesn't scream 'now we're even.' And Billy said the attackers told her to 'leave Ethan alone.' So, Los Leones Rojos were definitely employed by someone after Ethan."

"Right. And for a poor-quality street attack like that, anybody could have dished out a little cash under the table. I can't trace that."

"What about Quentin Hawkins—the man Lucius told me about?"

Claire looked despondent. "The man's a freakin' ghost. I've got nothing on him other than his military record, most of which is redacted—meaning he's all kinds of bad news."

Mica straightened and frowned. "So, we're stuck waiting for him to make a mistake or the original funding party to pay for another hit."

***

A SONG PLAYED in Ethan's mind. Something shadowy and unformed like black sand through fingers. The words conveyed darkness and hinted at a dubious deed, and the accompanying melody was tinged with anger an edge of fear.

Ethan replayed the shooting in his head—*the phone rings, it's knocked from his hand, he bends over, and the window shatters*. Had he been so close to death? To calm himself, he thought of the night Billy whisked him to safety in the elevator and kept him grounded with her body pressed against his.

"Morning, Ethan." Dan joined him in the rehearsal room.

"Morning." He tuned his guitar.

"You seem unusually somber," Dan said.

"You heard about Billy?" He didn't wait for a reply. "I've been singing, traveling, and off and on the road for twenty years. Not one of my team has ever been injured. Now in the span of a few weeks, I've been shot at with Claude right next to me, and last night Billy was attacked. And on my birthday, somebody tried to roofie me."

Dan nodded. "Scary stuff." He shuffled through sheet music in his briefcase.

"None of it makes any sense." Ethan continued. "Snipers, drugs, and street thugs. And why now? Why not when I was a belligerent drunk and maybe actually deserved it. Reckoning for the past?"

"Now, come on, don't be like that. The person attacking you is the one to blame. You can't blame yourself."

"Person or persons? Feels like there's more than one out to get me. The people I care about are in danger."

"Do you care about Billy?"

He cast a sideways glance at Dan. "I care about all of my bodyguards. They're my friends."

Dan sat down on a chair beside him.

"Yeah, I care about Billy," Ethan admitted. "Probably more than I should. And let's just leave it at that."

"Sure thing, boss."

Niko entered the room. "Let's get our practice on!"

"New drummer's made it another month," Dan teased.

Niko rolled his eyes as he sat down behind his drum set.

ETHAN DRANK a sip of water between songs. He and the band had been practicing for over two hours and had decided to take a break.

Niko stood from his drum set and plucked a soda from the cooler near the wall. "We heard about the roofie at your birthday party." Niko chuckled. "Poor *Chunk* was pretty distraught that night. After you left he was running around like a chicken missing a head, trying to figure out whodunit."

Edgar gave a humorous grunt.

"I mean," Niko continued, "it's pretty messed up that someone would try to do that to you, but Claude's reaction at not having noticed somebody spike the drink was flippin' funny."

"We heard Billy managed okay," Dan said, walking around the room, stretching his long legs as his shoes scuffed the carpet.

Ethan instantly saw visions of Billy's playful grin as she fumbled with his shirt buttons, followed by their lips pressed together. He hadn't told anyone about her behavior that night, but he suspected Pope told Dan, which meant everyone now knew. Still, no one knew about the kiss.

"Did she really get robbed the other night?" Niko asked.

"Robbed? Where'd you hear that?" Ethan asked.

"Uh, Alice, I think."

"Not robbed. She was attacked by street thugs and taught them a lesson."

"Right on." Niko pumped his fist in the air.

Edgar grunted in appreciation.

"Honeymoon period is over. How are Pope and the men taking to your new security?" Dan asked.

Ethan suspected his real question was if his men had any problems taking orders from a woman. "They're learning and adapting. And I half-suspect Billy Jean wouldn't hesitate to kick their butts back into tune if they get off-key."

Dan tossed peanuts from the snack tray in his mouth before chewing and swallowing. "Can't help but notice you like to look at her."

"She's nice to look at." Ethan wouldn't dismiss his friend's observation as that would only reveal his guilt in his attraction to her.

He didn't need his buddies ribbing him about a woman. They'd keep it tasteful, but since he actually liked Billy, he might not be able to hide it if they started teasing him.

"How long will Billy and Barry be with us?"

Until the job is done, Ethan thought.

"Through the season," he answered truthfully. He had already decided that if they cracked the case and stopped the attacks, he still wanted to keep the Rider team on board until they had sufficiently trained his team.

He wouldn't admit he also wanted to keep Billy around. Would she stay on when his case was closed? After all, she was there more for the investigation than security, wasn't she?

When he realized his crew was staring at him, Ethan cleared his throat and strummed his guitar. "Let's keep practicing."

BILLY ATTACKED the punching bag methodically. Jab, jab, hook. Jab, jab, hook. Every five repetitions she swapped her stance and dominant hand and every twenty repetitions she added in a few undercuts.

Fortunately, this particular hotel gym had a boxing bag in the fitness room.

Her phone played Ethan Storm's soundtrack—a mix she'd created of his fastest, most intense songs. With her earbuds in, she moved to the rhythm of "Angelic Demon," one of her favorites.

> *Demons lurk in the shadows*
> *Know yourself and know your foes.*

It vacillated between fast and slow, the lyrics a reminder of the good and bad in everyone. People weren't all good or all bad. Emotions warred with their decisions as often as logic did. People were complex.

She thought of the music video accompanying this

song. In it, Ethan was dressed in black, looking like Lucifer himself with a devilishly handsome smile. He walked the streets at night, watching robberies and violence. But during the course of the song, he would intermittently sprout digitally enhanced white wings and save someone.

How many people had Ethan actually saved with his music? How many people with his memoir? He'd shown fans they could overcome the worst parts of themselves. The self-destructive part. He conquered his demons and, through his lyrics, other people had been inspired to do the same. He was living proof that people could change. People could become better versions of themselves.

Billy could become a better version of herself, too.

She was pulled out of her boxing and daydreaming when Ethan appeared and held the punching bag for her. He wore shorts and a sleeveless shirt.

"What are you doing here?" she asked, glancing around, and tugging out her ear pods.

"I came to exercise. Don't worry. I'm not alone. Barry is outside dutifully guarding the door, but he told me he was anaphylactically allergic to robust physical activity and didn't want to come inside the gym." He winked at her.

Billy glanced at her watch. "I'm done with the cardio portion." She paused the music on her phone, keeping the screen out of Ethan's visual range and attempting not to look guilty that she'd been indulging in his music.

"What's next on your routine?" he asked.

"Squats and stretching."

"Join me over by the elliptical machine. I'd like to hear an update of the investigation while I exercise."

Sure, she could do that. Think clearly and critically while staring at his biceps and watching him sweat. No problem. She was a professional.

She unwrapped the protective gear on her hands as Ethan started the elliptical. Bending one knee, she grasped her ankle to stretch her quadricep. "I finished all of my interviews—if you can call them that. I tried to ask questions as casually as possible without looking like an investigator. Most people are genuinely worried about you. Alice especially. She was biting her nails the entire time. Most people don't find me or my questions intrusive or intimidating, so her behavior was odd." She moved to stretch the other leg. "Were you and she ever an item?"

"Alice? No. I mean, she's a nice girl—er, woman—but I've never dated staff."

"Which brings me to Meg."

"Haven't dated her either. Do you have any other motive besides ex-lovers? Because you won't find many."

"I don't mean Meg romantically. When I asked her about the shooting—was she there and is she worried about you? She seemed rather flippant."

"That sounds like Meg."

"Which is vastly different compared to the gushing worry she spews in front of the media." She released her leg and began stretching her arms across her torso.

Ethan's arms and legs pumped on the machine as he spoke. "Meg wears many hats. I'm not defending her behavior around you—her superficial personality can grate on my nerves. But our goals align. We both want to see my music make a profit, and we both know I don't have the skillset to promote my brand. She does. We have a strong history together, and she agreed to represent me when I made my comeback after giving up alcohol."

Although his words were slightly ragged from breathing a little faster with the exercise, his tone held the same casual vibe it always did. He wasn't upset at Billy's prodding, and he wasn't defensive of Meg.

"Anyone else?" he asked.

"No one with both means and motive. Hit men don't come cheap." She hadn't mentioned to him what Mica had told her about the identity of the sniper—ex-UK Special Forces with an impeccable reputation. "You have enemies—everyone in show biz does—jealous competition, another band wanting your spot in the virtual reality game, psychotic fans. But, again, no one who has both motive and means. Claire has done extensive research on everyone she could find." Billy leaned against the wall, facing Ethan. "And we have the problem of different methods."

"Right. I was targeted by a sniper, and you were attacked by thugs."

"I was referring to the roofie. The street attack on me may not be related. We don't have confirmation."

Ethan gave her an incredulous look. "You were attacked while on my payroll."

"I'm on Rider SI payroll."

"While assigned to me," he said, amending his statement, but in a tone that sounded more like, *you know what I meant.* "So, sniper, roofies, and thugs—different methods."

She didn't let the disagreement go. "The attack on me was while I was off duty." They had told her to leave Ethan alone, but Ethan didn't need the added stress of blaming himself for more violence.

"Have you ever been attacked on another assignment by something unrelated?"

"No."

"Uh-huh." His lips quirked.

"*Maybe* it's related," Billy conceded, mostly to wipe that expression off his face which caused a strange flutter and warmth in her lower abdomen.

ETHAN INCREASED the pace on the elliptical machine as he talked with Billy about his situation. She was holding something back, and he didn't understand why.

"Any headway on the roofie culprit?" he asked.

"Had to be someone who was in the club at the time. The prints on the glass were yours, mine, Meg's, and Claude's—all people we already knew had touched it. But someone can drop a drug in a drink without ever touching the glass."

Ethan admired Billy's thorough investigation of his situation. He also admired her form in her fitted exercise clothing. The suit she usually wore hid the curves of her bust and waist. Spandex hid nothing. Her toughness was attractive, and her contrasting softness equally enticing.

And she liked him. She attempted a poker face, but he could see slight body language changes that betrayed her attraction—cheeks intermittently turning pink when he cranked up the charm and rare lingering looks when he said something caring or insightful.

He wanted to repeat their kiss—except without her being under the influence. But he worried she'd interpret a romantic move as disrespectful. He definitely respected her and wouldn't want to cause her stress on the job. He needed more of a sign than a few indicators of attraction.

"How is Alyssa doing?" Billy asked.

"She's good. The West Coast part of the tour is harder because I'll be gone for a longer time and won't get to see her until May or June. I feel like an absentee father."

Billy fixed him a cup of water from the jug in the room and handed it to him. "From what I see, you provide a lot of quality time. That's indicative of a good father. The fathers I knew in the Marines missed their children terribly but made sure they provided quality time stateside. You can be home every day and suck at being a father." She paused, long enough for Ethan to deduce she'd spoken from experience.

"Anyway, travel doesn't make you a bad father. What you do with your time together is what matters. And when you can't be with Alyssa, you still video-chat several times a week."

He drank the water and placed the empty paper cup in the cup holder. "You're pretty good at being uplifting. You charge extra for your motivational services?"

She grinned. "Always."

After Billy left Ethan in the fitness room, he moved from cardio to stretching. Once upon a time, his exercise routines were about maintaining his image. Now, at forty, he was more interested in cardiovascular health than sex appeal.

He pulled his ear pods out of his pockets, inserted them, and called Mica Rider.

She answered the call immediately. "What can I do for you?"

"It's about the investigation," he said.

"I can assure you we are still working hard to find the perpetrator. We've been combing through data on everyone—"

"Easy. I'm not dissatisfied with the pace of things. It's not as though the police have made any progress. I expected you'd have a lot of suspects with a celebrity case." He cringed, not liking the way that made him sound so self-important.

He bent over, stretching his hamstring. "I'm worried how things are escalating—the roofie and then Billy Jean being attacked."

"We're not certain those events were related to the sniper shot."

"But they're all related to me." He politely pressed. "Billy Jean won't talk about the fight—other than to say she handled it and the Rider team is investigating it."

"Billy is very good at discretion."

"Okay, but I'm the client. I want to know more." He leaned sideways to stretch.

Mica sighed, but it was a sound of surrender, not frustration. The hesitation on her part led him to wonder if he wasn't going to like what she had to say.

"When Billy was attacked, they had a message for her."

Ethan straightened abruptly. "A message for *her*, not a message for *me*?"

"'Leave Ethan alone.' That was the message."

"Leave me alone? That doesn't make sense. She's my bodyguard."

"Ethan, is there any reason someone would think Billy meant more to you than just your bodyguard?"

"No." He started to pace the room. "Maybe. Damn." He continued to pace. Had his actions and emotions somehow put Billy in danger? Their kiss had been an isolated event, but others may have seen his subdued flirtatious behavior.

"Ethan?"

"Yeah." He rubbed a hand over his jaw.

"You have something tell me?" Mica prompted.

"I like Billy Jean," he confessed. "To be clear, I haven't made a move. I respect her too much for that."

"Does anyone else know how you feel?"

"I haven't told anyone except Billy Jean."

"Does anyone else know about this kiss?"

Ethan sighed, recalling the night Billy had drank the Rohypnol-laced drink intended for him. "No, absolutely not. She wasn't herself." He would have liked to think of that as their private moment, but of course, professional that she was, Billy had told her boss.

"It's okay. She's not in trouble. My point is that whoever hired the hit on Billy had reason to believe you two were involved or have the potential to become involved. This means it was someone close to you, especially if you didn't share your feelings or the kiss with anyone."

"No. No one." He gained some small measure of relief that Mica might be able to narrow her suspect list, but he couldn't stomach the thought that Billy could be harmed because of his interest in her.

"Mica, look—"

"Ethan, you don't owe me an explanation. Whatever two consenting adults do is between those adults. Billy doesn't have a manipulative bone in her body, so she'd never play you. If she has feelings for you, they're genuine. Conversely, you don't strike me as someone who would use his position as a client to seduce one of my employees. And if you had, Billy would have already outed you."

"That's quite a summary."

"I wouldn't be much of an investigator if I didn't know my team and my clients."

Ethan cleared his throat. "To be clear about Billy Jean—"

"I don't care if you see each other romantically. Billy won't compromise your safety. I guess you have to ask yourself if you're willing to compromise hers."

Although Mica's words were delicate, Ethan felt them like a punch to the gut. He liked flirting with Billy and had fantasized about kissing her again, but he couldn't do any of that if someone's jealous rage threatened to hurt her.

19

For two days after Ethan spent time with Billy in the gym, he holed up in his room—returning fan email, working on finances, and writing songs. Mica's words about compromising Billy's safety haunted him.

The following morning, Barry arrived at Ethan's room, not Billy. Was she upset with him?

By the time they were in the car driving to church, she still hadn't joined them. He'd been avoiding her. Was she now avoiding him?

"Where's Billy Jean?" Ethan asked Barry who was sitting next to him in the back seat.

"Family issue," Barry said.

"What family issue?"

The corners of Barry's mouth drooped. "Her dad died."

"What? When?" Ethan leaned forward. "Pope, pull over."

Barry continued, "Last night. They weren't close, but she's still going to pay her respects."

The car eased to a stop beside a sidewalk.

"Who's with her?" Ethan asked.

"What do you mean?"

"She doesn't get along with her family. Who's her support system? Who's she going to emotionally lean on at the funeral if you're here?"

Ethan had known Billy for almost two months now. As far as he could tell, she didn't have a close friend outside Rider SI.

Barry shrugged. "It's Billy. She'll be fine. She's tough."

"Nobody's tough enough to face the death of a parent alone. Pope, take us to the airport."

Obligingly, Pope typed in the new destination on the car's GPS and started toward the San Francisco International Airport.

"When did she leave?" Ethan asked.

Barry stared at him with a baffled expression. "Five a.m."

"Can you find out where she's going? Maybe we won't be too far behind her."

Barry slowly pulled out his phone. "Um. You want to go to her father's funeral? You can't crash a wake."

"She sure as hell shouldn't go it alone." She was tough, but she was also human.

He stared out the window. *For Pete's sake*, her father just died and she was flying back to West Virginia alone.

No matter what her father put her through growing up, the funeral would be hard. Even if she didn't mourn him, she would likely be bombarded by a slew of unpleasant memories.

If she'd told him, Ethan would have joined her. Of course, she wouldn't. He was the job, and nothing was allowed to compromise the job. Damn, he wished she'd let him in.

Barry began texting someone. "Your fundraiser is in three days."

"Then we've got time."

"She's going to kick my ass if I let you breach protocol for an unscheduled trip without a sufficient security detail."

Ethan could envision Billy winning that fight against Barry. She was faster and scrappier. "You send her my way if she gives you any grief."

Barry's phone buzzed. "Okay, Claire texted me the location of Billy's father's wake. Are you sure you want to do this?"

"If you can assure me she'll be surrounded by caring friends and family, I'll back off."

Barry pursed his lips. "I expect the welcome to be about as warm as Lake Erie during a January blizzard."

⸻

BILLY WALKED toward the funeral home wearing a black dress she'd purchased at an outlet mall after her plane landed in Charleston, West Virginia. She'd only had a few hours from the time she'd landed before visitation hours began. She'd thought about going to a local bar but opted for the gym instead. Her last solo bar excursion hadn't gone well.

She'd cleaned and dressed at a motel after her work out. Now, the late afternoon sun cast elongated shadows from the tall oaks around the building. In the warm, humid weather, she was relieved to be wearing a sleeveless dress rather than her work suit.

Once inside the funeral home, she slipped past people conversing in hushed tones as they stood near wreaths of flowers and sipped punch. She only recognized a handful of them, but, having not been a part of her parents' lives since leaving home at eighteen, she didn't expect to see many familiar faces. Nor would anyone recognize her now—no longer timid and broody but self-confident and even-tempered.

She walked up to the casket where her father lay. She planned to pay her respects and then leave. Ed looked at peace, and his color from the cosmetics looked better than the ashen state of his skin when she'd last seen him alive.

"What the hell are you doing here?" The room fell silent at Mac's outburst.

Billy's brother wore a dark-grey suit stretched so tight, she suspected he'd outgrown it a decade ago. His face was beet red and his eyes bloodshot.

"Paying my respects."

"You don't have any respect." He waved his him arms around dramatically. "Not for any of us. You think you're better than us."

"Just you, Mac."

Billy's gaze flickered around the room to see mixed expressions of sorrow, distrust, fear, and pity. She didn't feel any of those things. She felt at peace as she thought of the Shakespeare quote: "*He that dies pays all debts.*"

The years of anger she'd carried with her—the fire she'd thought she'd need to keep burning—had been extinguished. Foolish anger had only kept her from enjoying life.

She thought of Ethan's memoir and how part of his self-loathing had kept him from healing and kept him inside the bottle, looking out. When he accepted that the good and the bad in his life—the angel and the demon— were part of who he was, he was able to move forward and move past his addiction. The philosophy seemed sound enough to apply to her life as well.

Mac clenched his fists.

"You don't want to do this, Mac." She calmly stood her ground. He couldn't beat her. He'd be lucky to get a single punch past her defenses.

Still, she wasn't surprised when he charged at her from halfway across the room. She ducked, side-stepped and let his bumbling momentum carry him stumbling past her and into a wreath of red and white carnations.

He stopped, spun, and threw out a punch faster than she thought him capable. She moved to dodge it but still caught a glancing blow to the jaw. She didn't register any pain from the hit.

Boxing arms up, she made two quick jabs with her left fist followed by a right cross. Mac stumbled back as blood trickled from his nose. She didn't want to fight him, but she would defend herself.

"Stop! Both of you stop!" Their mother stepped between them. "Just stop it!" Grief and pain filled her voice.

Billy dropped her hands to her side. The last thing she wanted to do was cause their mom distress on the day of her husband's wake.

"Billy, I'm so tired of the fighting."

Then why didn't you stop it years ago? Billy wanted to ask.

But the past was over, and however fitting, they took their last swings at each other at the funeral of the man who'd started it all. Their family violence began with Ed, now it would go with him to the grave.

Her mother raised a hand in the air, silencing Billy before she could speak. "And, Mac, you're a grown man, start acting like one."

With the back of his hand, he wiped at the blood on the tip of his nose. "But, Mom, she doesn't care about us."

"Of course, she does," she snapped. "Who do you think has been paying your father's medical bills while you drank away your paycheck?"

Mac gaped at Billy.

She pursed her lips.

ETHAN HAD ARRIVED at the funeral home straight from the airport in time to see Billy's two-hundred-pound brother charge her. She fended him off like this was just another day at the office. When her mother intervened, Billy looked devastated to have upset her.

The emotion-drenched scene was heartbreaking to witness.

Billy turned and walked toward the exit, parting the crowd with her silent, calm stare.

Ethan walked beside her outside the building and toward the parking lot.

"How much of that did you see?" she asked, not making eye contact with him.

He placed a gentle hand on her forearm, stopping her. "Enough to understand why you keep your emotions so bottled up." He ran a thumb along the red spot forming on her jaw. She didn't push away or even move out of his reach. Though he wanted to hold her and comfort her, he wouldn't push his luck.

She stepped into him and wrapped her arms around his torso. Compassion flooded through him as he returned her embrace.

Her stiff, firm body relaxed.

There.

There was that soft side she kept hidden. They melted into each other, and he lost track of time as they stood entwined.

When she broke off the hug, he kept his arms loosely around her.

"Why are you here?" she looked up at him with big, brown eyes. Not a tear in sight even though she must have been a mess of emotions on the inside.

"I keep telling you, we're friends. Friends don't let other friends face funerals alone."

"It's a wake."

He gave an exasperated shake of his head. "Those either."

"Thank you for coming. It means a lot."

Ethan reached down and took her hand. "Come on. Barry hasn't eaten in six hours, and he's going to start chewing through the upholstery of the rental if we don't get him some lunch."

She chuckled and squeezed Ethan's hand. "Hey, I know better than to stand between that man and a meal."

As they walked toward the parked car where Barry waited in the driver's seat, Ethan took pride in the absence of tension in Billy. He'd done that—eased some, if not most, of the pain away. Maybe the reprieve was temporary, but there had been magic in the moment between them.

Healing magic.

AFTER LUNCH, Billy picked up her overnight bag, and the three of them went to the airport. They needed to get Ethan back to San Francisco to keep him on schedule.

The next morning, Billy woke, met Ethan in his hotel room, and accepted the cappuccino he'd prepared for her.

After two coffees to fight off jet lag, Pope drove them to the studio where Ethan would spend the day filming part of a new music video.

After Alice checked Ethan in at the studio, Billy's phone buzzed. Unlisted call.

She caught Barry's attention and raised a finger to her phone, signaling that she'd be back in a minute.

Barry nodded.

She stepped out the side door and accepted the call.

"This is Billy."

"I heard about your father," Maxine said.

Billy felt suddenly hot under the midday sun. Maxine wasn't calling about business. This was a personal call.

"Yeah, well, it wasn't a surprise. His health had been declining."

"Still. I know it'll churn a lot of old memories. Skeletons emerging from closets and all that crap that makes us stronger even if a bit bitter."

"I'm going to be okay. I think I've managed to lay those bones to rest."

"You've come a long way from the angry marine with a chip on her shoulder."

Billy snorted. "I suppose I have. I guess time really does heal wounds."

"Only when you learn to leave them alone and let them heal."

"Right. I'm letting all the hate go. It's past time. If accumulated events in my life—good and bad—led me to this moment, then I have to accept it all."

Maxine didn't reply for a long moment, and Billy could practically hear the gears turning in her head.

At last, she said, "You know, I thought the same thing at David and Mica's wedding with Vladimir at my side."

Billy knew the moment. Maxine had reconciled with her son, had gotten a daughter-in-law to take over the company, and had found love with Vladimir.

"Don't get too sappy. That'd be out of character for you," Billy said.

"I'm just wondering what helped you let go."

Billy ran a hand through her hair. "Friends. And I read a memoir about how the sum of our past makes us the whole person we are. If we reject pieces of ourselves, then we're just shattered glass. If we accept who we are and caulk the gaps, then we're a mosaic masterpiece."

"That's some profound shit you're spouting," Maxine teased.

"It's borrowed from someone a lot more poetic than I could ever be, but it resonated with me."

"Okay. Since I don't pay you to stand around talking on the phone, get back to work."

Billy grinned. "You don't pay me at all anymore."

"Yeah. Yeah. You know what I mean."

She meant, Billy knew, that she'd reached the maximum time allotment she had for empathy and senti-mentality.

"Thanks for calling," Billy said.

"Take care of yourself." Maxine clicked off.

Billy walked back inside and watched Ethan filming. In front of the camera sang the man who'd become her friend and helped exorcise her demons without even knowing it. Claire had once asked her to assign a number value of one to ten for the crush she had on Ethan; Billy would now have to give it a twenty.

Leaving, when the time came, was going to hurt. He liked her, and she could take that affection to the next level, but a romp between the sheets before her next assignment would only discredit her feelings for him.

She wouldn't disrespect Ethan or the feelings she had for him by making him a one-night stand. And they couldn't give each other any more than that, owing to their very different lives.

She thought of their hug at her father's wake. What would life be like if she could lose herself in Ethan's embrace whenever she needed it?

Fulfilling.

Amazing.

Impossible.

$\mathcal{E}$than rolled up his sleeves on his baby-blue shirt. He opted for blue jeans for this informal performance—a small gathering of about a thousand people.

"Maybe my concert didn't fall at a good time." He checked his watch. He was due on stage at the Billy Graham Civic Auditorium in five minutes to sing for the San Francisco Fire Department. This event had been booked months in advance—way before last week's apartment building fire in which SFD lost three of their own.

Billy had entered his dressing room at the ten-minute mark and waited by the door to escort him. "I disagree. You're probably exactly what they need to boost morale."

He turned to look at her. "You think so?"

"Music soothes the soul. They can mourn the loss and

celebrate life at the same time. And I saw the playlist you chose—uplifting. They need you tonight.

> *"'There are not more than five musical notes,*
> *yet the combinations of these give rise to*
> *more melodies than can ever be heard.'"*

"Another Sun Tzu quote?" he asked.

"You know it."

He chuckled. "You never cease to amaze me."

"Do you remember in your memoir when you wrote about singing in a park in Louisiana after the hurricane flooding? You had an overwhelming positive response and felt as if you'd given people hope amid disaster and light in a time of darkness. You're going to go out there tonight and give those heroes the same thing."

Ethan stepped closer. "Thank you." He reached out and gripped her arms.

She was always near him, but they had so little time actually alone together, especially after the roofie-fueled kiss, which they hadn't sufficiently discussed. Then she'd flown out to California alone. Next, the street fight interfered. Now, he didn't want to talk about a relationship too soon after her father died.

When would the opportune time present itself? He didn't want to wait for the end of his tour. What if she left before then?

"I like you, Billy Jean. I'm tired of pretending I'm okay seeing you every day and not touching you. I think you feel something too, but if it's my imagination, tell me to back off."

Her eyes were wide with big, dark pupils he thought he might drown in.

"It's not your imagination."

An ache in his chest eased at her words. "I want to kiss you again." He held himself back. She had to be the one to make the move. He wouldn't pressure her.

"It's complicated." She swallowed but didn't back away from him.

He felt the familiar pull toward her and heat spread through him, as if he was being sucked to the core of the earth. Still, he hesitated, thinking of Mica's words of caution.

The door to the dressing room burst open. "Ethan, they're ready for you. Oh, uh. Am I interrupting?" Alice's eyes darted back and forth between Ethan and Billy.

Billy used the opportunity to take Ethan into an escort. He walked beside her through the hallways and to the stage.

"They need this. They need you." Billy's voice was a soft whisper. She smiled and took two steps back to allow him to step onstage.

As he walked to the front and picked up his guitar, her words played in his mind.

It's not your imagination.

They would talk more, but for now, that was enough. For tonight, it was enough.

He stepped up to the microphone. "Thank you so much for having the band and me here tonight."

Whistles and cheers roared through the room.

"We have a group of heroes we've come together to praise—those heroes present tonight, those heroes on duty protecting loved ones, and those heroes with us only in spirit."

Another round of whoops and clapping reverberated through the room.

"Tonight, let's celebrate all of those we love and those we've loved and lost." He started picking at strings—beginning the melody. He glanced at Billy in the distance, watching the crowd and watching him. Normally, stage lights kept him from seeing into the crowd, but the intimate setting of the banquet hall gave him visualization of the entire room. "Let's let our light shine brighter than the darkness we feel when tragedy strikes."

The enthusiastic clapping of the crowd was interspersed with a few shouts of agreement.

He began to sing.

BILLY WATCHED as Ethan and the band began playing. The room was humming with excitement. Based on the uniforms, half of the crowd were male firefighters, ten percent were female firefighters, and the rest were spouses and children. Most people were out of their seat, tapping their feet and clapping their hands to the music.

The venue was less formal than the large arenas where he usually performed, but local police and security still took appropriate measures, checking bags as people entered and using wand metal-detector devices.

Billy, Wayne, JJ, Claude, and Barry kept to rotating stations in various locations behind the stage and in the crowd. About halfway through the performance, a firefighter in his dress blues approached Billy. She checked his title—chief.

"What station do you work for? I don't recognize you." He had tan skin and a blond buzz cut. Even through his polyester shirts, she could tell he was muscular and well-built.

"I'm working security for Ethan Storm."

"So, when does the job end? I'll stick around." His blue eyes sparkled with an invitation.

In the past, she would have taken him up on that offer—a one-night stand with a handsome man before she went back to work. Such was simplicity at its best.

But now she had strong, battling emotions for Ethan who had just told her he wanted something more.

"Job is over when the tours ends. That'll be in a few months."

He pulled out a piece of paper and scribbled something on it. "Well, if you happen to get a day off while you're in town, I can show you around the station."

He handed her the piece of paper with a phone number scrawled on it.

In the interest of being polite, she tucked it quietly into her suit jacket pocket. She wouldn't want him leaving Ethan's concert with bad memories. Instead, she called on the coms and rearranged the rotation, moving herself backstage for the rest of the event.

Backstage, her mind replayed Ethan's words.

I'm tired of pretending I'm okay seeing you every day and not touching you.

What would have happened if Alice hadn't walked into the room? Would Ethan have kissed her? Long seconds had passed, but he hadn't taken the opportunity. And what would Billy have done if he had kissed her?

She had power and control over every aspect of her life, but in Ethan's arms she felt powerless with the overwhelming urge to give herself over to him and enjoy the surrender.

"Yes, yes. Just like that," Ethan encouraged the band two days after the firefighter concert as they practiced. "Edgar, you keep the base slow and steady with a little swagger. Now, Niko, background symbols. Dan give me the finger snaps."

Dan set the electric piano to the tempo of Ethan's song.

The fund raiser had gone well, and today Ethan had the band trying out a new song he'd written.

"Excellent. And lyrics in one, two, three, four." As Ethan sang, he listened to the harmony and made mental notes on how to augment it. He spiced up the end with extra guitar chords.

"Well, what do you think?"

"It's cool," Niko said.

Dan scratched the stubble on his chin. "It's very good. It's a love song."

Ethan's mouth twitched. "Yeah. We've been known to sing a few of those."

"I know. You just haven't written a new one in a while."

"So?"

"This isn't the start of a midlife crisis we need to worry about now that you're forty, is it?" Dan asked.

Ethan scowled. "No."

Edgar grunted.

Ethan looked at the large man in khaki overalls. "You're taking Dan's side?"

"Nobody is taking sides, man," Niko said.

"I can't write a love song?" Ethan set his guitar down.

"Course you can—as long as there's no deeper meaning we need to know about."

Damn. Was he such an open book to Dan?

"I'm not having a midlife crisis," he grumbled.

"Okay. Who is the song about?"

"Who says it's about anybody?"

Dan shot him a don't-bullshit-me look.

"Billy Jean," Ethan confessed.

Edgar grunted his surprise.

"You and Billy are—"

"No, we're not," Ethan interrupted Niko. He turned to Dan. "But I have these damn feelings bottled up for her, and it helps to write and sing about them."

Dan pulled a toothpick out of his pocket and stuck it between his lips. "You're planning to woo her with a love song?"

Ethan snorted. "One does not woo a woman like Billy Jean with a love song. The song is for me, so I can sort out how I feel."

Niko cracked his neck from side to side. "Are you planning to woo her?"

Ethan sighed. He hadn't intended to have this conversation with his band, but they were also his friends.

"She doesn't want to be wooed."

"What does that mean?" Dan asked.

"I mean she doesn't want a relationship. She thinks we're too different, and she ruminates on the whole bodyguard job. There's some line there she doesn't think she can cross."

"So, she never said she didn't want you, specifically?" Dan asked with a hopeful tone in his voice.

"No, in fact, I'm certain she's attracted to me, but intentionally holding back. And—"

"So, woo her anyway," Niko said.

"How? She's not exactly a wine-and-dine sort of woman. I'm not telling her the song's about her, and I don't think she'd be impressed anyway." Was he honestly having this conversation with his band buddies?

They knew his greatest failures and his greatest success; they might as well know his feelings for his bodyguard. "Once upon a time, all I had to do was invite a woman up on stage to win her over. But I need to find Billy's interests if I'm going to develop a relationship of substance with her." Even if he succeeded, he still had to battle the additional worry Mica had added in mentioning he might compromise Billy's safety by being in a relationship with her.

Dan stood and walked to the door. He swung it open. "Barry, can you come in a minute?"

"Are you shitting me?" Ethan asked. "You can't bring Barry into this."

After Barry entered the room, Dan closed the door.

"What's up?" Barry drew out the words as he looked around the room, all eyes on him.

"Ethan likes Billy," Dan said.

Ethan glowered at Dan.

Barry scratched the top of his balding head. "Oh, okay. I didn't see that one coming. I mean, I know you like each other, I wasn't expecting a public declaration. What do you want—my blessing or something?"

"No," Ethan snapped. And this was hardly a "public declaration."

"Your advice," Dan said calmly to Barry. "Ethan doesn't know how to court her since she's ... unique."

Ethan paced the room. "Courting? What is this? The nineteenth century?"

Edgar gave a hearty laugh.

Barry snorted, ignoring Ethan's grumblings. "Unique, sure. But she's not hard to read."

"I know standard tactics aren't going to work," Ethan said. "Flowers and jewelry aren't going to sway her."

"No. She's a no-bullshit kind of woman. All you have to do is be genuine."

"I am genuine. She won't break her bodyguard code." Ethan waved a hand at Barry.

"There is no bodyguard code. But she does have walls. Those walls were erected over decades, and they aren't going to come down overnight."

"Well, how do I blast through a marine's wall?"

Barry shook his head. "You don't."

Ethan rubbed his temple.

Barry continued, "You don't blast it or ram it or scale it or dig under it. You have to dismantle that wall brick by brick, right out in the open." Barry sighed. "You know you've already been doing that, right? The morning coffee. The Rider concert trip. The funeral. It's all working even if making the connection with her isn't at a pace you're satisfied with."

"It's working?"

"Yeah. Maybe not as fast as you want it to, but it's working."

Ethan grinned. "It's working."

Billy waited backstage outside the dressing room as Ethan prepared for the concert. The hum of eighteen thousand fans waiting for him reverberated through the walls.

She didn't like the layout of the Chase Center, owing to the security difficulties. The stage was directly in the center of the arena, which meant fans—and potential threats—were seated a full 360 degrees around Ethan. But she had experience with most layouts and had prepared accordingly.

Ethan opened the door. He wore a silk navy-blue shirt and black slacks. Her heart thudded a few beats. Would her body ever stop reacting to the sight of him—such a masculine exterior surrounding a soft, creative interior?

"Ready?" she asked.

"One minute. Can you come inside?"

She glanced at Barry who suspiciously avoided eye-contact as though he knew what this was about.

When she stepped into his dressing room, Ethan placed gentle hands on her shoulders and squeezed once. "I believe that when tragedy strikes, it's a reminder to celebrate life."

"Okay."

He dropped his hands and took a step back, enabling her to breathe again.

"I've done something without your permission, and I hope it doesn't upset you."

Something Barry knows about? she pondered.

"We're not deviating from tonight's schedule," she said. Ethan's safety came first.

He smiled. He might have been able to melt her heart into a puddle with that look, but she wasn't breaking protocol.

"It's nothing like that," he said. "I brought your family to tonight's concert. I thought they needed to make some enjoyable memories this year after their loss."

She blinked at him. "They came?"

"Alice says they're all here: your mom, Mac, and Hugh with his family."

"You brought them to your concert?" She considered the logistics—plane flights, hotels, tickets.

"Barry knows their suite number if you want to see them. You're not obligated to. This isn't me trying to force a reconciliation with your family. I don't meddle. I'm not a meddler."

She thought of her nieces walking in awe into the large open atrium before taking the stairs up to gaze through the glass at the wide bay view. Hugh's wife would love the art on display throughout the Chase Center. Her mother would be speechless, basking in the luxury suite with its posh seating and incredible view of the stage.

She looked into a pair of cloudy green eyes. He was worried, she realized, that he'd overstepped his bounds.

"I'm flabbergasted. Thank you. They'll have a wonderful time."

He looked relieved, but still carried some tension. She wasn't sure what else troubled him, but she didn't want it interfering with his performance. Under the circumstances, what would Ethan do if she needed reassurance? The answer came easily. She stepped forward and hugged him.

"Knock 'em dead," she whispered in his ear.

He held the hug a beat longer than friendship allowed. When he pulled back, he was all gleaming-white smile, with that familiar flirtatious glint in his eyes.

He planted a quick but firm kiss on her lips. "Let's go."

She stood for a stunned second before following him out the door.

Claude took the lead with Billy and Barry in the rear.

"I don't think I've ever seen a dumbfounded expression on your face." Barry's voice was an amused whisper.

Still in shock, Billy didn't reply. Barry would assume her reaction was from Ethan's amazing gesture. This time, she'd keep the kiss to herself.

"You knew about this?"

"Yeah, he wanted my opinion on a scale of one to ten about how pissed off you'd be."

"Why would I be upset?"

"He was afraid you'd think he was using your family to win your affection," Barry explained.

"It didn't cross my mind. I don't think he's capable of manipulating anyone like that."

And he already has my affection, Billy didn't add.

"Your family's in town for the week, if you want to take time off to see them."

Her partner understood her, knew that she wouldn't take time off to stop by and see her family in the suite tonight. If she was going to see her family while they were in town, it would only be when her client was in a secure location.

"Thanks, Barry."

THE CONCERT HAD TRANSPIRED SMOOTHLY, and Ethan was enjoying a day of rest in his hotel room. Billy used the downtime to go for a walk but spotted Mac in the lobby.

"Billy."

Her world tilted on its access at the sound of Mac's voice—uncharacteristically soft and containing something reminiscent of remorse.

She faced her brother and stood ramrod straight, waiting for whatever terrible news he'd come to deliver.

Mom. Please, God, don't let it be about Mom.

She'd flown all this way to go to the concert. Had something happened?

Mac wore blue jeans and a faded Pearl Jam T-shirt. His hair was combed, and he squinted at her. "I owe you an apology."

"No one's hurt?" she asked.

He frowned. "No."

"Everyone is okay? Mom? Hugh?"

"Yeah, yeah. They're all good. They loved the concert."

She felt her anxiety ebb. "How'd you find me?"

"Your assistant told me. I called your company and told a real nice-sounding lady I needed to talk to you."

"Claire gave you my location?" Billy was stunned. Claire knew better.

"I told her how I needed to mend bridges. She made me do this crazy, lengthy verification thing before she finally said what hotel you're staying at. She wouldn't tell me your room number."

Claire had given up Billy's location? That was against protocol. She should have alerted Billy—who damn well wouldn't have told Mac where she was.

"I'm sorry," Mac said, tucking his hands in his pockets.

Dammit, Claire. Mac had given her some sob story, and she'd caved. Now Billy was forced to deal with him.

"Sorry for what, Mac?" Billy crossed her arms, waiting for her older brother to chide her about something.

"Being an ass, mostly—I mean, growing up all that was just kid stuff. When you ran off to the military and didn't come back, I thought you'd abandoned us. I didn't know about the money."

Billy ran a hand through her hair, then relented. "Walk with me."

They exited the hotel and strolled down Turk Street. She could smell the salt water of the bay even if she couldn't see it from here.

"You weren't supposed to know," she said. "I swore Mom to secrecy. Anyway, I did it for her—to help *her*."

He shrugged. "That's good enough reason for me. I didn't think you gave a rat's ass about any of us. Helping Mom is enough to know you cared."

"Money was enough? You're no longer mad I didn't visit more?"

"Not the money itself. Just knowing you didn't forget about us. Hell, after you've seen the world and fought in wars, why the hell would you want to come back to our dump in the woods?" He lifted his eyes to hers. "The money shows you didn't abandon us. You still cared. You didn't have to help Mom. I know she didn't ask for it, but you gave it anyway. So, thanks. And I'm sorry for picking fights when you did come visit."

Billy considered all the anger she'd harbored for her family over the years. So much wasted emotion.

She lightly punched Mac in the shoulder. "Old habits die hard?"

He gave a crooked grin. "Yeah, I guess they do." His brow furrowed. "You know why I was so hard on you growing up, right? I always knew if I kept you down, Dad wouldn't."

"You were protecting me?" she asked incredulously.

"I swear to you, his punches were harder than mine."

He rubbed his neck as if recalling some old injuries. "It's juvenile, I guess. But I was mad you never thanked me."

"For bullying me?" She blinked at him.

Mac sighed. "I learned early on that if I protected you—stood up for you against Dad—we both got hurt. But if I roughed you up some, then he left us both alone. I thought you understood that."

"No, I didn't."

They walked into a park with a playground and benches.

"Dad calmed down not long after you left. About the time his breathing went down the crapper. Hugh grew up in a different environment than the rest of us. He had a better childhood, I think."

That was of some comfort, Billy thought. It also explained why Hugh never understood Billy's perspective.

"Well, you came all this way. We might as well have dinner tonight," she said. Ethan didn't have plans, so she could take the night off. Tomorrow he had practice with his band at a rented studio.

"Okay, but none of those highfalutin restaurants you're used to."

"What makes you think I go to fancy restaurants?"

"Ethan Storm picked you up from our father's funeral. A *freaking* rock star. He could probably rent out an entire Ruth's Chris Steakhouse for a date night and not bat an eyelash. Then, he flies all of us out here, and we get a suite to watch his concert."

"I'm his bodyguard, not his date."

"So *you* say. A man don't look at his bodyguard the way that man looks at you."

Mac's teasing words send a thrill through her.

"Oh, yeah? What the hell do you know about it?" She challenged him playfully like when they were kids—little sister to big brother.

Mac chuckled. "Relationships? Not a damn thing."

MICA SAT AT HER DESK, staring at the profiles of her latest hires. She'd conducted her interview of the Alonso brothers at a gun range and had been impressed. They not only had weapons skills but interpersonal skills. They were willing to travel and seemed genuinely excited about the prospect of helping people. Most of Rider SI was comprised of former military. Mica hoped breaking the mold wouldn't come back to bite her in the butt.

Claire burst into the room. "It's Meg Martin!"

"Okay. Deep breath." Mica put her computer screen to sleep to give her full attention to Claire. "Sit and explain your outburst."

"Meg hired the sniper," Claire declared as she dropped into the vacant chair in Mica's office.

"Walk me through your discovery." Mica believed Claire, but she wanted to make sure she understood all of the details herself in order to present it to Ethan Storm. She suspected the singer was going to want some hearty proof if Mica accused his agent of being the perpetrator.

"Meg keeps an electronic ledger on her computer that downloads monthly statements and consolidates them in one location. Very organized. I could access it thanks to the spyware Billy planted. Anyway, nothing seemed concerning when I went through it last month. Sometimes chunks of money get moved to pay for a vendor. But, two days ago the download showed a large sum went out to an organization she'd already paid. I smelled something fishy. I looked into the account holder. *Et voilà!* Shell corporation."

"So, probably our sniper."

"Yup."

"And he just got paid again." Mica felt a sickening lump form in the pit of her stomach as a question formed. "Is the second payment the final installment for the attempted hit in March, or is this the next payment to finish the job and kill Ethan Storm? There shouldn't be a follow-up payment this late. She must be paying for a new service."

Claire's expression morphed from glee at her landmine discovery to dismay that the sniper might strike again. "And the latest payment was twice the first. I don't know if it has some special significance. We have to inform Billy."

Mica nodded. "You call Billy. I'll call Special Agent Eddie Finch."

It was time to loop in the FBI, and since Mica had worked with Eddie once upon a time, he was always their go-to agent. Technically, the sniper case belonged to local police, as it wasn't a hate crime or organized crime, which would have warranted FBI jurisdiction. But the case hadn't been solved by local police, and Mica wanted the FBI involved in something as dangerous as a scenario involving a contract killer now that they had more information.

None of Claire's illegally discovered information was permissible in court but, Rider SI could still point the FBI in the right direction.

"Where is Billy now?" Mica asked.

Claire grimaced. "With Meg and Ethan."

22

Billy stepped outside of the recording studio room in downtown San Francisco to take a call from Claire. She left Ethan in the back room practicing guitar with the rest of his band, who were accompanied by Claude and Barry. Meg sat in the front room, working furiously on her computer. Alice was near her, on the phone making calls about dinner reservations a week from now. Pope was waiting by the car.

"Claire," Billy said, greeting her colleague.

"Billy, I've had a breakthrough. Meg had two transfers to a shell corporation. Alone, the funds don't look like much. Combined, it's seventy-five thousand dollars."

Billy's stomach clenched. Meg was inside the building with Ethan. Her mind spun with questions. What did

Meg stand to gain by killing Ethan? She'd had a dozen opportunities to hurt Ethan, so why hire a sniper? Why hadn't she attacked him directly?

Maybe Meg wasn't capable of her own violence. Or was she? Billy recalled how Meg had briefly touched Ethan's glass the night of his birthday party. Had she spiked the drink? To take out Ethan or to take out Billy? Drugging Billy and having part of the team take care of her could have created an opportunity to harm Ethan. Maybe Meg hadn't counted on Ethan leaving *with* Billy. No theory provided an adequate explanation.

"Mica's going to call in Eddie, but I haven't obtained much the FBI can legally use yet," Claire said.

"I understand. I'll call you back." Billy disconnected the call and set her phone to record as she walked back into the studio.

Single exit. One window.

Alice, Claude, and JJ were in the front room now. Alice and Meg worked on their laptop while Claude played Candy Crush on his phone. Behind the closed door, the band rehearsed.

Threat assessment: Meg wasn't armed, though her purse was within reaching distance if she had a weapon in there. She was at the opposite end of the room from the door to Ethan, so she wouldn't be able to reach him before Billy could.

"What's up?" Barry asked as he stepped out of the rehearsal room and into the entry room, eyeing Billy.

Billy kept her voice low. Over the sound of the band in the other room, she was inaudible to anyone but her colleague beside her. "We need to separate the band from this establishment."

Barry scowled and followed Billy's gaze. "Meg?"

Billy nodded. "Meg."

"We're sure?"

Billy shot him a look.

"Okay, we're sure." Barry walked to JJ. "How about you take the gang out for lunch? There's a burger joint two blocks from here."

Billy would prefer if Ethan evacuated with his band, but she knew he wouldn't be sidelined.

JJ gave a momentarily confused expression but obliged. He stepped into the doorway separating the two rooms. "Hey, Dan, Edgar, Niko, come with me. We'll stretch our legs and grab lunch."

"I'll take a chicken salad," Meg called after them, oblivious to the changing mood of the room.

As Billy watched the exodus, the tension eased slightly. She didn't know how volatile the situation would become when they confronted Meg, and fewer bystanders meant fewer people to protect.

Ethan had silently watched the evacuation, not making a fuss. "Billy Jean, is everything okay?" He set his guitar aside and stepped into the entry room.

Billy set her phone on the table near Meg before approaching Ethan and taking a protective stance beside him. Barry casually stood near Meg.

"I just got off the phone with one of our investigators," Billy announced to the room.

Meg looked up from her laptop, finally taking notice

of the new dynamic and thickening tension. Alice's head jerked up and she ended her phone call abruptly. Claude stood blocking the door.

"We found several wire transfers to multiple accounts, which were closed shortly after the deposits were made. The sum total would be within range of affording a professional sniper." Perhaps slightly on the low end, but that wasn't pertinent to this discussion.

"From Meg?" Ethan gave a nervous chuckle. "No way." He looked from Meg to Billy and back to Meg. "Meg?"

Billy waited. Meg seemed to be weighing her options, glancing at the door. Her face paled as she seemed to realize running wasn't one of them. Meg's hesitation, rather than an immediate declaration of her innocence, spoke more than words.

"Ethan," she implored, standing but unable to move toward him due to Barry blocking her way. "Ethan, it isn't what it sounds like."

"It sounds like you took a hit out on me." He stood, clenching his fists.

"No. Not a hit. Just a scare. Just one shot where no one was injured."

"There was a crowd of people. Someone could have been injured by your stunt. Someone could've been killed."

She delivered an incredulous stare. "No one was hurt. And your ratings soared. Your concerts sold out, and you got three more interviews because of my *stunt*."

Ethan paced.

Billy kept quiet. Ethan was going to get more of a confession out of Meg than Billy ever could.

"Reckless," he hissed. "You don't take that type of risk with people's lives."

"I'm no amateur," Meg snapped back, her lips contorted in a snarl. "You're not young. Not hip. You dress too conservatively. Honestly, the drop in your ratings forced my hand."

"Not like this." He clenched and unclenched his fists.

"You celebrities," Meg scoffed. "You're all the same. You want your agent to do all the gritty promotional work for you because you need it, but you lack the spine. I get my hands dirty, and you take the high road. Well, now you know the ugly truth."

"Yeah. Real ugly." Ethan ran a hand through his hair. He turned a hardened stare on Meg. "You honestly paid to have someone shoot at me?"

"Yes. And it worked." She raised a hand to gesture at Billy and Barry. "I didn't know you were going to hire extra security, but they've been a waste. You're not in any danger. You never were."

Claude watched the exchange in stunned silence.

"Danger from you."

Meg flinched. "No. Ethan—"

"And the roofie?"

"Roofie?" she looked from Ethan to Billy. "I don't know anything about that."

Meg looked sincere, but Ethan's eyes were filled with distrust.

"And the attack on Billy?" he demanded.

"That wasn't me, either. Really, what's next?" Meg threw her hands up in the air. "Am I going to get blamed for Barry having indigestion?"

Ethan hardened his glare.

"Ethan, don't be angry." She took two pleading steps toward the singer before Barry's belly came between them.

Glass from the window shattered. Billy dove for Ethan, taking him down to the carpeted floor with her. On the ground, they were safe from further shots through the window. And that certainly had been a gunshot.

She looked over at Barry and Meg. Meg was limp, and both of them were covered in blood.

"Barry! Status?" Billy stayed on top of Ethan.

"Meg's dead." Barry's face fell in dismay.

"Meg?" Ethan tried to get up, but Billy kept him pinned down.

Claude began to crawl across the floor, but Billy signaled him to stay put and remain near Alice, who was screaming wildly.

Billy tapped her ear com twice to activate it.

"Pope? Meg's down. We've got a shot fired at the studio. What's your status?"

"Turning the engine on," Pope said.

Barry crawled low over to her and Ethan.

Billy continued to give orders, "I need the car around back. Now."

"Yes, ma'am," came the reply.

ETHAN STARED at Meg's body crumpled on the floor. His ears still rang from the gunshot—or maybe the sound of the window shattering, he wasn't sure. Billy was barking orders, while Alice sobbed hysterically.

Ethan tried to move when Billy shifted off of him, but then Barry's bulbous body took Billy's place holding him down.

"JJ, get the band back to the hotel," Billy said into her coms as she crawled to her phone and pocketed it.

Ethan's heart pounded, but Billy's calm demeanor helped him keep his cool.

With her gun in one hand, she nodded to Barry.

"Move!" Barry barked at Ethan.

Ethan shoved to his feet. They dashed outside with Ethan wedged between Barry and Billy.

Ethan caught one last look at Meg—eyes fixed and unmoving at the ceiling. He'd never seen a dead body before—outside of the context of a wake or funeral—and certainly not one of someone he knew.

Claude and Alice joined them as they left the building. Pope had the Tahoe on the curb. Billy yanked the door open, and Ethan was thrust inside with Billy on top, keeping his body pressed to the floorboard. Barry and Alice climbed into the back seat and hunkered down. Claude rode shotgun.

As Pope pulled away from the curb, the car behind him honked irritably. The Tahoe lunged forward into traffic. Barry got on his phone and started describing the incident—presumably to the police; Ethan wasn't sure.

Two blocks later, Pope pulled over. Everyone readjusted to sit upright and pull on seatbelts. Alice and Ethan were wedged between Barry and Billy.

Ethan noticed that Billy had holstered her gun at some point. She was sweating, but she managed to catch her breath quickly.

As the car pulled into traffic, he gave Billy a grateful look. She placed a hand in his, and he felt the weight of her unspoken reassurance. Steady Billy. Just another day on the job.

She looked at Ethan with concerned yet calculating eyes.

"What is it?" he asked. "You're analyzing the attack?"

She ran a hand through her short, dark hair. "Just the obvious. If Meg had arranged the first attack, who arranged this one?"

He thought about the bullet trajectory. "Was Meg the target or me?"

"I'm not sure. I think Meg, but you took a step as the shot was fired. I need time to think it through."

His phone rang.

Billy moved to withdraw her hand, but he wasn't ready to let go. He pulled the phone out of his pocket with his free hand.

"It's Alyssa," he told Billy, which he knew she'd understand meant he was going to answer it.

"Hey, hon." He was surprised by how calm his voice sounded after events.

"What happened?" Alyssa asked. "Somebody sent a Tweet that you were shot at again."

Sometimes he hated social media. "There was another shooting, hon. I'm fine. I'm safe in the car."

"Who did this?"

"I don't know yet."

"But you're okay?"

"I'm okay." He would tell her about Meg later.

"Did Billy save you?"

Ethan mustered a grin as he looked at the bodyguard beside him. "She sure did."

23

———

illy didn't think she saved Ethan. She replayed events at the studio in her mind. Ethan had been pacing. Making him or Meg the harder target?

A good sniper wouldn't have missed Ethan and landed a kill shot on Meg. However, Billy wouldn't have the advantage of Claire being able to review video footage, since there hadn't been a crowd of fans with mobile phones watching and recording this time. Perhaps Claire could devise a schematic of the buildings and sort out a shot angle based on information Billy provided her.

"Where to, boss?" Pope asked.

"North, toward Napa Valley." Billy pulled out her phone. Six minutes and twenty-seven seconds of Meg's confession was safely recorded—along with the gun shot that killed her. She needed to get this to the police, along with an explanation for why they'd left the scene of the crime.

Billy needed to call Mica, but she didn't want to have the conversation in front of Ethan. He was already shaken. She began texting instead.

Billy: *Another sniper hit. Asset is fine. Meg is dead. Taking Ethan to secure location then I'll call you.*

Mica: *Dead? But she was our suspect.*

Billy: *And she confessed before her death. She took a staged hit out on Ethan. Who took a real hit out on her? We're back to square one.*

There was no way the sniper was just eavesdropping to take Meg out if she confessed. Executing someone from a rooftop or balcony took time and planning. Ethan's concert schedule was public but not his practice sessions. Someone knew he and/or Meg would be at the studio. Meg had been in the corner on her computer and away from the window ... until she took steps toward Ethan.

Mica: *Both snipers. And funds went to the same source.*

Billy: *No way she paid for her own execution.*

Mica: *Call me as soon as you can.*

Billy concluded the exchange by giving Mica the "thumbs up" emoji.

"It'll be an hour and a half, maybe two-hour drive, with traffic," Billy told Ethan.

"Where are we going?" he asked.

"Safe house."

Aurora Meridian's family—the in-laws of one of the

Rider SI team—owned a vineyard in California wine country. They could spend a few days there for safety.

Maybe she could piece together what the hell happened at the studio—and who was responsible.

FORTY-FIVE MINUTES in and a slew of text-message planning later, Pope pulled the Tahoe over to fill up on gas while Billy stretched her legs. A rental car Mica had arranged met them there.

"Barry and Pope are going to take you and Alice to the safe house in the rental car," Billy explained to Ethan.

"Why in the rental? What's wrong with the Tahoe?"

"I need to make sure it's not being tracked. Someone knew you were at the studio, so either there's a bug—and the vehicle is the only thing we don't have eyes on at all times—or someone told the shooter where you'd be."

Ethan pursed his lips as he took Billy by the elbow and led her several feet from the car away from everyone else.

"What about you?" He kept his voice low.

She looked down at his grip on her but didn't move out of his grasp. "I need to go back and handle the situation. Local police won't be happy we took off."

"You'll be careful?"

She grinned. Wasn't his worry adorable? She'd never had a man worry about her well-being the way Ethan did. "I'm always careful."

"I know." He let go of her elbow with an expression of worry as if he thought he'd offended her. He continued to crowd her personal space—so much that she began having X-rated thoughts about him which were completely inappropriate for the setting and situation.

"I know you're careful," he repeated.

"Nobody's after me," she reassured him. "It's you we need to get to safety."

"What about the guys who jumped you that night? We still don't know who did that or if they'll send more."

She had a strange urge to kiss away the worried look in his eyes, but Alice, Claude, and Barry were watching their exchange from a distance. And Ethan was a client—though she felt like that excuse was wearing thin.

"I'll be back this evening."

"Text me."

"You won't have a working phone. All mobile devices need to be deactivated, so you can't be tracked to the vineyard. Barry will have a burner. I'll send updates to his phone."

Ethan's brow furrowed, though he nodded. "I need to let Alyssa know."

"Call her again. Tell her you'll be out of touch for a few days. I'll call Tamika and Moody and explain the situation. I don't know if the shooter is hired to hurt people close to you. Under the circumstances, Mica is putting protection on them."

He swallowed. "I'd like that. It would mean the world to me."

You mean the world to me, Billy thought.

Jeez, she was getting soft. Must've been all those sappy ballads of his she'd been listening to. But, damn, the music was as alluring as his luscious eyes.

She squeezed Ethan's shoulder, turned, and climbed into the Tahoe. As she started the engine, Claude and Ethan hugged out a goodbye.

"You want to hug?" Claude chuckled as he sat in the passenger seat. "You look like you could use one, too."

"I don't hug." She pulled onto the road and took I-80 back toward Berkley. She realized this was the first time she'd ever been alone with Claude.

"I noticed. You have that don't-touch-me vibe."

"Mostly, I go for the don't-mess-with-me vibe." She shot him a half-grin so he'd know she was only half-kidding.

Claude laughed. "Oh. You've got that, too. I've never seen Ethan *not* hug someone, and he does *not* hug you."

Billy thought about the song Ethan had improvised on the second day of them knowing each other.

> *Billy Jean is not my friend*
> *She's just a guard to keep me out of the sun*
> *She says I can't have fun*

"I'm his guard," she countered. And they had hugged, she didn't add—a few wonderful embraces that were some combination of agony and ecstasy and rarely done in front of other people.

"So am I."

"You've been friends a long time."

Claude shrugged, a comical gesture with his large frame folded in the seat. "Ethan's friendly with everyone. Hugs people he's only just met."

"It's important to have walls." Was he going to talk during the entire drive back?

Claude grunted. "Maybe if you're China."

Yup, lots of talking. Well, at least if she was talking to Claude, she wouldn't be thinking of hugging Ethan—shirtless ... in a jacuzzi.

ON THE DRIVE back to San Francisco, Billy relayed all events of the shooting to Claire and Mica. By the time Billy presented herself to SFPD, Claire had the entire report with schematics typed, converted to a PDF file, and sent to Billy by email. She had even included the audio file of Meg's confession from Billy's phone.

After several grueling hours with the lead detective, going over her role, the event, and her contact information, Billy retrieved Ethan's guitar from the studio. Next, she went to his hotel room where Claude had already packed Ethan's belongings, checked out of the room, and had the Tahoe packed.

In the garage, Claude handed her the keys.

"Thanks," Billy said, rubbing at an ache in her neck. She wasn't looking forward to the drive back to the safehouse, but the longer she was away from Ethan the more she wanted to see him. As much as she tried to tell herself her feelings were the result of simple bodyguard instincts, she knew she was lying to herself. Every part of his charisma had seeped into her bones.

It was as though he'd gotten stuck in her head the

way his songs stuck in his fans' heads. How do you get a song out of your head? Listen to it in its entirety.

Except applying that to Ethan meant giving into her desires. Another kiss, but one in which they didn't stop. Fingers into flesh. Skin on skin.

"Billy?"

"Yeah? What'd you say?" She looked from her tight grip on the car door handle to Claude who gave her a quizzical look.

"I checked the Tahoe. No bugs."

"Great. Thanks, Claude." She glanced in the back seat where Ethan's coffee maker was carefully strapped in. The sight of it made her smile.

He stepped toward her.

"We're not hugging," she said as she climbed into the driver seat.

Claude stepped back and walked around to the driver side. "Okay. Okay. But you need some downtime after what happened."

She scowled. "Thanks, Dr. Phil."

Sitting beside her, Claude gave her a pointed look.

She punched his arm lightly with a grin and started the engine. "Not my first rodeo."

"Yeah, okay."

"Good talk."

When Billy arrived at the vineyard, Claude snorted awake from his nap in the passenger seat.

He took in the vineyard along the long, paved driveway. "Whoa. The safehouse is here?"

"We're borrowing the bed and breakfast on the property. It belongs to a former client. They were nice enough to vacate at our request."

A sea of green grape vines spread out in every direction. The landscape seemed to sparkle under the light of the setting sun.

After she parked the car, Barry greeted her outside the house. "Ethan and Alice are sleeping. She's upstairs in the bedroom, and he's on the couch."

Claude stood and stretched with a grunt.

"What's the plan?" Barry asked.

Billy pulled her luggage bag out of the back of the rental. "We'll lay low for a couple of days. Mica is going to pull Mason and Dorian in to watch Alyssa and Tamika in DC."

"Okay. I'll make a grocery run. Back in an hour. Text me if you think of anything you need."

Billy handed him the keys, left Barry with the Tahoe, and walked inside the cabin, careful to close the door quietly since Ethan was sleeping on the couch. She was envious of the tranquil moment of rest. She wanted to close her eyes, too. It was only mid-afternoon, but the day had already been a taxing.

Claude excused himself and went upstairs to lie down.

She walked toward the sofa, intending to pick up the empty water glass when Ethan's eyes snapped open.

"Billy, thank God." He rolled off the sofa and onto his

knees where he wrapped his hands around her waist and hugged her.

She stood in shocked silence at the embrace. She was at a loss for what to do next. The side of his face was pressed against her abdomen. Despite her long moment of hesitation, he never let go.

Ethan's arms around her felt phenomenal. He held her so tight, as if he was holding on for dear life. The raw emotion and vulnerability emanating from him shattered what was left of her walls.

She plunged both hands into his thick brown hair. Warm. Soft. Tugging gently at his hair, she tilted his head back, giving her full view of the compassion and desire on his face. She bent over and kissed him.

The blissful merging of their lips had excitement coursing through her.

Ethan pulled her with him onto the couch, their lips never breaking contact, and she adjusted her body so that her thighs straddled Ethan as he leaned against the back of the couch.

He kept his arms around her, but instead of leaving them locked in place, he used them to move and explore her body.

She lost herself in his sensual touch. Everything felt good. So damn good. And so damn right.

She'd never been with a man where such tenacious emotions had entwined themselves around her core so completely that the physical experience of intimacy was enhanced by the emotional depth of their feelings for each other.

Billy wasn't sure how long they kissed and held each

other, but she was sure there were entirely too many clothes separating them.

ETHAN LOST himself in Billy's intoxicating embrace. The kiss was everything he'd known was hiding beneath her calm, collected surface—passion, desire, need.

Oh, yes. Now he had undeniable confirmation he'd been right about her attraction to him all along. She wanted him, and he was prepared to give himself to her while taking his fill of her.

The click of a door handle from one of the upstairs bedrooms snapped Billy back to awareness. She rolled off Ethan and, in one graceful motion, pushed to her feet. She straightened her shirt just as Alice emerged from the upstairs bedroom.

Ethan sat motionless on the couch, feeling his heart race.

With red-rimmed eyes, Alice glanced at them over the balcony before walking to the bathroom and closing the door without a word.

"Has anyone spoken to her?" Billy asked. Her voice held a twinge of breathlessness Ethan took pride in having caused.

Ethan stood. "Yeah. She and Pope talked on the ride here. She's shaken about Meg. She'll need some time to handle it."

Too fast, Billy was cooling off. But now Ethan knew what lay just beneath her composed exterior, and he knew how to access it.

"Billy Jean—"

She turned, unzipped the outer pocket of her travel bag, and pulled out a laptop. "Claire and I set up a secure connection so you can do a quick video chat with Alyssa. She needs to see your face and know you're okay."

He moved toward Billy and cupped her face in his hands, holding her gaze so he could look into her eyes. Did she love him? Who would be so thoughtful as to arrange a video conference with his daughter?

He planted another kiss on her lips but kept it brief. "Thank you."

She set the laptop down on the table and started the video chat. As soon as Alyssa was in view, Billy stepped out of view.

"Daddy!"

Two minutes, Billy mouthed.

"Hey, Pumpkin." His heart melted at the sight of Alyssa's smile. He'd never done anything worthy of having this gem in his life, but there she was with those adoring eyes.

"The shooting is on the news, but Mom won't let me watch it."

"Your mom's a smart lady."

"When are you coming home?"

"I'm not sure. I'll call you in a few days when this is over." Would it be a few days? One could hope.

"Is Billy there?"

"Right here." When he extended a hand toward Billy, she took it and let him pull her into view of the camera.

"Billy!" Alyssa beamed. "You're okay? I was worried about you."

Billy's smile radiated reassurance, and Ethan

wondered if Alyssa had the power to override Billy's no-hugging rule. "Of course, I'm okay. It's my job. I eat danger for breakfast."

The moment of levity lightened the gravity of the situation. But almost as quickly, tightness settled over Ethan's chest. Meg was still dead. Her killer was still out there, and whoever hired him or her.

When Billy sat beside him on the sofa, she let him keep hold of her hand.

Alyssa noticed. She looked at their hands before her smile widened.

Tamika came into view. "You okay, Ethan?"

She blinked at the screen a moment, but Billy didn't try to move away from him. Maybe she was rethinking her "no dating the client" policy.

"I'm okay. Alice is pretty shaken. Pope, Barry, Claude, and Billy are looking after us."

"You be careful. And give us updates. Alyssa has stayed up past her bedtime."

Ethan leaned forward, looking at his daughter. "Goodnight, Pumpkin."

"Night, Dad."

The video disconnected.

illy watched Ethan stare at the blank screen where his daughter's face had been. He stood and walked to one window, peeking through the curtains.

Her heart ached for him, but she'd done what she could.

"She's safe," he said, as if convincing himself, still facing the window. "I'd go out of my mind if anything happened to her." He turned to look at Billy, green eyes tinged with sorrow.

"She'll be in good hands. Mason will guard over her with his life until this is over."

"Over? I don't understand." He rubbed his neck with a sigh.

"We have our team working to make sense of it." Billy gave a dry swallow. "I think this is the part where a bodyguard gives you firm reassurance that there will be an end to this, and a friend gives you hug."

Ethan turned toward her with a perplexed expression.

Billy continued, "The former seems superficial, and the latter, well, I don't know if I can stop at a hug."

He gave her a slight grin, but it still held the worry he felt for his daughter. "You say that like it's a bad thing."

"Sleeping together will complicate an already complicated situation."

"What if you're wrong? What if it simplifies everything?"

"Relationships never simplify anything."

"But they can strengthen people. I like you, Billy Jean. I've liked you since the day we met. And I've wanted my hands on you every day since the first time you pressed against me in that elevator." He eased into the gap of a few steps between them. "Simple or complicated, I don't give a damn. It feels right. Everything with you always feels right."

He didn't move, didn't touch her. But the passion in his voice cast a warm net around her, pulling her closer. A siren's song enticing her to surrender.

She didn't usually overthink sex, but she'd never considered the act with someone she respected and cared for as much as Ethan. She didn't want a fleeting one-night stand. More than anything else, that realization terrified her. Because where could this go?

Billy stepped closer and arched her body up to kiss him. He wrapped his arms around her, claiming her with a scorching kiss that set her entire body alight. His tongue teased her mouth open and promised tantalizing things to come.

When his hands slid under her shirt, their calloused texture made her feel small and feminine. She matched his intensity with her own, deepening the kiss and pressing her body firmly against his.

"Billy Jean." His voice was ragged when he broke away from the kiss.

She looked around, noticing that they'd managed to kiss their way into the downstairs bedroom. She sat on the edge of the bed, untied her boots and slid them off.

Looking up at Ethan, she took in his vibrant eyes, disheveled hair, and kiss-swollen lips. He tugged off his boots and shirt. Before she could finish unbuttoning her shirt, he pulled her into his arms and toppled her onto the bed.

He kissed her again, this time so slowly and deeply she felt him touch her soul.

ETHAN PULLED AWAY to look into Billy's eyes which smoldered with desire. Desire for him. How had he ever won over this amazing woman?

He felt around her sports bra to discover two perfectly proportioned breasts. He closed his hand around one as he buried his face in her neck. She ran fingers along his bare back as she whispered his name.

Had he won her over?

Doubt had him pulling back to inspect the soft features of her face. She smiled at him, sending warmth radiating through him.

He knew he needed to clarify his intentions. "This isn't a fling, Billy Jean. If we do this, we're entering a relationship—one with communication and trust. We're in this together."

He felt the temperature of her mood plummet.

She relaxed back on the bed and stared up at the ceiling. "I hear you. And what you're offering sounds like what I want. But it also sounds like a fantasy. We're worlds apart, Ethan. And you have a daughter. I'd protect Alyssa with my life, but I'd make a terrible parent. If you're asking for an honest appraisal of our long-term potential, I have my doubts."

"The fact that you would protect Alyssa with your life makes you a great parent already. And your interactions with her have all been stellar. I'm not asking you to predict the future, I just want an honest statement that you're ready and willing to try a relationship with me."

When she didn't answer immediately, he drew her into his arms and pulled the throw blanket around them. He pushed the aching need for intimacy with her into the back of his mind. He would have to resign himself to a longer waiting period since she obviously wasn't as ready as he was.

"I don't know how to make it work." She relaxed her body against his.

"Then we're not ready," he said softly.

He couldn't be upset with Billy's honesty. It was one of the traits he admired in her. He was a little angry at himself for pausing their activities in search of clarity. But the fact that his questions halted their intentions to sleep together meant he'd done the right thing.

Besides, Mica's words of caution about starting a relationship and putting Billy in danger echoed in the back of his mind. Was he being selfish in wanting Billy, under the circumstances?

They lay together for several minutes. Then Ethan heard the soft, slow breaths of Billy sleeping. He hadn't considered how exhausted she must be after everything she'd done that day.

For now, he was content to hold her while she slept. His sleeping angel. She watched over him while she was awake, but he could watch over her while she slept.

BILLY WOKE to the smell of coffee. She was alone in bed and still wearing her slacks and sports bra. The bed smelled like Ethan. She remembered falling asleep in his arms, cocooned in the warmth and security of his body. She could get used to sharing a bed with that man—and it would only be better when they finished the events they'd started last night.

Events she'd ruined.

She scrubbed her hands along her face as she sat up. Technically Ethan had ruined the moment, being all decent and chivalrous by laying out what was at stake.

He was right, of course.

She liked him enough that intimacy would equate to more than mere sex, and she needed to be prepared for the next steps. Which were what, exactly? The only next step they needed to focus on was finding Meg's killer and keeping Ethan safe.

She found her phone on the charger and her suitcase in the room. Wasn't he thoughtful? And how had she slept through all of that?

She cleaned, dressed, and shot Mica and Claire secure text messages to check in.

When she emerged from the bedroom, Ethan was in the kitchen—still shirtless. He'd brought his kiloton coffee maker in from the car and set it up. He handed her something frothy and potent-smelling.

She took a sip. "Divine."

He smiled. "You could have been saying that last night. And you showered without me. Maybe I'm losing my sex appeal."

She cleared her throat. "You definitely haven't lost that. And parading around shirtless is cheating."

With a cheerful shake of his hips, he poured batter from a mixing bowl into a skillet. "My terms haven't changed. When you accept them," —he gestured to his bare torso—"all of this is yours."

Billy groaned into her coffee. "You're insufferable."

"I think you mean *adorable*."

He sure as hell was. She bit back a smile so as not to encourage him.

He flipped the pancake. Snuggling and coffee and breakfast? Was this his new tactic? She sat down at the stool by the kitchen counter to watch him cook.

The tactic was working.

He placed two pancakes on a plate before her along with utensils. The syrup dripped over the edges of the pancakes as the sweet smell of maple rose into the air.

She cut into them and took a bite. "You're weakening my defenses."

Ethan smiled. "You don't stand a chance."

"Billy doesn't stand a chance against what?" Barry asked, entering the kitchen from behind Billy.

Billy choked on her second bite of pancake before washing it down with coffee. "You're up?"

"Of course I'm up. I've already done a perimeter check. Can I get a cappuccino?"

Ethan nodded. "Coming up."

Barry continued, "It was very thoughtful of you two to share a room so that I could have my own and not the couch."

"We slept," Billy replied emphatically.

"Right," Barry drawled.

"We came to an understanding," Ethan said.

"I need some fresh air." Billy took her coffee and went outside the back door onto the cabin porch.

The California sun kissed her cheeks as the aroma from her coffee filled her nose. She took in the view of the vast expanse of vineyard from this house on a hill. So many different grapes for so many different purposes— wine, raisins, juice, and jam.

She sighed. She wasn't ready to talk to Barry about her feelings for Ethan. Whatever those feelings were. She'd very nearly slept with him in a house full of people. What had she been she thinking?

"I CHECKED on Alice a few minutes ago," Ethan told Barry as he prepared his coffee. "She's pretty shell-shocked. I think we need to get her some medical attention."

Barry frowned. "Her mental health is going to have to wait until it's safe to leave. We can't have someone who knows your location leave the safehouse and risk a breach."

Ethan contemplated explaining how Alice wouldn't betray his location, but the Rider team had their protocols. He could respect them.

"What understanding did you and Billy reach?" Barry asked.

Ethan handed Barry his coffee as he considered how best to answer Billy's partner's question. Barry slid into Billy's vacated chair and began eating her abandoned pancakes.

"I want to date Billy, and I made my intentions known. I'm working on dismantling that wall we talked about."

Barry snorted. "She keeps her emotions bottled pretty tight."

"I noticed." Ethan scraped more batter into the warm skillet.

"If it's any consolation, in all the years we've known each other, I've never seen her look at a man the way she looks at you."

Ethan gave a chipper smile. "That is a consolation actually. Thank you."

Barry shoveled more pancakes into his mouth, and then spoke around the food. "What's the hold up? You like each other."

"She is afraid our career paths are too divergent." He over-simplified the situation so as not to dive too deep into the list of his worries.

"Is she right?"

Ethan placed the next pancake on the spatula and flipped it onto Barry's plate.

"This is my last big tour. After this, I'll do a few gigs, but I won't be gone for any length of time. I want to be home for every holiday and school break Alyssa has. I wouldn't expect Billy to stop working no matter how serious we get."

"Yeah, that wouldn't go over well." Barry smeared butter on and added syrup to the last pancake.

Ethan turned to wash the dishes. "Well, if you feel so inclined, put a good word in for me."

"Eligible millionaire bachelor with three homes, ten hit songs, writes romantic lyrics, makes killer coffee, and cooks pancakes. If that doesn't sell itself, I'm not sure a few words of encouragement from me are going to salvage things."

"Well, you two are friends."

"Yeah. Yeah. I'll talk to her. No guarantees."

"There never are in life."

"Except death and taxes." Barry chuckled before eating another forkful of pancake.

"Except those."

"And you can't control the family you're born into," Barry added as he chewed.

"True, but why is that relevant?"

Barry pointed his fork at Ethan. "You look at Billy, and you see a woman confident in hand-to-hand combat, handguns, problem-solving, and keeping people safe. What you don't see is that this woman has never been told she's relationship material. She's never had someone dote on her and make her feel beautiful. *Feel it*—not words. Words are cheap. The confidence she has in her work doesn't bleed over into her self-esteem in other aspects of her life. People don't realize that their own emotions can be silos. She had brothers who convinced her she was an ugly duckling amid dysfunctional parental dynamics."

"She told you all of that?"

"No. She'd never be forthcoming with that level of personal information. I pieced together enough of her comments over the last five years to assemble that summary. So, you're welcome. Five years in five sentences."

"Thank you." Ethan had a lot to contemplate now.

"Thanks for the grub." Barry stood and walked out the back door.

Claude lumbered down the stairs. "Do I smell pancakes?"

25

———

illy, Barry, Claude, and Pope took turns walking the perimeter throughout the day.

Billy was winding her way through the vineyard when Barry joined her.

"Any news from Mica?"

Billy shook her head. "No. You?"

"No. Pope's doing weapon's inventory. Claude's taking a nap so he can cover the night shift. Alice had a sandwich before slinking back to her room. I think she helped herself to a Meridian Chardonnay, too."

Billy pursed her lips. "Crap. We need everybody sober and sharp in case we need to move in a hurry. And she'd better not be mixing her benzodiazepines with wine."

"I'll talk to her next time she's out of her room."

"How's Ethan?" Billy asked.

"Worried about everybody but himself."

Her lips curved in a half-smile.

"Are you going to talk to him?" Barry asked.

"Should I?"

"He's worried. He's hurting from Meg's betrayal. And he's in love with you."

Billy took a shaky breath. "Yeah, clearly he's not firing on all cylinders."

Barry didn't laugh.

Billy sighed. "We are very different people."

"So are Mason and Aurora, Ryan and Jenna, Claire and Drake. Being different doesn't doom a relationship to failure."

"He has a daughter."

"Whom you adore. Alyssa already has a mother, but I bet but she'd like a cool friend who could teach her a little self-defense. Think about how great Ryan and Jenna's son get along."

"Why do you care if I'm in a relationship?"

"That's a helluva thing for you to say," Barry snapped.

"Easy. I didn't mean it an unfriendly way. We've been partners for seven years—"

"Yeah."

"And we've never discussed relationships."

"I didn't know you were missing out—or I didn't realize it until I saw what you're like when you're in one."

"You're not making any sense."

"You may not be in a romantic relationship in the traditional sense. But you get up in the morning and spend the day with a man you admire and adore—don't pick apart my verbs, just listen to what I'm saying. Your time with Ethan has revealed a side of you I didn't know was there. You smile more. You hum his songs. You complain less—not that you're much of a complainer. You even shrugged off the chip on your shoulder about your family. So, yeah, we haven't talked about relationships all these years because I didn't know there was a man who could dismantle those walls of yours."

She let his words sink in and discovered she couldn't find fault with any of them. "Okay. I hear you." She realized that at some point she'd turned them back toward the house. "But be honest." She nudged his elbow playfully. "Ethan put you up to this."

Barry held up his hands in surrender. "He may have asked me to put in a good word. And I may have complied so as not to hinder my daily fix of his awesome coffee."

When Billy reached the front of the house, she took the porch steps two at time, nodding to Pope on the rocking chair as she passed. He must have finished weapons inventory.

She walked to the back bedroom, playing a conversation out in her head. She would explain her feelings to Ethan, and they could have a responsible discussion about the logistics of a relationship.

When she entered the room, she saw a pile of clothes on the floor and heard the shower running. Her mouth went dry, and her pulse quickened. She closed and locked the door as she kicked off her shoes.

So much for conversation, she thought as she stripped naked. *Go big or go home*. Wasn't that the saying?

ETHAN WASHED IN THE SHOWER, wishing he could wash away images of Meg's death. They'd worked together so long that he couldn't believe she'd been that reckless. He'd have to tell the band and Alyssa. Alyssa and Meg knew each other and, although they weren't close, this was probably the first person Alyssa knew in her young life who'd died. At least in all of this, Alyssa was safe.

Alice was a wreck. When he'd knocked on her door to check on her this morning, she declined breakfast. Maybe she and Meg had been closer than he'd realized, or maybe Alice was traumatized by the shooting. Or both. He planned to try to get through to her again tonight.

For now, he closed his eyes beneath the hot water and let the soothing moisture wash away the worry.

Ethan finished rinsing soap from his hair when he heard a knock at the door.

"Can I come in?" Billy's voice sounded more tentative than he'd ever heard it.

"Um. Yes. Everything okay?" But he knew there was no danger. She would have used a very different tone for warning.

When she pulled the curtain aside, Ethan's heart kicked up a notch. His abdomen clenched at the site of Billy, naked, stepping into the shower with him.

"You are so beautiful," he said on an exhale.

He hesitantly reached out to touch her, wondering if his eyes deceived him. When his fingers sank into flesh, he pulled her to him, meeting no resistance. Crushing his mouth to hers, he delighted in her soft, hungry lips. He wasn't gentle. He was too starved for her to show tender-ness. But she took his fervor and reciprocated with her own.

Their bodies melded as he deepened the kiss—or had she deepened it? She kept so much passion concealed beneath her controlled surface. Knowing he could pull that passion out of her gave him a thrill that turned him on even more.

He pressed his fingers into her hips, taking his fill of her as he gave as much pleasure as he took. Her soft flesh was an exquisite complement to the harder side of her resilient personality and fighter instincts.

If he could have found the lyrics, he would have tried to express the depth of his emotions, but his mind was overrun with raw desire that escalated with each of her encouraging moans. Maybe he could wax poetic sipping an espresso and watching the sunrise, but lost in Billy, he had no words for the beauty of their lovemaking.

When she called out his name, he let the ecstasy wash over him until they were both spent and panting. They clung to each other beneath the spray of water, holding on for dear life.

BILLY LAY beside Ethan under the covers in stunned, speechless delight. She'd never given her body over to another person so completely and surrendered control while simultaneously basking in the glory of sharing herself so thoroughly.

"So, I hope you took that as my intention to give us a try," Billy said.

"We can make this work, Billy Jean. You're an amazing woman. I want to get to know all of you inside and out."

"I'm not made of sugar and spice and all things nice."

He grinned. "I don't care much for sugar. I'll take a spicy chorizo omelet over a doughnut any day."

He stroked a lazy finger along her collarbone, sending tingling delight through her.

"I feel as though you unlocked a part of me I didn't know was there. And I don't mean just the sex. Your music, your memoir, they've been an inspiration. I hope that doesn't make me sound like just another fan."

"I'm flattered a woman of your caliber appreciates my creativity as well as my feelings. I bared all in that memoir. I have no other secrets, except for the feelings I've been harboring for you."

When she glanced at the clock on the bedside table, she felt Ethan stiffen beside her. "It's my shift soon. I still have a job to do."

"I expect nothing less. What time do you go back on duty?" he asked.

"Twenty minutes."

He rolled on top of her and nuzzled his nose into her neck. "Then if we allow five minutes for you to get dressed, I have fifteen minutes to remind you what's waiting for you when you're off duty again."

When he pressed his hard body against her, she was instantly aroused. She arched up to meet him and pressed her lips to his.

In contrast to the hungry, grasping need in the

shower, this time he kissed her slowly. Knowing he had this passionate softer side took the emotions within the lovemaking to deeper levels. He was slow and deliberate as if he hadn't a care in the world and nothing mattered to him but her.

MICA'S PHONE RANG. She pried her eyes open and looked at the caller ID.

"Everything okay?" David asked as Mica sat up in bed.

"It's Claire."

Mica's husband reached over and turned on the bedside lamp.

"Alice Lee," Claire said when Mica answered the phone.

"Alice is dead?"

Was Ethan Storm's team dropping like flies?

Mica shook out the sleepiness in her mind as David placed his hand in hers. She appreciated his support.

"No, Alice is the one who hired the assassin."

"I thought she was in the gray column."

"She is," Claire said. "I found nothing for motive and she certainly doesn't have the money, but she wasn't using her funds. She was using Meg's."

"Okay. Good work." She kissed David on the cheek and rolled out of bed to dress. She would need to make some phone calls. Alice was at the vineyard with Billy.

"I'll make coffee." David tossed his covers aside.

So much for going to bed early. Mica was grateful for

David's support. As an ER physician, he didn't complain about her late-night calls or odd work hours.

"Mica, there's more." Claire's tone was grave. "Another payment left Meg's account. Three total payments."

"*Sh... sugar.* Who's the third target? Ethan again or someone else?" And if Lucius was right, Quentin Hawkins didn't miss.

Fear and frustration roiled inside Mica. She couldn't logically wrap her mind around the situation. According to Meg's confession, she bought the initial attempted hit on Ethan. According to Claire's new intel, Alice paid for the hit on Meg—actual murder this time.

Claire said, "I discovered Alice was the perpetrator because 'dead' Meg was still sending emails. After Meg was killed, I continued to watch her accounts and email. I even programmed her laptop remotely to automatically turn on the camera and start recording the minute the computer was in use. Guess whose face popped into view?"

"Alice. That was... brilliant."

Claire didn't retort with her usual peppy "I know" response which made alarm bells ring in Mica's ears.

"Do we have any motive for why Alice would kill Meg? Or any clues as to who the next target might be?" Mica pulled on blue jeans and a pink Atlanta aquarium T-shirt.

Mica realized Claire had fallen silent. "Claire?"

"Yeah, I know the next target. Are you near your laptop?"

Mica wound through the house, pulled her laptop out

of her briefcase, and opened it. It lumbered out of sleep mode. "I am now."

"I emailed you copies of the emails Alice sent from Meg's computer. They can both be traced to the same IP address," Claire said.

Mica pulled up the first email dated three days before Meg's assassination.

TARGET: Meg Martin
FUNDS RELEASED

The email included the details of Meg's schedule in San Francisco. Mica continued to read the email. The next one was dated yesterday.

TARGET: Billy Jean Parrish
CURRENT LOCATION: MERIDIAN
     VINEYARDS
FUNDS RELEASED

"Oh, my gosh," Mica gasped. "Billy? Why Billy?"

"I don't know, but now the killer knows exactly where they are."

BILLY SET the table while Ethan cooked.

The view from the window revealed the sun setting over the fields of grapes. Golden light over a landscape of green turned into a plain of darkness under a starlit sky.

Pope and Claude were in the other room watching

television. Alice was up in her room, probably still mourning Meg's death. Ethan, Claude, and Pope had checked on her periodically throughout the day.

"My next concert is in three days," Ethan said.

Billy sensed the worry in his voice. If he cancelled the concert, he'd have thousands of angry fans. But he also wouldn't push to have the concert and put everyone at risk if the threat was still real.

"I know." Her words came out more like an apology.

"I can't believe Meg did this. I can't believe she's dead. We were friends a long time. It's hard to mourn the loss of a friend who betrayed you." He diced tomatoes.

"Under the circumstances, I think it's normal to feel conflicted. You shouldn't feel bad for mourning the loss of your friend—even if it seems you lost her before she actually died."

He rinsed his hands and dried them with the kitchen towel he'd slung over one shoulder. "You're right. I don't know when I lost that friendship. At least months ago, if not longer." He began wrapping asparagus in prosciutto and arranging them in rows on a baking pan. "When Meg confessed, I had a moment of relief—like maybe all of this was over and I wouldn't have to fear when the next bullet would strike. Now that she's gone, I don't know what to feel. Is it even over?"

"We're trying to figure that out." Billy set the last piece of silverware on the table.

When she turned around, Ethan stood in front of her, drying his hands again. "When this is over, we still have to figure out you and me."

Her heart sped faster at his proximity. At what point

along the way had she fallen for him? Did it matter? She'd stopped fighting it.

"Yes, we do. I love you, Ethan, and I'm not above admitting that that scares me."

He smiled and pulled her into a hug. She relaxed into his strong arms and warm body.

Her phone rang. Pulling away, she plucked it off the counter. "Mica."

"Claire uncovered who hired the hitman. It was Alice Lee."

"Alice?" Billy repeated, incredulously. She didn't doubt the accuracy of the information, since it came from Claire, but she couldn't fathom why Alice would have Meg killed.

Ethan threw his towel down on the table and stormed out of the room. He'd been close enough to the phone to have heard Mica's statement about Alice.

Billy kept the phone to one ear as she walked toward the living room. She snapped her fingers to get Pope and Claude's attention. When they turned to look at her, she pointed a thumb in the direction of Ethan stomping up the stairs. Pope jumped up and followed him.

Mica was saying something about an email trail. "And, according to the email, you're the next target."

"Me?"

"You remember I told you who the sniper is?"

"Quentin Hawkins. Ex-UK Special Forces."

"He knows your location. Billy, we need to get you moved."

She heard shouting from upstairs. Ethan's shouting.

"I'm on it," she told Mica. "Barry's outside doing a

perimeter sweep. Call him and tell him to prep the cars to go. I need to diffuse a situation here."

She hung up the phone, pocketed it, and pulled on her suit jacket before dashing upstairs.

Special Forces turned hitman. He wouldn't be a human being—he'd be the hollowed-out shell of a man. A weapon focused on his mission. A man who didn't see failure as an option.

An assassin who would die before he accepted failure was the scariest opponent of all.

26

*E*than's blood boiled after overhearing part of Billy's conversation. He was sick and tired of lies and deceit and people getting attacked. He was fed up waiting for someone else to solve his problems. He'd climbed the stairs two at a time and burst into Alice's room without knocking. Now, he stood facing the unlikeliest perpetrator he could have imagined.

Why, Alice?

"You hired the sniper?" he demanded.

Alice startled at his intrusion and loud accusation. She looked haggard, with bags under her eyes and her mascara smeared as though she'd been crying. As she stared at him, unblinking and not refuting his accusation, he felt no sympathy for her current state of distress.

"I did you a favor," she sneered. "Meg had me help

her hire the shooter the first time. Do you realize you could've been killed? She risked your life for a publicity stunt."

"Why didn't you just out her? You could've told us what she'd done, and we would have made sure it didn't happen again." He paced the floor as he clenched his fists.

"She would've fingered me as an accomplice. Or she would've said I did it myself. It would've been my word against hers."

"Then why didn't it stop there? What about the roofie and the attack on Billy?"

Pope entered, but Ethan held up a hand to halt him.

Alice sat hunched on the side of her bed. "The roofie was for you from me."

Ethan shook his head. "I don't understand."

Alice scoffed. "Of course, you don't. You honestly don't remember us, do you? I shouldn't be surprised; you were so damn drunk."

Claude entered the room and stood beside Pope.

Ethan's stomach twisted as he stopped pacing to focus on Alice's words. Had something happened between them? If it had happened when he was still drinking, had Alice harbored animosity toward him for all these years? She would have been eighteen or twenty so long ago—much too young then, as now.

"You turned me down, Ethan. Even when you were a babbling drunk, I wasn't good enough for you. So, I thought I would loosen you up with a roofie on your birthday." She shook her head, dark, scraggly hair swishing around her face. "It took so long to work up the courage, but I knew if we just had one night together you would realize what you'd turned down and what you've been missing out on all these years. But then Meg was on you that night like a cat in heat."

She snorted and wiped at her eyes. "As if she hadn't just tried to kill you weeks ago. Then your bodyguard drinks your drink and the jokes on me." She unleashed a bitter laugh. "The irony! You screw Billy after she drinks the roofie I bequeathed to you. Then, you have me fly her family to a concert—arrange hotel and suite seating. The works! So now I know you're not above sleeping with the hired help. You're just above sleeping with *me*."

The barbs in Alice's voice had Ethan flinching. He wanted to shake some sense into her, but she'd plunged so far off the deep end there was no saving her.

"You hired the street hit on Billy?"

Alice shrugged. "I figured if Meg could get away with it, why couldn't I? They weren't going to kill her, just beat her up a bit. Send a message. Ugly up that button nose of hers."

"And you hired the sniper to take out Meg."

"She pieced together what I'd done against Billy. She had the nerve to criticize me when she still hadn't been punished. She needed to be punished."

Billy enter the room and stood beside Pope and Claude.

"Ethan, we need to get you out of here," Billy said.

"Alice–" he started to say.

"I know. We'll deal with her later."

"What do you mean? What's the urgency?" Ethan felt

his pulse rising. Billy looked nervous, and nothing rattled his Billy Jean.

Before Billy could answer, Alice unleashed a hysterical cackle. "Billy's next. No more street thugs. Only the best for Ethan's whore."

Ethan's mouth went dry. He grabbed Alice by the shoulders and shook her. "What have you done?"

Pope pulled him off Alice, and he and Claude dragged Ethan out of the room. Alice's grating laughter felt like a thousand pin-size icicles pricking his spine even while it faded as they entered the hall.

When everyone was out of Alice's room, Billy pulled the door shut. "Pope, get Ethan in the Tahoe."

"Like hell," Ethan said. "We need to get *you* out of here. You're the next target."

"Yes, but you're still the client. You can't be a casualty at my execution."

Pope and Claude started to drag Ethan down the stairs.

"Wait a damn minute!" he protested. "I'm your boss. I'm ordering you to protect Billy."

"You're top priority," Pope said.

"Sorry, boss." Claude said. "Sometimes we have to protect you from yourself. We've always known that, too."

Ethan looked back up the stairs at Billy as he was forced in the opposite direction.

With a grim, determined look on her face, she pulled out her phone and started talking to someone. Her expression held no hint of apology for the way she was treating him.

Only one brief flash of concern told him she had

doubts about her ability to survive an encounter with the assassin.

Guilt rose inside him—vile and acidic. His feelings and need to express them had put Billy in danger. She could die because of him.

Billy watched Pope and Claude haul Ethan away. The rock star's hard, angry look didn't soften her resolve. Livid and pissed at her was better than dead. Since she was the new target, she needed to distance herself from him.

Feeling a vibration in her pocket, she pulled out her phone and took the call.

"Barry's not answering his phone," Mica said.

"Shit." Billy rushed down the stairs. "Change of plans!" she called down to Pope and Claude. "He's here. Take Ethan to the cellar."

"Screw that!" Ethan tried to get free of his friends but failed. "We leave together."

Billy shook her head. "Turn your phones back on in case we need to communicate." They didn't have time to turn on and don the earpiece communications they used during concerts and outings.

The lights went out, plunging the living room into darkness.

"Go now!" Billy commanded them. She heard them shuffling away from her.

"Billy!" Ethan roared.

The cellar door opened and closed.

Barry. She needed to find Barry. He'd been on perimeter sweep. If she could keep the assassin outdoors, she could keep Ethan safe. That left him inside with Alice, but she was no threat with Pope and Claude protecting him. And based on her pupil dilation, she was helping herself to her benzos, which should keep her mellow.

Billy pulled out her gun; the heft of thirty ounces of firepower provided a comforting sense of security.

Then she walked right out the front door. She wanted the assassin to know she wasn't inside the house, but she wasn't going to make herself an easy target. She pulled the front door closed behind her, dove off the front porch, and disappeared into the vineyard.

ETHAN STEWED in the darkness of the cellar as Pope called the local police and Claude checked the locks on the tunnel that lead outside to the vineyard by the light on his phone. They had memorized the layout of the property. His team had come a long way from the rooftop storm chaos in which he'd first met Billy.

The cellar was filled with barrels of aging wine and racks of bottles. A musky smell mixed with an aroma of oak and sweet fermentation.

Ethan raked his hands through his hair. He was stuck in here, sitting on his ass while Billy faced an assassin. Alone.

Alone or with Barry?

Ethan would feel better if it was two against one. Except Barry had been outside when the lights went out, suggesting the hitman had gotten past him. Past him or through him?

Ethan swallowed the taste of bile in his throat. "When this is over, you're both fired unless you go help Billy." He could make out their nonplussed expressions by the light of their mobile phones.

Right, that was hardly a threat he would actually carry out. "Fine. Only one of you needs to stay here with me, right?"

Pope and Claude exchanged looks.

"If I promise to stay here like an obedient dog, will one of you go help Billy?"

A long silence stretched before Pope and Claude seemed to come to some type of agreement.

"Yeah, okay," Claude said. "I'll go."

Claude pulled out his gun and headed down the tunnel toward the exit leading to the vineyard.

After he left, Pope locked the door behind him. Ethan sat heavily on the floor and leaned against a barrel. Billy's words echoed in his mind.

You can't be a casualty at my execution.

THE HALF-MOON GAVE Billy the barest amount of light—enough to avoid running into poles, fences, and vines. It was too dark for her to try tracking footprints in order to turn the situation into an offensive hunt for the killer.

Let your plans be dark and impenetrable as

*night, and when you move, fall like a
thunderbolt. — Sun Tzu*

She weaved through row after row of grapevines as she circled the house looking for Barry. She stepped lightly, keeping the crunch of her boots barely audible on the ground. She worked to control her breathing and dampen her fear.

Assassin. UK Special Forces.

She'd never gone head-to-head, one-on-one with a trained killer. But she was no amateur.

When she spotted Barry's body in a crumpled mound, she froze, resisting the urge to run to the aid of her friend.

Please be alive. Please be alive.

Billy pulled out the thinnest of cords from her bracelet. She ran the nearly invisible material from one fence post to another one foot off the ground—a nice trip wire in case the attacker came from behind her.

She scanned her surroundings as she crouched behind a dense cluster of fanning grape leaves. Barry's unmoving form was out in the open.

There were no elevated locations across the field of rolling hills to set up a perch to fire a rifle. That, coupled with the fact that Quentin had to be near the house to cut the power, meant the assassin lay close by in wait.

And Barry was bait.

She'd have to take that bait to check on her partner, except, she intended to show Quentin he'd reeled in a Marine-issue barracuda, not a floppy flounder.

Emerging from her hiding place, she kept her gun

high as she swept the area. Adrenaline honed her focus razor-sharp as she crept toward Barry. Constantly keeping her gaze scanning her surroundings, she bent silently and felt for a pulse.

Relief washed through her. Injured but alive. An assessment of his injuries could wait.

A faint rustling noise had Billy rolling backward, away from her fallen friend. She heard the spit of gunfire from a silenced weapon followed by the *thunk* of a bullet where she'd been crouched seconds before.

She stayed low, taking aim toward the spot where the sound of gunshot originated, but a sudden punch to the ribs threw her backward.

She fired her gun, yet knew the shot went wild. The noise rang through the undulating hills of the vineyard as Billy landed on her back.

Staring at the starry sky, she sucked in breath against the pain.

Damn, he had good aim in the dark.

Her bullet-resistant suit had prevented the projectile from entering her body and killing her, but the impact felt as though it had cracked a rib.

A shadowy figure loomed over her, raising his weapon.

27

———

The bitter irony, Billy thought, as she stared down the barrel of the gun.

She'd finally fallen in love, and it would be the death of her. Obviously, Alice had made some blundering assumptions earlier, but, ultimately, Billy had loved Ethan and he loved her. She'd do it all again if given the choice.

From the direction of the house, gunshots rang out in rapid succession. Billy watched a large form firing widely as he ran toward the assassin.

Crap, Claude, save some damn ammunition.

She used the distraction to raise her gun and fire at Quentin.

He saw her move and dove to the side, causing her bullet to hit his leg rather than his torso.

Claude, out of bullets but still firing up until impact, plowed into the assassin as he reeled from the gunshot wound. With the size difference in the men, the collision was like a linebacker hitting a tight end.

Still, she couldn't assume the tackle would slow Quentin for very long.

Gritting her teeth against the pain in her side, Billy forced herself to her feet. Her knees felt weak, and her gun hand shook. The sensations were from pain and adrenaline, but they still pissed her off. She wasn't weak. She needed to get herself under control if she was going to beat Quentin.

She tried to take aim, but the tumbling men and limited light gave her no opening to take a shot.

Quentin used the strength of his arms and legs to shove the heavier man off him.

Claude launched backward, stumbled, and struck his head against a pole in the vineyard. He fell to the dirt.

Billy took aim at Quentin, but the man was too fast. He'd already ducked into the next row of grapes when she fired.

He seemed to have lost his gun in the tussle with Claude, but an assassin would likely have another weapon.

When a shadow moved, she turned and fired again. She had a decision to make—stay there, stand her ground, and protect her friends, or chase Quentin and stop his next attack. With his leg wound, he could decide to bolt, regroup, and attack again later—tonight, tomorrow, or sometime in the future.

A rustle of leaves sounded to her right, and she

turned and sprinted after the assassin. She followed the sounds—shuffling here, the crunch of dirt there—until they fell silent.

She stilled herself into stealth mode, catching her breath and listening. Only the sound of her own thudding heartbeat filled her ears.

The shadow materialized out of nowhere and lunged at her.

She fired, but the trajectory was off. When she hit the ground, her gun sailed out of her grasp. Pain flared through her side where the bullet had struck her earlier, but she couldn't afford a moment's hesitation.

She ducked her head and began pounding her fists into Quentin's ribcage—a rapid-fire series of uppercuts as though he was her punching bag. Since he was on top of her on the ground, she couldn't get as much power behind the punches as she would have liked—all arms and no hip rotation. Still, the man could only block defensively.

Quentin rolled off her and sprang to his feet, frighteningly agile for someone with a bullet wound to his leg.

But he hesitated for a moment, giving Billy time to stand and the satisfaction of knowing she'd hurt him enough that he needed a few seconds to compose himself.

She thought about the knife in her boot, but with the rib injury, she'd be too slow to bend and pull it out. Quentin could strike again before the knife was out.

The assassin launched himself at her, kicking and swinging.

Billy sidestepped, ducked, and then jabbed. They

danced like this for a few minutes, Billy aware of her escalating fatigue.

Her defense faltered, and Quentin landed a blow to her shoulder and then her back. He pounced and was once again on top of her, this time with his powerful hands around her throat.

Seconds.

She only had seconds before he would strangle her to death after crushing her larynx. She had to stop him, but how?

Claude appeared—the assassin's gun in his hand. He pulled the trigger, but nothing happened. "What the—?"

The distraction gave Billy the seconds she needed to draw her leg up and pull the knife out of her boot. She thrust it up, under the hitman's left armpit.

His grip around her throat slackened.

She shoved him off her and got to her feet, gasping for air.

Quentin lay sprawled out in the dirt as his punctured brachial artery dumped blood onto the ground around him.

Claude panted, gaping at the dying man.

Billy sheathed her knife and smacked him on the back. "Thanks, Claude."

"I can't believe it didn't fire. I had him."

Billy turned the gun in Claude's hand and showed him the biometric sensor. "Fingerprinted to the user. Not your fault. They don't even make these in the US. I'm betting this was entirely custom-made, with a silencer."

Claude gaped at the gun handle. "Does Rider SI use any of these?"

"No. Too much room for error. Batteries can die. Temperature or moisture can ruin the electronics."

Billy inspected the spot on Claude's jacket where he'd been shot.

"I'm glad we got the bullet-resistant suits," he said.

In the distance, the sound of sirens approached.

Claude sighed. "It was a pleasure working with you, Billy."

"You, too." She gave him a quick, one-arm hug.

"Maybe the guys will stop calling me Chunk when you leave."

Billy chuckled. "Since you saved my life, I forgive the roofie oversight. I'll put in a good word for you with Ethan's crew." Clutching her side, Billy walked to the front porch and sat heavily.

The job is finished, Billy thought.

Ethan was safe. But what exactly did that mean for the two of them?

Billy tilted her head back. The twinkling stars appeared calm and peaceful. Serene. Her job had been a success. The killer was dead, and no one else would be injured. Alice would go to jail—it would've been only a matter of time before she turned her rage on the object of her affection and harmed Ethan. Now, she couldn't.

"I should tell Ethan and Pope it's safe to come out." Claude looked like the last thing he wanted to do was move from his seat on the porch. Poor guy had probably done more tackling and cardio tonight than he'd done since his football days.

"Let's wait until the cops arrive and secure the scene. I want Alice in cuffs before Ethan's out of his hiding spot."

"Okay. I'll just text that the sniper is dead so they won't worry anymore."

Billy summoned her remaining energy and walked over to Barry. She sat in the dirt beside him and pulled him upright into her arms as her side protested in pain.

Barry grunted and stirred. His skin color looked good and a pulse check revealed it was strong. She assessed his injuries and found only dried blood matted to his hair. When she inspected the wound, it appeared to be a gash, but, by the faint moonlight, she couldn't tell if it was from a blunt-instrument blow or a bullet. In any case, Billy was relieved.

The sound of the sirens grew louder as Barry gained consciousness.

"Damn, Billy, never expected to wake up in your arms."

She helped him sit upright. "Somebody had to save your sorry ass," she joked.

"Did we win?"

"Yeah, we won."

"Okay. I'll go back to sleep." He started to close his eyes as he leaned against her.

"Oh, no you don't. You have to suffer police interviews right along with me. I'm not doing all the heavy lifting while you nap."

He grunted but watched with her as the flashing lights bathed the vineyard driveway in red and blue.

"CLAUDE TEXTED. The assassin is dead and everybody else is alive."

Ethan leaped to his feet at Pope's words. "Let's go!"

"I don't know." Pope stared at his phone. "I think that was just an FYI and not permission to leave the cellar."

"Pope, if the shooter is dead, it's safe. Let's get a move on."

He chewed his lip. "Yeah, okay. But I'll go first."

Ethan nodded and gestured to the door impatiently. He didn't give a damn who went first. He needed to lay eyes on Billy. Sitting in the dark had probably only lasted twenty minutes, but the wait felt like twenty hours. He needed to see Billy safe and whole.

He followed Pope to the cellar door, up the stairs, and through the main floor of the house. When they passed through the front door, Ethan saw Claude, Billy, and Barry by the faint moonlight. Police cars had already started the journey down the long driveway, their sirens growing louder.

Claude was hunched over on the porch steps, looking haggard and as if he'd rolled in the dirt.

"Are you hurt?" Ethan placed a hand on Claude's shoulder.

"No, boss. I'm okay. But can I get the same twenty-four hours off duty after a fight that Billy and Barry get?"

"You bet."

Billy and Barry were seated in the dirt on a backdrop of dark grape leaves edged in a silver glow. Barry held his hand to his head.

When Billy saw Ethan, she pushed to her feet with a

grimace that told him she'd been injured. Whatever her wounds were, she was still ambulatory.

Ethan rushed to her side, gently wrapping his arms around her. "Are you okay? Is Barry okay?"

"He took a hit to the head, but he's awake. That's a good sign, but he needs to go to the hospital to get checked out."

Ethan squeezed her tighter to him, trying to warm the cold dread that had tentacled around his rib cage while he'd waited in the cellar.

Billy stiffened in his grasp and sucked in a breath. "Easy."

"Where are you hurt?" He pulled back slightly, eyes roaming her body but unable to see anything in the dark light with her dark suit. Were those red marks around her neck?

"Just bruises. Lots and lots of bruises. Now if somebody asked if I've ever been shot, I have to say yes."

"You were shot?"

"Yes, but the suit did its job. I don't have any holes in me, though I feel like I was punched by a gorilla."

Ethan cupped her face in his hands and pressed his forehead to her. "Thank you. And thank God you're okay."

She tilted her head up and pressed her lips to his for a brief kiss. The simple gesture melted his heart. He felt as if she was reaffirming her feelings for him even after this ordeal. The assassin threat was over, but their relationship was just beginning.

"I'm glad it's over," he said. "It is over, right?"

"Yes, it's over. You and your crew are safe."

Mica adjusted her back-support cushion as she sat in her office chair. All felt right with the world.

Billy had navigated her first investigative role and was ready for more, though if Mica had known Ethan's case was going to be so difficult, she wouldn't have chosen it as Billy's first. Yet, she'd wrapped it up and, surprisingly, was also entering a serious relationship.

Mica's nursery was finished, ahead of schedule, and complete with crib and a rocking chair for nursing.

And lastly, Mica had met with the Alonso brothers per her father's request. They were bilingual, knowledgeable about weapons, and had an advanced maturity for young men their age. She suspected their streetwise, jungle-hardened savvy came from their international experience and unusual upbringing.

She agreed to a six-month trial period of employment. Each Alonso brother would be paired with more experienced Rider employees who would evaluate their performance and report back to her.

Rolling her shoulders, Mica moved her mouse toward the power-down button on her desktop computer. An email message dinged. She recognized the sender—one of Lucius Titan's minions, a man named Hoyle. He was the same one who had emailed her last time to let her know Lucius was ready to see her again with information about the sniper.

Sh-sugar.

She knew visiting Lucius in the first place was a slippery slope. She had no desire to be in regular contact with the man.

With a heavy sigh, she opened the email.

Lucius has information pertaining to Lautaro Fernandez he believes will be of value to you. Please return to Lucius's current establishment at your soonest convenience.

—Hoyle

Mica tapped a finger to her lips as she reread the email. None of her clients were remotely involved with the Argentinian drug dealer. What could she possibly learn of value from Lucius?

Nothing.

He wanted to see her so he could rope her into some larger, probably more dangerous, scheme of his.

Pressing the trash icon, she deleted the email. She absolutely wasn't going to visit Lucius Titan in prison ever again.

———

THREE MONTHS LATER

BILLY MOVED to the beat of the song, following the motion prompts on the images before her. She stepped and swung her hips in rhythm. At least she thought she was staying in rhythm. Alyssa had set the game to an easy level, but even then, Billy wasn't hitting any high scores.

She pulled off the headset when Ethan's song ended. "How'd I do?"

Alyssa's face told her all she needed to know.

"That bad, huh?" Billy looked at the mounted screen where her score for the virtual reality dance game glowed in neon letters.

"If you're going to date a singer, you'll have to be able to dance," Alyssa said solemnly.

Billy chuckled. "Is that so?"

"I'll teach you." She grinned.

"Okay. But if you teach me to dance, I have to reciprocate and teach you something."

"Teach me to shoot a gun."

"Um. No. I want to continue to date your father." She didn't think teaching Alyssa to shoot would go over well with her parents. "But I can teach you boxing and self-defense."

"Cool! Then we can combine them into dance fighting."

"Dance fighting?" Billy arched a skeptical eyebrow.

Alyssa laughed.

Ethan walked into the room as he dried his hands on a kitchen towel. "Turkey's done."

The doorbell rang.

"I'll get it!" Alyssa dashed out of the room.

"You ready for Thanksgiving dinner?" Ethan asked Billy.

He looked worried, she noted—as if a few hours with his ex-wife would damage their relationship. But there was nothing fragile about the love they'd forged. Besides, Billy found Tamika and Moody's company pleasant. While the Thanksgiving would be a little unconventional, Billy knew she would enjoy it.

"Ready." She smiled.

"Mom and Moody are here!" Alyssa hollered from the other room.

"I have a lot to be thankful for." Ethan grinned, the concern fading from his face.

"The truly awkward meal will be tomorrow with my family," Billy said.

"I get all the dirt on young Billy Jean. It'll be fun."

"It'll be something." She hadn't had a meal with them in over a decade.

At least, she'd already reconciled with Mac. She was looking forward to reconnecting with the rest of her family. Maybe Ethan's cool demeanor would help keep her relaxed through it.

She leaned forward and kissed him.

"Come on! Thanksgiving dinner!" Alyssa called.

Ethan took Billy's hand as they walked into the dining room. He greeted Tamika and Moody with hugs. Billy wasn't sure she'd ever soften to the point of hugging everyone, especially when a handshake sufficed.

"Billy, we're excited you could join us." Tamika's wide, white smile radiated warmth.

"Thank you for having me."

Ethan began carrying food from the kitchen to the dining room table, and Moody joined him.

"I'm going to teach Billy to dance, and she's going to teach me to fight," Alyssa said.

Tamika stared at Billy as she cleared her throat with a cough. "Self-dense," Billy clarified. "I offered to teach her self-defense."

Ethan stepped beside her and wrapped one arm around her waist. "That's a great idea."

Billy followed him into the kitchen, planning to help bring food to the table, but when they were alone, Ethan's eyes shifted to a smiling, seductive green. He snapped the kitchen towel around Billy's waist, grasped the other end, and pulled her to him.

She surrendered to the motion. "Alyssa is less than impressed with my dancing skills."

"There are numerous other reasons I fell in love with you." He gave her a teasing kiss. "You're everything I want even without dancing. Besides, you have many other noteworthy skills." He moved to nibble her ear.

She wrapped her arms around him, intent on never letting go. He'd been patient and persistent—everything she needed in order to be able to take the plunge into a relationship. "I love you."

<<<THE END>>>

The Dr. Whyte Series:

Black Gold

Whyte Knight

Gray Horizon

SAMPLE CHAPTER: GRAY HORIZON

Gray Horizon is a 2019 Readers' Favorite Bronze metal
award-winning thriller novel

CHAPTER ONE

Lillian heard shouting from across the hallway and
looked up from the imaging screen. A red-cheeked, burly
man jabbed a finger toward one of her residents in irrita-
tion. A bulge in his jacket pocket suggested the presence
of a gun. She had seen too much violence in her lifetime
to think it could be anything other than a weapon. Too
bad the emergency room didn't have metal detectors at

the entrance. The slight sway of the man's rotund body indicated some degree of intoxication.

He was trying to force his way to the bedside of a woman who had been brought in earlier after a car accident. She had multiple injuries, old and new, none of which matched a low-impact fender bender.

Lillian's gaze roamed the emergency room to gauge the level of the threat. The bustle of activity was fairly standard for evening traffic. The waiting room was twenty people deep. Resident physicians, respiratory therapists, phlebotomists, and nurses bustled to and fro, while paramedics wheeled in a stretcher with the newest emergency arrival. In one corner, two policemen were helping subdue a psychotic patient until chemical restraints could be implemented.

This was a normal day at the office, except that this woman's inebriated husband might reach for his gun and open fire at any moment.

Lillian leaned over to Mary, one of the nurses. "Please ask security to meet me at bed four. *Discretely*."

Mary looked up from her computer screen and stared at Lillian. Her mouth fell open in alarm. "Bed four. Yes, Dr. Whyte."

The escalating situation couldn't wait for security to finish with the psychotic patient. Lillian needed to intervene, especially since the man was armed. The hair on the back of her neck stood on end as she approached the shouting. She steeled herself for the confrontation.

The young resident looked terrified, but stood his ground to protect his patient.

"Let me see my wife, you damn punk!"

Lillian stepped into his direct view. "Hello. I'm Dr. Whyte. Can I help you with something?"

The man scrutinized her black scrubs and red hair. "You can get this kid out of my way, so I can see my wife," he snarled. He gestured to the closed curtain.

Lillian could smell the schnapps on his breath and see his bloodshot sclera. She positioned herself between her resident and the man.

Although her heart thudded in her chest, she kept her voice calm. "She's resting. If you want to wait in the lobby, we can let you know when visitors are permitted." Her senses were on high alert, watching his every twitch and shift.

"I'm not a goddamn visitor! I'm her husband!"

In a quiet but sharp tone, Lillian said, "Then would you also be the man who broke her wrist, cracked three ribs, and bruised her neck?"

A deep scowl settled on his face causing his bushy eyebrows to nearly touch over the bridge of his beefy nose. His eyes became obsidian. Lillian imagined she was seeing what this man's poor wife had seen time and time again.

Despite sensitivity and leadership training, Lillian's mouth seemed to land her in hot water. She had angered him and was now the object of his wrath. Better her than his wife or her resident.

Events in her Lillian's life over the last decade had propelled her into learning advanced self-defense. She had more training for combat than most people, yet her previous experiences did nothing to dull the adrenaline coursing through her.

The man's knuckles cracked under the force of restrained fury as he balled his fists. "She tell you that?"

Lillian looked him directly in the eyes. "She didn't have to."

The man snapped. He roared and lunged at Lillian.

Time seemed to slow as she watched every motion and took evasive measures. She twisted her torso to the right and dodged him, letting him collide with one of the beams holding the curtains partitioning the room.

He swore and spun around to find her.

Several nurses and emergency room technicians turned to stare. The police were still on the opposite side of the emergency room.

Lillian knew what would come next—the gun. Multiple homicides would be followed by either suicide or the police taking him down when he ran out of bullets. She needed to end the fight before anyone conjured the idiotic idea of coming to her rescue.

The man drove his hand into his pocket and jerked out the gun. The flash of metal glinted in the fluorescent light of the emergency room.

Lillian was already moving closer. She grasped the revolver and launched a knee into the man's upper abdomen. As he bent over with a grunt, she twisted the gun out of his hand.

He took an enraged swing. His tree trunk of an arm barreled toward her. Stepping back, she avoided the blow then kicked at his knee hard enough to shred ligaments.

He unleashed a howl of pain and crumpled to the linoleum floor. If he knew what horrendous germs and bodily fluids lurked on the floor, he might not linger there.

She looked down at the revolver in her hand. It was loaded. She opened the cylinder, swung it out, and dropped the bullets on the counter. With her heart pounding, she laid the gun beside the bullets and stepped back from the counter.

Two police officers scurried over and began restraining the man even as he complained about the assault and the pain in his stomach and leg.

Lillian sighed. Now she had created an extra patient in the already crowded ER. At least nobody got shot.

Ivan Kleist splashed water onto his face from the public restroom sink before inspecting his bruised, swollen jaw. He ran his tongue over his chipped molar. He had spit out the bloody tooth fragment during the fight two days ago. If only the German tooth fairy—*Zahnfee*—still paid in gold coins, Ivan wouldn't have to work so hard for fifty thousand Euros.

Verdammt.

He had retrieved the file, no easy feat. But the beating he'd taken would ache for days. Maybe he was getting too old, too slow. Crime had many financial advantages, but sometimes the physical cost seemed steep.

"*Tu va bien?*" Renni asked.

Ivan looked in the mirror at the Frenchman standing behind him. "*Ja.*"

Renni Durand hadn't escaped unscathed either. Ivan

wouldn't be surprised if his colleague peed blood for the next week from the punches his flank had sustained. He had a cut on his cheek above his stubbled jaw. One brown iris was encircled with blood.

Renni wiped his face with a damp paper towel. "Ze exchange is in one hour. We've got to move."

As they left the bathroom, Renni lit a Gauloises and took a drag. "Somezing felt off about zis job." A wisp of smoke twisted into the air.

Ivan had no interest in smoking, but at least the smell of the French tobacco was more reminiscent of a cigar than bleached American and Canadian cigarettes. German smokers often smoked American brands unless they enjoyed the German F6. Just like his country to pick a practical name—nothing sexy or luring.

"You say that about every job." Ivan ran a hand through his short, spiked, pale blond hair.

"This one is different."

"You say that too."

"*Zut*," Renni swore.

"So don't go to the exchange," Ivan offered as they walked the Ring Road away from the Beijing Railway Station. The enticing aroma of chuan'r—roasted meat, charcoal, cumin, and pepper—from street vendors filled the air.

"If I don't go, who has your back?"

Ivan couldn't argue with Renni's logic. They knew little of the individuals who had hired them except that they wanted this flash drive and its contents in mint condition, and they wanted the previous owners of the USB in the grave. The previous owners put forth a stronger fight than expected. They had been surprisingly averse to dying. As a result, Ivan's jaw still ached.

The men they fought had claimed the attack was a double-cross. Ivan and Renni had done the job they'd been hired to do. They were not told of the contents of the USB drive, so they couldn't possibly be double-crossing anyone. The men went to their graves thinking someone had betrayed them.

Perhaps someone had, but Ivan had no way of knowing the details. It wouldn't be the first time he had been hired to eliminate someone previously in cahoots with whomever had hired him. Business was business. If nothing was fundamentally different in this job compared to others, why did he feel the need to be hyper-alert? Now that they had the USB, the job was almost finished. They would make the exchange.

After that, Ivan planned to take the week off and go back home to Germany to recuperate.

Ivan and Renni took the stairs to the third floor of the office building under rennovation. The steps creaked under their weight.

Ivan was accustomed to secretive meetings in secretive places. This particular exchange was no different. Except that it *felt* different.

Renni Durand—the cavalier, nicotine-addicted Frenchman—seemed on edge as well. Or was Ivan projecting his own emotions? No matter. They weren't a couple of amateurs. They could outmaneuver any opponent.

Ivan and Renni exited the stairwell on the third floor.

Battery-powered LED lanterns dimly lit the room at the end of the hall.

"Are you the cook?" Ivan asked a tall, bearded man sporting a CZ 75.

The sleek, 9mm semiautomatic pistol had been made in the Czech Republic. It was a respectable weapon, but it appeared out of place in the hands of a man whose ridged brow and jutting jaw made him look like he belonged in the Paleolithic era. He needed a club, not a gun. Another man who could have been his twin stood a few feet to the right of him.

The first caveman grunted in amusement. He stepped aside to reveal a petite Asian woman.

"*Annyeong hashimnikka.*" The woman bowed.

Ivan mimicked her bow but was at a loss on how to acknowledge her greeting. He was fluent in German, French, English, Dutch, and Russian, but he knew scant Korean.

"I am the cook," the woman said in English.

Ivan straightened. "I—" he began, but she turned and walked away from him.

—am insignificant, apparently.

This was not his first encounter with arrogance. The people he worked for often thought they were better than him. Ivan knew the truth. The contractor of a thief was no different than the thief himself—or herself. He didn't discriminate as long as he was paid well. And he didn't feel the need to explain the lack of distinction to those who employed him. They could stare down their nose at him as long as he walked away with a bigger bank account.

His gaze followed the cook as she walked to a tiny metal desk with an open laptop.

She extended an open palm. "The package?"

Ivan withdrew the flash drive from his pocket and handed it to the cook. His eyes caught a glimpse of burn scars on her hand. After turning and sitting at the desk, she plugged it into the laptop.

One of the men stepped between Ivan and the cook, blocking his view of the computer screen. He could hear her small fingers as they moved over the keyboard rapidly. She would be opening file after file skimming through document after document long enough to confirm he had provided the stolen information she sought. Ivan had already examined the flash drive and knew what terrible secrets it held, but he kept his expression neutral.

Ivan glanced at his partner Renni, who kept his position, standing back far enough that he was near the exit and could see the cook and her two guards clearly. Ivan had no doubt his partner would ensure their safe escape should the cook intend a double-cross.

The woman nodded in satisfaction. "*Joh-eun.*"

Although none of the gunmen had drawn their weapons, a window shattered. Behind Ivan, Renni collapsed with a grunt.

Sniper.

Ivan dove to the floor and rolled. He didn't hear a second sniper shot. Of course the shooter wouldn't want to risk hitting the computer and drive.

With the rustling of fabric, the cook's men drew their guns.

Ivan lurched behind a metal rolling cart with construction supplies as bullets erupted around him. When he drew himself into a tight ball, his joints protested with pain. He positioned his fingers to draw his weapon.

The noise of gunfire and ricocheting bullets filled the room. His ears rang from the deafening roar as his heart, amped up on adrenaline, thudded in his chest. His opponents had the clear advantage. Three against one. Ivan planned to at least put up a good fight.

The hair on his neck stood on end as a trickle of icy sweat ran down his spine. He was accustomed to fear and danger in his work—dark people doing dark deeds—but the contents of the encrypted documents they had stolen for the cook sealed his death warrant. After they had stolen it and before this delivery, Ivan had seen what terrible information was on that flash drive. He had debated the consequences of not making the delivery at all, but that would have certainly made him a target.

Now he understood he had indeed been hired to double-cross the men from whom they had stolen this information. The men he had killed. Just as he would be killed.

When the cook's men had emptied their semiautomatics, Ivan came up shooting.

The cook was already exiting via the stairwell, laptop tucked under one arm. Ivan didn't have much time. Once she was out of harm's way, the sniper could open fire. In fact, when she was out of the building, the whole place could be incinerated if they felt so inclined. He needed to get outside.

He darted across the room. A sniper's bullet grazed his arm.

"*Verdammt*," he growled.

Judging by the timing of fire, he was up against a bolt-action sniper rifle. At least it wasn't an automatic weapon. At fifty, he wasn't as agile and fast as he used to be. He suspected the sniper was positioned in the building adjacent to this one.

One of the cook's guards stayed behind, and Ivan heard him reloading his gun. Ivan faced bullets from two sides. He slid under a vinyl curtain tacked to an unfinished wall, partitioning the room.

Glass rained down as the sniper continued to fire through the windows.

Ivan crawled along the floor, ignoring the shards of glass biting into his bare forearms. He reached a gaping hole in the floor where wires and pipes crisscrossed haphazardly. He squeezed his battered body through the opening, slipping on his own blood before falling into the darkness of the room below him.

Pain shot through his back as he struck a metal beam lying across the floor. He grunted and rolled over, listening for motion as his vision adjusted to the darkness.

The gunfire had ceased, but it was only a matter of time before they found him. His escape routes were limited. The stairwells were not an option; they would be watched. The elevator shaft would be the next logical place for them to lie in wait to execute him. He was too high up to jump without breaking a leg—or worse.

Ivan recalled the construction waste chute on the side

of the building. He had spotted it when he and Renni arrived and first inspected the building. Since the chute was on the other side of the building, it would not be visible from the sniper's vantage point.

Gritting his teeth through the pain in his back, Ivan pushed himself to his feet. He wound his way out of the room, down the hall, and toward the rear stairs. As he pressed his face to the glass, he looked outside the building. Streetlights faintly illuminated the forklifts and cranes outside the window. He looked up and noted the chute's opening was two stories above him. It ended in a large, rectangular trash bin. No doubt it would be filled with jagged chunks of concrete, shards of fiberglass, and twisted rebar, because that was the sort of day he was having.

He cringed when the door to the stairwell moaned. Straining to listen over the sound of his own thudding heart and panting breath, he heard no footsteps or voices. He took the stairs two steps at a time up two stories.

He found the chute.

Judging from what he had seen from the stolen drive on the laptop, he would have a permanent target on his back. He needed to go into hiding. He could trust no one, because the bounty the cook would put on his head would be high.

Such a thought made him remember Renni was dead. With a pang of guilt, he softly apologized to his friend. *We should have been more careful.*

Ivan hoped he wasn't such a bastard that he would have ever betrayed Renni. Perhaps he would never know.

His only hope of survival was to hide and change his

identity. He had the money and resources for both. Except he couldn't hide.

Based on what he had seen in those files, he couldn't cower and let events unfold. With that thought, he leaped into the chute and hoped to hell it could withstand the weight of an eighty-five kilogram man.

⁂

Lillian showered and crawled into bed. The adrenaline rush of her ER confrontation had long since worn off. Now she needed rest.

Warm arms enveloped her. The comfort of them eased the tension in her body.

"You're home late," Sean said, scooting close behind her and burying his face in her hair and into her neck.

She had called him to let him know she'd be late, but one hour late turned into three.

"I had to give a statement to the police. And then there was the documentation." The paperwork was never-ending for a physician. Since she had gotten into an altercation, more paperwork presented itself.

"What'd you do this time?"

"Hey." She rolled toward him. "Why would you assume it's my fault?"

He chuckled as he repositioned to keep her close.

She looked into his warm, brown eyes. Small crow's feet crinkled at the edges. She liked to think all of their laughs and fun times together over the years had created those character lines.

"Okay," she conceded, running a hand through his

brown hair and along his firm jawline. "Yes. It was my fault. I turned a wife-beater into a patient."

Sean arched an eyebrow at her. "You think a taste of his own medicine will make him repent and turn over a new leaf?"

"No. But he was harassing my resident, and I wasn't going to stand for that."

He pursed his lips. "Is this something we're going to need legal representation for later?"

"No. It's all on video. He attacked me, and then he drew a gun." She tapered the last few words into a quiet tone as she cringed, waiting for Sean's response.

She felt his body tense around her.

"A gun?"

"A little snub-nose Colt."

"Probably a Cobra."

"Which I identified on him early and was prepared for the draw."

Sean sucked in a deep breath, but kept his voice calm. "I didn't give you combat and weapons training so you could pick fights with belligerent wife-beaters. You should let the police and hospital security handle trouble in the ER."

"I would have, but they had their hands full. If I hadn't intervened, I would have been on the other side of the ER when he opened fire on my resident."

Sean squeezed her tight. She could feel the strong and steady thump of his heart. Her cheek rested against his warm neck.

"I would prefer you on the other side of the room when violence erupts."

"That's not who we are."

He didn't reply, but she felt his throat bob in a swallow. She hadn't meant to make the events of Montreal resurface, yet she knew Sean would be thinking of the day she had been shot. The day she nearly died in his arms.

"You're okay?" he asked.

"I'm okay." She nuzzled her nose into his neck.

"Do you want to talk about it?"

She kissed his neck and the stubble along his jaw brushed her cheek. "Done talking."

He massaged a thumb along her back in small circular motions. "You're still tense."

"What does my secret spy suggest I do about that?" She nipped at his ear.

He sucked in a sharp breath as he pressed his firm body against her. "*Former* spy."

"Sure. Whatever you say."

"I suppose I could share my top secret, for-your-body-only techniques for tension reduction."

She wriggled out of her nightgown. "Show me."

⁂

DEPARTMENT OF DEFENSE
TOP SECRET
NUCLEAR THREAT INVESTIGATION

CASE FILE: 8966B20
Deputy Director: William Austin
Re: Dr. Lillian Whyte and Agent Sean Jennings

TRANSCRIPT:
DEPARTMENT OF DEFENSE INQUIRY

DOD: You've been involved in quite a few violent altercations in the last several years.
DR. WHYTE: Being an emergency room physician isn't for the faint of heart.

DOD: Do most emergency room physicians disarm gunmen?
DR. WHYTE: Not that I'm aware of.

DOD: But you do.
DR. WHYTE: I've had training.

DOD: After Kenya?
DR. WHYTE: Kenya and Montreal.

DOD: Much like those events, you were face-to-face with international criminals again in this most recent incident.
DR. WHYTE: Was there a question in there?

DOD: It is intriguing and confounding that a civilian with no known ties to the criminal underworld would be entangled on three separate events in international crises.
DR. WHYTE: Agreed.

DOD: Would you say there were any abnormal events prior to your trip to Iceland?
DR. WHYTE: None.

DOD: Not even the detonation of a nuclear weapon out to sea by North Korea?

DR. WHYTE: I wouldn't categorize that as abnormal, no.

<<<END SAMPLE CHAPTER>>>

To purchase full book , CLICK HERE